HONORABLE ROGUE

LINDA J. PARISI

CITY OWL
PRESS

HONORABLE ROGUE
Blood Rogue, Book 2

CITY OWL PRESS
www.cityowlpress.com

Cover Design by Mibl Art. All stock photos licensed appropriately.

Edited by Tee Tate.

For information on subsidiary rights, please contact the publisher at info@cityowlpress.com.

Print Edition ISBN: 978-1-64898-076-3

Digital Edition ISBN: 978-1-64898-075-6

Printed in the United States of America

For Diane

Praise for the Works of Linda J. Parisi

"This book hit the mark, amazing characters, suspense, and the mystery behind the rogues. I loved every second of the book and read it in one sitting, now all I have to do is wait for the next book in the series which hopefully won't be too long." – *Paranormal Romance Guild*

"Stacy and Chaz light up the page together and are downright unforgettable. Plenty of steam and just enough danger to keep the plot zipping along at a fast, thrilling clip combine to make this a phenomenal read in the vein of JR Ward that fans of paranormal romance will adore as much as I did." – *April the Book Dragon*

"A charming story that was a nice derivative of a standard vampire story…I loved the drama and danger throughout the book. The insights into vampire politics were fascinating. Well written and very easy to read and understand, it was a great start to the series, and I'm looking forward to what happens next." – *MP Book Reviews*

"The story was well written in a way that the reader could stop after this book and not be disappointed. A great read for a cold weekend." – *Readers Favorite*

"Blood Rogue took me on a journey filled with suspense, danger, humor, and romance." – *Totally Addicted to Reading*

"The debut novel to a new paranormal series, Blood Rogue, is a fast-paced, action-packed fantasy from page one…It is an entertaining story readers can devour in no time." – *InD'tale Magazine*

"With a gritty urban backdrop and plenty of intriguing clan dynamics, Blood Rogue is a perfect vampire romance. Plenty of steam and just enough danger to keep the plot zipping along at a fast, thrilling clip combine to make this a phenomenal read." – *Kat Turner, Author of Hex, Love, and Rock and Roll*

"Blood Rogue is a well-crafted, smart adventure of the unlikeliest of lovers...reminiscent of lore's age-old heartbreak, how can two beings that belong in separate worlds ever be together? A great read!" – *M. Kate Quinn, Author of Endangered Diamond*

Author's Note

This book deals with loss, pain, and grief. This book also deals with healing. No one can ever truly know what another person feels but to me, there can be no better aspiration than to try and understand. A broken heart will never heal the exact same way it was before. Just remember that the people who love and care for you will always be there. No matter how many repairs have to be made, they will always be your glue.

Chapter One

ONLY ONE CITY IN THE WORLD MOVED CONSTANTLY, JUMPING AND jiving much like the dancers in the ballroom behind him and much to the same beat—driving, frenetic, and unstoppable. Only in the hours just before the faint rays of the sun peeked out over the ocean would New York mellow, going from *hip hop* to cool jazz, and allow that much-needed breath before beginning a new day.

Hunter Pierce knew behind him, even in the dim light, past the lavender-and-white neon, past the glitter of the disco ball attached to the ceiling, past the delicate white flowers encased in glass on each table, they danced straight into an uncertain future.

And not just Charles and Stacy—all of them.

Yes, the future was uncertain. But for nearly two thousand years Hunter had watched humans build cities and watched those cities rise and fall. He'd seen civilizations ravaged by plagues and become decimated by war. Yet this was his home, the bedrock of his soul.

He sank his weight into the ground, ready to fight. A vampire plague, a pestilence of rogue vampires, threatened all he had built. For a split second he knew the hollow of fear, then he felt the rock of the Palisades beneath his feet and drove that foundation deep into his psyche. No one would take this home from him. Not even his maker.

Hunter shook his head. He had so many misgivings. Despite the tenuous times, he applauded Charles and Stacy and their courage, for even if humans and vampires survived the war to come, what could they have together in this beautiful marriage, sixty or seventy years?

While people lined up outside the ballroom to fill their plates with food, too many scents assailed his senses. He found the aroma of the food heavenly but the mixture of alcohol and perfume distasteful. And the deep bass of the music pounded away at the inside of his ears. But, most of all, he couldn't get rid of his sense of unease which made his escape to the hilltop inevitable.

Crisp, cool, and dry, he enjoyed the brilliant night. Once he compartmentalized, there was perfection in the silence, a stillness which took the breath away. A valley of diamond lights spread out before him until the land rose and the distance gave way to the greatest skyline in the world. Hunter breathed deeply, caught once again by the sheer magnificence of a sight he'd never have been able to conceive of as a human and had never gotten used to as a vampire.

He settled his shoulders as he stared and marveled at man's ingenuity and then, with a slight huff, scolded himself for not appreciating one of the pleasures life had to offer. There were so few left. And so, he wondered. Was sixty or seventy years of happiness worth the pain? Was this amount of bliss all this life had to offer his friend now?

Life? Life meant only one thing: the river of blood. His mouth watered, and he chided himself again. After nearly two thousand years Hunter thought being in a crowd of humans would have been easier to bear. But there would be the blood and there could only ever be the blood, as it was at the beginning and as it was now.

He swallowed again and tamped down his thirst. He was glad to be at this wedding, even though their anonymity was at stake. What would happen to his people? What would happen to these two people who he now called friends? Stacy had earned his gratitude for her courage, even garnered his respect, not lightly given. Together Charles and Stacy had fought a rogue. Not just any rogue, Mikhail Kirilenko, a Paladin, a vampire cop whose job was to hunt and kill rogues. He hoped they would use their courage and be able to survive the inevitable, for the only true constant in this life was time and its companion, change.

Hunter moved to the edge of a patio with a slight shake of his head, watching the humans in the ballroom jump up and down, their arms waving and hips twisting to music that seemed to keep getting louder. For thousands of years, humans had been dancing as a part of celebrating, and he couldn't get used to their frenetic gyrations nor the assault on his ears.

He preferred the cocoon of darkness, the perfect stillness of the night and sank into the silence to find the peace eluding him, but then a muffled choke broke that peace. He looked down at the terraced grounds to find a woman standing on the grass below him. She seemed to try holding back a shivered sigh but failed, and the sound reached inside, surprising him. He cocked his head and stared. Tall, with auburn hair swept up into a Grecian knot, she wore the same dress as the other women who'd stood by Stacy as she'd married Charles.

He hadn't really noticed her before, and Hunter wondered why as he found himself walking toward a small set of stairs. Charles had surprised him by asking that he stand with him during the ceremony. Saying no still seemed the best course of action. But now he thought perhaps not, as he would've shared time with this willowy beauty. Something about this woman tugged at him. And in blocking out the incessant noise from the crowd, he couldn't hear her thoughts. He continued until he was on the grass, then standing beside her. She smelled fresh and clean, of citrus and herbs, a scent he'd enjoyed as a human.

She seemed…sad, and he wondered what sadness could intrude on such a festive occasion. "Apologies. The night is beautiful, the silence self-explanatory. May I?"

She turned. Her brown eyes reminded him of amber glass, bright in the moonlight which made him think of being alive and unfettered. Yet her gaze held the vulnerability of a doe and the threads of a pain he could only guess at. "Free country." She turned back to the skyline. "Friend of the groom?"

"Yes. For quite some time." Hunter bowed his head. "Hunter

Pierce at your service."

The line of her mouth softened from straight to curved. "Chaz said those very words the first time we met," she murmured. "I always wondered how far he'd go with it." She seemed to start, as if just realizing she'd spoken out loud. "I'm Tori. Tori Roberts. Friend of the bride."

She moved a small pocketbook to her left hand and reached out with her right as if to shake hands. Hunter backed up a step. In an awkward response, she stepped back as well.

"I gathered by your dress, although I was a little late for the ceremony," he remarked, trying to cover his faux pas. "Do you disapprove?"

"What?" She seemed startled by the question. "Of Chaz and Stacy?" He nodded, and she shook her head. "No, never. My God, you can see how much they love each other."

"I do. And yet you seem upset. So I thought...well, if I may be candid?"

"Go right ahead," she dared.

"You might be jealous."

Her gaze turned from horrified to amused in less than a second. "Boy, is your radar off. Way off. We're sisters. I couldn't want anything more than for Stacy to be as happy as she is right now."

Hunter frowned. "Stacy didn't mention any siblings."

Tori laughed softly, and Hunter enjoyed the sound. "Sorry. Not by blood. We're sorority sisters. Best friends."

"Ahh. Then I beg your pardon. My assumption was incorrect."

"You know what they say about assuming anything, don't you?"

Hunter nodded and thought of Sam and Charles and the bond that had grown between all of them because of the menace they faced, a bond that wouldn't exist under normal circumstances. Vampires tended to be loners and very territorial. "Would you like to sit?" He indicated a stone bench nearby.

She faltered, and Hunter found her hesitation unsettling. But then she agreed, which he found to be even more unsettling. She placed her pocketbook on the bench. "Not too long, otherwise they'll send out a search party."

"You have nothing to fear," he replied, scanning the area one more time. "The grounds are secure."

"Nice to know. But from what?" Her gaze caught his as she tried to read his meaning. He made sure she didn't succeed. "Chaz seems to be in some kind of security business for some kind of pharmaceutical company."

Surprise had Hunter answering a touch too quickly. "Why do you say that?"

She paused, seeming to notice, but then continued anyway. "Because Stacy asked me some very vague questions regarding scientific method but wouldn't answer *my* questions because of a nondisclosure agreement." He raised a brow to indicate she should go on. "Are you in the same business as Chaz?"

Hunter nearly laughed. She didn't know who or what they were, which was good for her safety. He had no wish to threaten her life as he had Stacy's. "No." Her face fell. "I own the business."

"Really," she huffed. "I'd never have thought." She rose and stared down at him with an eagerness that had concern filling his insides. "Perhaps you can explain."

He shook his head ever so slightly. "You know I cannot answer."

"Of course." She swallowed as if to contain her curiosity, but the movement only brought his gaze to the tiny pulse fluttering in her neck. He stared, mesmerized by the sight. "But you'll find I can be very persistent when I want information."

Her words brought him back to the present. "I've withstood worse." The corner of his mouth lifted.

She set her chin and shoulders as if ready to fight. "I'm tempted to take your words as a challenge."

Pleased, he retorted, "I would welcome such a contest."

"I'll bet you would." She glanced toward the ballroom windows, then back at him. "If you'll excuse me? As much as I would love to continue this conversation, I really need to get back."

Hunter stood as well. He wondered how someone so astute could be so sad inside. So he asked, "A question before you go?" She lifted her chin, almost a dare to continue. "Why are you so sad?"

She reached for the small pocketbook sitting on the bench. The movement caused her shoulder to hide part of her face. Hunter knew all about hiding.

"How do you know I'm sad?"

"Part of my business is reading people. Can you tell me a few moments ago you weren't?"

She stepped back, trying to put distance between them. "I'm not sure that's any of your business."

"Agreed." Hunter approached her as he would a doe, trying to suppress the predator inside. "You wear a mask, and if I may be so bold, I think your friends would prefer you didn't."

"Really." Her brows drew together. "Was this part of your 'service'?"

"Apologies," he said, inclining his head. "I've found most people prefer the truth—eventually."

She bit her lip, paused, and then blurted, "What's your truth?"

Hunter found he had to hold back a bitter guffaw. "I'm a vampire."

"Wow." Her mouth opened, no sound came out, and then laughter burst from her lips. "That is the first time anyone has ever used being a vampire as a pickup line on me. Incredibly inventive."

She clapped her hands together lightly. Whatever had possessed him to tell her his most guarded secret? Nonplussed, he answered, "You asked for the truth. I gave it."

"Right," she answered. "I wonder what Chaz would say if he knew." She clapped again, but the sound faded as he drew even closer.

For the first time in a very long time, Hunter found himself completely engaged by a woman. He stepped forward, and this time, she didn't step back. He lifted his arms to circle her body and said, "He would say business and pleasure should not mix. He would tell you I have no business thinking what I'm thinking."

She lifted trembling fingers and tucked an errant strand of hair behind her ear, yet her lips lifted with an almost-roguish smile. "Would he now?"

Hunger filled him. Her heartbeat thumped inside his ears, slow and oh so enticing. Then a picture from the past flashed through his mind, and he stepped back, filled with confusion. "Forgive me. I'm sorry. I shouldn't have been so forward."

Her eyes scrunched up and relaxed, her gaze turning gentle. "I wasn't saying no."

"Weddings," he shrugged. She stepped back again, the moment and the opportunity gone. "Perhaps we might talk later?" He bowed and left, not giving her the chance to say no, but remained hidden in the shadows watching. Always watching, yet wishing he could be part of the play.

Footsteps rang on the stones of the patio a few moments later. He turned to see a young woman approach. "Tori. There you are. They're ready to cut the cake. C'mon."

"Yeah, sure. I'm coming."

A picture of her doing exactly that in his arms filled his head. He banished the idea immediately and, as penance, circled the entire estate to make sure his soldiers were ready for anything. Although Mikhail was no longer a threat, the young vampires who'd attacked Charles and Stacy bore no sense of reason. They might try anything. And they could go rogue at any time. The happy couple deserved a night free from worry. Besides, this was his territory. What kind of leader would he be if he let something happen on their wedding night?

After making his rounds, Hunter walked back into the ballroom. He watched Samira Anai Se-Bat, the oldest of their kind, jump up and down and twist and whirl with the rest of the guests in wild abandon. Sam seemed to be enjoying herself immensely, a side of her Hunter had never seen before. He found himself smiling at one point, enjoying her antics.

Time waited for no vampire or man, and soon the party reached its conclusion. Hunter said goodbye to Charles and Stacy, wishing them good fortune and great happiness. Then he walked over to Tori. She'd changed into a shirt and jeans, and he found her outfit so much more disappointing than the dress that fit her like a second skin. "May I escort you to your car? It is late, and the parking lot isn't well lit in places."

"I—I suppose." She shivered and threw the sweater she was

carrying over her shoulders against the chill. "You really are in the security business, aren't you?"

"I do not like leaving things to chance." He started walking with her, matching her stride for stride.

"Are you always this uptight?" she asked.

Uptight wasn't exactly a description he'd use for what he was feeling at the moment. "I'm not used to social gatherings."

She seemed to sense his truth so she answered with her own. "Neither am I. I haven't been to a wedding in a long time."

"People make me...nervous." Wrong word, right idea. They made him thirsty.

She quirked her lips. "The dead don't."

"The dead?"

She nodded. They walked up to the first parking lot, and she stopped by a silver car. "Not such a long walk. I dropped off my car earlier. Primo spot." She looked around. "Even under a light."

Hunter nodded, wishing for a few more moments with her. Time. Ever a friend. Ever an enemy. "Perhaps you can give me a lift to my vehicle, then? I was not so fortunate."

"Sure. Get in."

He walked around her car to the passenger side and got in. "Ahhh. Your license plates. You're a doctor."

"Yes. A pathologist."

"Now I get the humor." She drove them up through several levels, up to the last parking area on the grounds. "There." He pointed to his SUV all the way at the end of the lot. "Tori. Tonight while you looked out at the lights, you called me inventive. Perhaps I am. Bold, even. I wanted to ease your sadness. I can, if you wish."

Her eyes widened. "Thanks for the offer, but no thanks. I'm not really all that pitiful. "

"I thought no such thing," he exclaimed, hoping she believed he was telling her the truth.

"Well then, your words make me feel better, sort of," she told him. "But the answer is still no."

Hunter bowed his head. He'd hoped she would tell him no and respected her for not taking the easy way out. "A kiss, perhaps?"

This time she didn't say no, so he leaned over and nuzzled the shell of her ear. His mouth watered as his lips grazed the tantalizing pulse in her neck. His incisors grew, but he pulled them in as he lifted back and simply pressed a kiss onto her cheek. "I am very pleased to have met you."

She smiled, a hint of pink suffusing her cheeks. How incredibly inviting. How very hard to deny his need and let go. "Good night, Tori."

"Good night."

SAM APPROACHED HIM AS HE LEANED AGAINST HIS CAR, WAITING FOR her. "You should've gone with her."

He drew his brows together. "I have duties to perform."

"Really, Hunter. You're allowed a night off once in a while. You do the same for your soldiers, don't you?"

"Of course." He threw her a look. As much as he tried to keep the sneer out of his tone, he couldn't. "You seem to have taken advantage of the evening."

She whipped her head around and stared at him. He watched her mouth open and thought he was to be scolded, but she shook her head. "Because I understand the need to have fun, Hunter." She turned and stared into space for a moment. "When I was a little girl my people would dance until the sun began to rise in the sky. That's why they're called celebrations."

"Fun is an illusion." Her hand reached out. He moved away slightly. "I don't want your pity."

"Fine. I won't give it then. Your will is your own. But maybe it's time for you to change, to indulge in a few illusions. Go after her."

He pushed off the car and opened the door for his friend. He would take Sam back to the compound, put Mercedes in charge, and, to his eternal regret, do exactly what Sam had told him to do. Go after Tori.

Chapter Two

DR. VICTORIA ROBERTS YAWNED. SHE TRIED TO LIFT HER HEAVY eyelids. The road blurred for a split second, then came back into focus with startling clarity. A slither of fear raced through her veins. She gripped the steering wheel tighter and shifted in her seat. Time to stop and get some caffeine.

She pulled into the Forked River rest area, noting a pit stop wouldn't hurt either. She wondered if she wouldn't have been better off staying with the rest of the guests in the hotel. As she washed her hands, the jolt of cold water woke her up.

No help for that now, she thought. Besides, home was less than a half an hour away. And the coffee was strong enough to help her stay awake for the rest of the ride.

Tori pushed open the double doors of the rest stop with her elbow, a habit all doctors had from not wanting to touch door handles. She took another sip, grimaced as the strong brew seared down her esophagus, and stopped dead in her tracks. The long, black, and very sleek limousine was hard to miss in the nearly empty parking lot, as was the driver's obvious right to park the vehicle anywhere he pleased.

"Umm. Excuse me. Your limousine is blocking in my car."

A blond-haired man leaned against the hood of the limo, wearing dark sunglasses even though it was the dead of night. Without answering, he walked over and opened the door to the back of the limo.

Did he really think she would get in?

Tori backed up toward the double doors of the rest stop. She'd seen a state trooper buying coffee just before she had. She prayed he was still there.

"I would suggest you get inside." The man had the look of a bodyguard even though he swept his hand, palm up, toward the back of the vehicle.

Fat chance. Not only did Tori have a cup of hot coffee in her hand, she had pepper spray in her bag and a ton of self-defense courses under her belt.

"They won't help you," he added.

"Really."

Wait a minute. How did he know what she was thinking?

The next thing she knew, the man was in her face and she hadn't even had time to draw in a deep breath.

"I'm not quite sure I want to ask again."

He leaned into her neck, moving up and down as if he was an animal and she possessed a scent he couldn't resist. "Delectable," he murmured.

Tori tried to pull away. His grip tightened. She brought her heel down on top of his shoe as hard as she could. He yelped as he let go.

Tori whirled and got her fingers on the door handle of the rest stop, then thought her hair would pull right out of her scalp. "Arrahhh!"

"Hold!"

Despite the pain radiating through her skull, Tori recognized that voice. The man from the wedding. Chaz's boss. The one who'd told her he was a vampire.

Tori lifted her free hand and tried to pry away the fingers fisted in her hair. Cold. Impossibly cold. Cadaver cold. *What the—?*

"Rolf."

"Hunter."

Tori knew the sound of two alpha males circling one another. She listened to it all the time in the hospital.

"What are you doing here?"

Relief. Sweet, sweet relief as the yanking fingers ceased their dirty work and let go. Tori shook her head and rubbed her scalp with her fingertips, massaging the abused skin.

"I could ask the same of you, except, wait a minute," the blond fiend tapped his forefinger against his cheek. "You live here, don't you?"

"Nice of you to remember."

Hunter. Hunter Pierce was his name. He owned the security company Chaz worked for. And he had a really unique pickup line.

Tori didn't hesitate. While they were engrossed in finding out who was top alpha, she reached out, grabbed the door handle again, and pulled it open. She had only one intention, to find the cop inside or get someone to call one.

"Uh-uh-uh." The blond wagged the same finger as he yanked the metal out of her grip. She moaned as he tightened his other hand around her biceps.

"Let her go, Rolf. I won't ask again."

"Rolf!"

The blond straightened. He threw her arm away as if she were poison and sauntered down the steps to the limo. Suddenly, Hunter was beside her, pushing up her sleeve to examine her arm. A low growl issued from his throat.

"Rolf. Get in the car. Now."

Blond Boy obeyed.

"Miklos."

An older man climbed out of the limousine, leaning heavily on a pearl-handled cane. He had salt-and-pepper hair and a rugged face which was lined with living. His suit looked to be Armani, but she wouldn't exactly know Armani without looking at the label. She wasn't that rich. But the suit simply fit as if it were made for him.

"Hunter."

"What is the meaning of this?" Hunter asked. Tori heard anger threading his tone but also disbelief.

"I felt it necessary to keep an eye on the human. She was seen talking with Stacy."

The human?

"In my territory?"

Hunter sounded…astonished. No more than Tori, though, with talk of territories and humans. What the hell was going on?

"I feared you wouldn't be impartial. And Sam…well, Sam has a weakness toward them."

Them? What the hell did that mean?

"How dare you!" Now Hunter sounded like a very insulted alpha number one.

The older man nodded and sighed. "Under the circumstances, I thought I—"

In her entire life, Tori had never heard words come out of someone's mouth so cold as Hunter said, "There are no circumstances, Miklos. None. I could call you out right now."

"You could. A challenge is your right. But the fight would not be fair."

"What about your pretty boy lapdog?"

"Yes, then the fight would be fair, but the redemption of my honor would still be lacking. I prefer to fight my own fights."

Fight? Really?

Hunter stiffened beside her. "You counted on that fact when you decided you had the right to come here and check up on me. Without permission. You are a snake and a bastard, and someday, there will be no hole or clump of grass for you to hide in."

"Perhaps. But I protect my people, Hunter. What do you do?"

"I give them the caring and respect they deserve, something you seem to have forgotten. You don't own them, Miklos."

The elder man shrugged but seemed to lean more heavily on his cane. Even in the dark, Tori could make out the tension of his knuckles around the handle as his breath hissed inward.

Without thought or hesitation Tori said, "Sir, I'm a doctor. You need to get your weight off your leg before it gives way. Let me help you."

Tori put her coffee down on the top step and rushed down the rest to put her shoulder under his arm. Just in time too, as his weight fell onto her. No sooner did she feel her knees buckle than Blonde Boy was there to help.

"I've got him."

Blondie had taken off the shades. Instead of derision, Tori found caution and respect in his gaze as she followed. He helped the older man into the car, but the gentleman shook his head when Rolf went to close the door.

The old man motioned for her to approach. "Doctor, eh?"

"Yes. Your leg doesn't look sturdy at all."

The man grimaced. "A lion tried to make me his dinner. I won but paid the price." He lifted his pants leg. The leg was missing literal chunks of muscle from the calf. She couldn't imagine what his thigh looked like.

"Jeez," she breathed.

All of a sudden she felt Hunter beside her. There was a long silence between the men, almost as if they were talking to each other. Then the old man said, "First it's one. Then two. And three. Then there will be no end."

"Perhaps. But we have more pressing problems requiring our attention. Their numbers are growing."

"They are a pestilence."

"And like the locust, they will destroy so much before they are done. Take care of your own home, and I will take care of mine."

"See that you do, Hunter. See that you do."

Blond Boy made to close the door, but Tori stopped him and asked, "May I do anything for you?"

The man smiled and shook his head. "Thank you for your kindness." He turned to Hunter and added, "You know what must be done. Use the Lethe."

"Yes."

Tori watched Hunter and Blond Boy stare at each other again, then Rolf got in and the limo drove away. Once it was gone Hunter asked her, "May I follow you to your home to make sure you get there safely?"

"What's 'Lethe'?"

"Nothing." He walked up the steps, picked up her cup, and handed her coffee to her. "Will you allow me?"

Tori considered. He seemed okay. He was Chaz's boss. And he'd just come to her rescue, although she wasn't quite sure what kind of rescue it had been.

"All right. But once we reach the police station, you make a left at the light and follow the signs back to the parkway."

He didn't answer. He simply followed her to her car, held the door open for her, and leaned in once she was seated. He waited for her to place the coffee in the cup holder and leaned very close, so close she thought he might kiss her. Instead, he did the same as Blond Boy and ran his nose along the line of her neck. He leaned closer. There was a pinch, and an instantaneous warmth filling her groin. Then everything seemed to float from far away. What a night.

No way. No way in hell. There was no way in hell she would ever drive home in this condition. Tori sat up in her car, waiting for the world to stop rolling. Her stomach clenched, and she drew in a deep breath, letting out the air in short staccato huffs. Then her eyes widened. She knew her body. The antsy yearning in her core reminding her she hadn't had sex in a very long time had been replaced by immense satisfaction. Indeed, she hadn't felt this relaxed in years.

Tori groaned. The wedding. Stilted pictures that turned fuzzy and gray raced through her brain, pictures of fingers undoing her jeans, lifting her shirt out of her pants, slipping aside her thong. She strained to remember, then wondered if she really wanted to as a sinkhole grew wider and wider inside her belly. *Oh no. No, no, no, no, no. Please tell me I didn't make a complete fool of myself.*

She shook her head. Nausea consumed her as her stomach flipped, and Tori stilled until the waves stopped creating havoc. She rubbed her temples with her fingers, but not from pain, simply to try to right the world. Dear lord, had she made an absolute spectacle of herself?

Completely and utterly mortified, Tori let her head fall and rested her forehead on the steering wheel. She banged it lightly on the plastic over and over again, very good at heaping blame on herself, not very good at letting go of it. She'd opened her heart a smidge for Stacy and Chaz, let their love inside and ended up with the sadness consuming her again. *My own damned fault. So stupid. So incredibly dumb.*

Doctor that she was, Tori couldn't help the thoughts flying through her brain. Had there at least been a condom involved? She strained to remember. The pictures ended up even more muddled. Would she have to get tested for STDs? She opened the door of her car and stepped out, stopping herself just in time before she slammed the damned thing closed and woke up the entire complex.

No matter how foolish her actions, Tori was extremely grateful that at least she'd made it home in one piece. As she stood there, trying not to sway, she thought back to the wedding, and warmth crept back into her heart. She banished the nonsense with the picture of Stacy and Chaz saying their vows inside the gazebo, her heart filling as she'd watched her best friend get married. Feeling something so warm could never be wrong, so she'd just have to deal with the aftermath of her own recklessness.

Thick ocean air spread like a blanket over her, and she forced herself to focus. She closed the car door and breathed in the warm, sultry late-September night. She walked toward her town house, releasing the air in a heartfelt sigh. With the soft ocean breeze caressing her skin and the slight echo of the waves beating against the shore, Tori realized this was the kind of night to fill the void of hurt that could never be filled. Between the beauty of the night and the need she'd denied until it had exploded in her face, somewhere inside the hangover that didn't hurt, inside the satisfaction of release, somewhere lurking in the back of her mind, there'd been a man, a linebacker. No, a soldier with short, dark hair and clear, gray eyes that saw right through her. They'd turned smoky with heat, and he'd made the pain inside go away.

She continued walking toward her townhouse, and the pictures started to come into focus. Tall with massive shoulders, he seemed to want to protect her. Tori slowed, her footsteps faltering. Son of a gun.

He was in security. He owned the business Chaz worked for. Hunter. And when she'd asked who he really was, he'd told her he was a vampire. Can you imagine? Of all the things to say, he'd given her the best pickup line she'd ever heard. A vampire.

Tori picked up her pace again and continued through the parking lot, smiling in bemused disbelief. Vampires and sex all in one night, just like in one of those B horror movies. Who'd have thought?

Suddenly, Tori froze.

"Run!"

She couldn't. She kept telling her feet to move, and they refused to obey. Someone tried to tackle her, but she ducked. Her next breath made her gag. What the hell?

Tori stared as the man who'd tried to tackle her attacked another man in the parking lot.

"RUN!"

Wait a minute. She knew his voice. The man from the wedding. Hunter.

As if his name was a magic word, she unlocked, turned, and sprinted towards her townhouse. She could hear her heart pound in her ears, her lungs pistoning for all they were worth.

She reached the steps and her front door, and then she heard a scream. Not a scream for help, not a wail of agony, a screech as if someone was being thwarted, denied their very existence.

Tori turned. A man lay on the ground.

Without thought, Tori ran back to help, choking on the foul air. She found Hunter lying there, his gaze full of accusation.

"I thought I told you to run."

Chapter Three

VENATORIUS.

A name Hunter had not heard in nearly two thousand years.

Venatorius.

His skin rippled under the whisper of death, the nerve endings beneath bowing under the weight of remembered pain.

I own you.

A debt long since repaid yet still seeking that last tiny piece of his soul.

Do you remember?

A different time and place seeped into his bones, an older time, a time when life had been worth less than a few coins, a place filled only with death. Phantom fire had filled his back. Blood had seeped from the marks of the lash. A buyer for his body had made no effort to hide his lust. The scene shifted, and the weight of leather and steel had felt at home upon his body, the haft of his sword a familiar friend to his hand. The sand of the arena had spread beneath his sandals as he'd twisted and turned, the clash of steel upon steel ringing in his ears.

Hunter Pierce shook his head to dispel the images and sat up. The scent of the dying filled his nostrils, leaving behind an old and bitter taste. Or were those just his thoughts?

He rose to his feet and found Tori backing up and away from him, horror filling her gaze. Looking down, he found his shirt covered in blood. He lifted the cloth and found the gash already healed.

"No. That's impossible. No one can heal that kind of cut that fast."

She practically stumbled in her haste to get away. Then she straightened. And he knew she was about to faint.

Faster than the human eye could see, he sprinted over to the doctor, catching her just in time. He lifted her legs off the pavement, and her head lolled against his arm, exposing her long, tanned neck.

There was only one winner in this game, no matter the past, and could only ever be one winner. Blood.

"Sir?"

His best lieutenant ran to him, gulping in deep breaths of air as she halted by his side. Her short, modern haircut seemed at odds with the wicked knife in her hand. As did the tiny diamond-stud earrings in her earlobes. Her heart hammered in his ears. Her concern for his well-being was appreciated but misplaced. Still, he softened as he settled the doctor deeper in his arms.

Looking down he said, "I'm fine, Mercedes. Unharmed. So is she." His gaze shifted off into the distance. "Did you find it?" Mercy nodded. "You cut off the head? Set the fire?" Mercy's shoulders slumped a little, but she nodded again. "These vampires were newly made, and their bones may not burn completely, so make sure to bury any that might be left, and then scatter the ashes. Have your men follow the other two vampires who were with this one. They haven't turned rogue yet. I fear they will soon. Once you're finished, report back to me. Number forty-six."

"Yes, sir."

He stared at her hard to make sure she knew she'd disobeyed orders. "You shouldn't have followed me. I left you in charge of the mansion."

She stared back at him without remorse. "The lady Samira gave me leave to follow."

Hunter nodded and lifted the woman in his arms high up into his chest. In his mind he could see her gaze just before she'd fainted, dark, almost accusatory, letting too much in and nothing out.

What a combination. So smart and yet so cautious, she'd proven so very brave. No one could have been more surprised when she'd run to help Miklos in spite of Rolf's treatment. He blew out a deep breath. She'd run back to help him too.

Beauty. Daring. Courage. Such a lethal combination.

How lucky for her they'd been able to destroy the rogue—unlucky for him. For now, she'd become a part of this mess whether she wanted to or not. His fault for starting the game to begin with. He should never have listened to Sam. He should never have given in.

Red-gold strands glittered in her auburn hair as it fell over his arm. She weighed more than he'd expected, yet her tall, willowy frame suited her. Statuesque. But with curves in all the right places.

His gaze followed the long line of her chin, the high cheekbone, the nose perfectly placed. Not a blemish or a mark. How incredible.

Hunter shook his head. He'd had no business admiring her beauty at the wedding, nor what had come after. He should never have satisfied his hunger with her. Not under these circumstances, not while rogue vampires threatened anyone and Miklos threatened everyone connected to him.

And now, hearing a voice he thought long dead? Dredging up the past, especially making it public? Unease draped across his shoulders like a well-worn blanket. His past was no one else's business but his own. Hunter frowned. Seemed as though he'd have no choice but to let his history become public knowledge now. The voice inside his head was not his imagination. Therefore, he could only believe that the attack was part of a long-standing vendetta.

Her head lifted. "You can put me down now."

So deep was he in his thoughts, Hunter started and nearly dropped her.

Her eyelids fluttered open. "I can walk," she added.

As deep and as dark as they'd been before, now her eyes were soft like melted caramel and chocolate. He wanted to sink inside their warmth. But her gaze carried too many questions he couldn't answer.

"Are you certain?"

She nodded, so Hunter stopped walking and let go of her legs. She slid down his body, awakening fiercely controlled emotions. She must've felt them too, for her eyes widened. Then they narrowed. Her gaze flared, then slipped into sultry. And her thoughts? Too loud and too enticing, to be sure.

"Be careful what you wish for," he murmured.

"I beg your pardon?"

"Nothing." She leaned back, tilting her head up to his. He stared at the pulse fluttering beneath her skin. He swallowed hard. A fierce battle raged inside, a battle he'd come to hate. Lips or neck. Lips or neck.

"I know you."

"Hunter Pierce."

She rubbed at her temple with her fingers. "The wedding," she whispered and digested the information with an innocent curiosity that tugged at his insides. "You told me you were a vampire. I laughed."

Hunter certainly wasn't laughing now. He looked around. Although late, a car could drive by. So could the police. He didn't like standing out in the open. "Yes."

"You were attacked. So much blood. Yet you healed. How is that possible?"

So many years of hiding. So many years alone. So much better for both of them to stay this way.

"Such a foul odor," she continued. "What kind of man smells like that? Even corpses don't smell that bad."

The mist swirled in the lamplight, creating a natural cover—but would never cover up tonight's mess. "Not a man," he answered. "This is all very hard to explain. It would be easier to do so inside your house."

She paused and cocked her head, her hands resting on her hips. "Who says I'm inviting you in?"

Taken aback, Hunter paused a moment. Then he responded with honesty. "It would be safer if you did."

She didn't reply. But her body did, leaning in whisper close. "Maybe. Maybe not." She paused as if something occurred to her.

"What did you do to me?"

Do to you? The scent you're giving off right now is begging me to repeat our last meeting. "Nothing. We met at the wedding. I'd gone out onto the patio for some air. You were standing on the grass. We talked."

She frowned. "I don't remember you. And yet I do. I was looking at the lights."

"Dr. Roberts," Hunter insisted. The last thing he wanted was for this evening to blow up into a circus. Mercy's men might circle back, and his lieutenant was certainly close enough to catch some of this discussion. "Tori, please. Can we at least continue this conversation inside?"

She nodded, turned, and began walking. Hunter followed her down the sidewalk and up the steps to her townhouse. Admiring her gait from behind, he remembered. Voluptuous. Large, ripe breasts falling into his waiting palms. Her soft moans and her slick core. Swallowing her screams, then the taste of her blood. So rich and vibrant, and so full of life.

That tiny, hidden piece of him wanted to know more about her, drawn to her along with her blood. But he'd given her the Lethe as Miklos instructed so she wouldn't remember him. Because he had to. As a rule, Hunter stayed away from humans. Tori had been a rare indulgence. One he now regretted—really regretted. Because she was no longer enthralled and was way too smart to let him try again.

She opened the front door. For a moment he feared she'd close the damned thing in his face. He wondered if it wouldn't be better that way.

Instead, she waved him inside and shut the door. She followed, her thoughts chaotic, tumbling one on top of another, and her emotions following so close he couldn't separate them in his head.

"All right, Mr. Pierce. We're here. I'm safe, I think. And you're alive. I think. So, start talking. You told me you were in security. Who are you really? And for the love of God, why was that man trying to kill you?"

"Not a man. A very powerful and very, *very* dangerous creature. A rogue vampire."

She'd crossed her arms over her chest in consternation or disbelief

—he wasn't sure. He watched as they unfurled slowly. "Creature? Really? He looked…" Her voice trailed off, and Hunter heard the words inside her head. She'd been about to say *human*. But humans couldn't decay like in such a manner and live. And humans couldn't make a gash so deep heal that fast. "What did you call it? A rogue vampire? What does that make you?"

Very well. She wanted direct. So be it. "I'm a friend. I've known Charles for about eight hundred years."

"Eight hundred. *Right.*"

He ignored the sarcasm. "The creature was a rogue. A killing machine. A vampire ready to drain every human it can." Her lips parted, and the corner of her mouth lifted. There it was, that familiar human reaction of disbelief, the huff of disdain. "And me? I'm your normal, everyday…" Hunter couldn't resist pausing for emphasis, "vampire."

She burst out laughing. "You said that before."

Hunter frowned, and his brows drew together. Was she mocking him? "I assure you," he continued. "There's very little humor in this situation."

"Right."

Her laughter continued to bubble, making him angry. He stiffened. "I do not lie."

"Really? You say you've known Charles for around eight hundred years. Well, I'm a doctor and I happen to know that's physically impossible. You really need to stop playing with me."

He paused wondering if he dared answer. "I'm not playing with you, Tori. Nor am I really alive."

She burst out laughing again. Suddenly she stilled as if something occurred to her. "The grounds at the hotel. The wedding. We sat on a stone bench. The night. So crisp and cool, a perfect autumn night." Her voice trailed off, but her thoughts pounded at him. *My car. The front seat. Fire filling your cool, gray gaze. Need filling my belly. Your arms drawing me close.*

"That's impossible," she whispered.

His mouth quirked despite himself. What he thought was forbidden, but deep inside Hunter knew he wanted every moment of those forbidden thoughts. "What is?" he asked.

"I woke up here, in the parking lot." Without conscious thought, her fingers traced her lips. "My car."

He shrugged. Time to take back command of himself. "Too many humans. I was thirsty."

She stilled and winced, her hand clasping her upper arm. She pulled her fingers away and saw they were coated red. As she lifted her arm up to look, he saw tiny scrapes on her skin. She walked into her kitchen and washed off the blood. His mouth watered as his gaze followed each and every thread snaking down her drain. Her body slumped, and he watched as she leaned her forehead against a cabinet above the sink. A desire to protect her filled him as he watched her massage her temples once again, a desire that scared him almost as much as the rogue that had attacked them.

She frowned as she strained to make sense of the night, and he commiserated with her, which scared him even more. "And what was I?"

There was only one way to end this. He had to sever the connection between them. "Convenient."

"Really? Whoa. Okay, I admit it. I was a little drunk, and I was really tired. I remember buying a coffee. We had sex, didn't we?"

Without skipping a beat, he replied, "You had an orgasm. I had dinner."

All the air rushed out of her lungs. She tried to draw in a breath, but the air locked tight in her throat. She shivered, rubbing her good arm to ward off the chill, and he lifted his gaze to catch hers, turning about as cold as she felt. He had to in order to fight the words and feelings flying at him like swords.

Oh my! I remember every moment now. The incredible fire. The sensations racing though my body. The moment of reaching a peak I've never, ever reached before. "That was cruel."

He dared not show the least bit of remorse. "I'm not known for my tact, Dr. Roberts. The sooner you understand that, the better. You asked for the truth. I gave it."

Her gaze narrowed. "Bastard."

By birth? No, not actually. By deed? Much worse. "Another truth."

She pulled down a paper towel and wet it, then patted her arm dry. She repeated the action with a fresh towel, and he saw no more blood. The wounds had been superficial, thank goodness. She threw the used towels into the garbage. Reaching into a drawer, she grabbed some antibiotic ointment and smoothed some on the scratches. Then she turned around. She was angry. Damned angry.

"I just witnessed someone try to kill you."

"Something," he corrected.

"He came after me too. We should call the police."

Hunter knew her anger was better aimed at him, so he remained unaffected by her ire. She folded her arms across her chest and cocked her head, daring him to continue.

He chose not to. Instead he bowed and swept his arm in front of his body, indicating that he wanted her to sit down in the living room. "I told you. Not a 'he.' A rogue vampire. And involving the police would be a waste of time."

"A waste of time?"

Hunter lifted a brow. "They won't find any evidence."

"My goodness. What was I thinking? Of course. You can just make bodies disappear."

Not happy with being truthful he replied, "In this instance, yes. They burn. Quite easily."

She opened her mouth to retort, then closed her lips. A tiny muscle in her cheek twitched. Finally the words blurted out. "Because he was a rogue vampire and you're just an ordinary one. Gotcha. Fine."

She straightened items on her counter, putting a few pieces of silverware into a drawer. The attempt to distract herself was obvious. "There's only one way to truly prove who you are besides the name I just called you—which, for the record, should be a lot nastier—and I hate to call Stacy on her honeymoon. But Stacy's the only one who can tell me the truth." She put her hand into her pocket, ready to pull out her cell.

Hunter shook his head. "There's no need to bother them."

Tori lifted her chin, and he could feel the ice inside her matching the chill of his gaze. It was pretty obvious. She wanted to know how he had known what she was thinking. Her whole body locked. "I think you'd better leave."

"I can't." A flash of regret ran through him. "The rogue wasn't alone, and you're a target now. Whether you want to be one or not, I'm duty bound to protect you."

"Fine." He felt the thread of anger as it filled her belly and would have admired her fortitude if the circumstances between them had been less dire. "I can take care of myself. I release you from whatever obligations you feel you carry. Leave."

Hunter smiled. Strange. He didn't feel sad. Nor angry. Responsible? Absolutely. Guilty? Without a doubt. Resigned? How could he not feel this was entirely his fault? Had he left her alone at the wedding, had he not taken Sam's advice, she wouldn't be a target now.

"I can't." He shrugged out of his coat to reveal the huge blood-stain on his shirt. "I seem to have a bit of a problem."

He swayed a bit as he put the garment on the couch. He turned, and Tori motioned if she could lift his shirt. He nodded.

His gaze followed hers. There was no wound. Just a wide expanse of pale skin. No mark. Nothing. Her fingers grazed the skin of his belly, and he sucked in a deep breath.

He swayed again.

"You need to sit down," she told him.

This time Hunter's smile turned sad. "No, Doctor. What I need is your blood."

Chapter Four

"EXCUSE ME?" WHAT HAD STARTED OUT AS A NIGHT SHE WANTED to remember had now turned into a nightmare. "I don't think so."

Tori pulled her cell out of her pocket. She didn't even have time to blink before her phone was plucked from between her fingers. Stunned, she asked, "How did you do that?"

He ignored the question. Instead, he addressed the giant issue filling her mind. "Stacy explained to me I have no clotting factors in my blood. Which means I bleed a lot when wounded. However, I heal very quickly. As you just noticed."

"'Stacy explained,'" she muttered, trying to wrap her head around what was happening. *'Stacy explained'?* Her heart pounded, and she took a deep breath. She could feel her hands trembling and decided fear wasn't acceptable. So she donned her scientist hat. Second question first because the scientist in her became fascinated. She'd deal with her human half later. "Explained what?"

"Since I don't make my own blood cells..." he continued. "Well, you can see my predicament."

Predicament? Stacy? Tori shook her head. Vampires. Boogeymen. Childhood nightmares. Television shows. Now there was a thought.

True Blood. Bill and Eric and Sookie all sitting in her living room having a party.

Back up a little bit, Tori, and try to be fair. Wait a minute. Fair? After the way he's behaved?

He stared at her, his posture almost military but his shoulders hunched and his features resigned. Okay. Not the nicest—whatever—in the universe. He'd taken her privacy and made a mockery of it, he'd taken advantage of her body without her permission—, although she'd kind of asked for it—but, thank goodness, didn't mock it. And he had been trying to protect her, trying to save her life, even if it was his fault she'd been in danger. But damn, it would be nice to know what the hell was going on before she offered up what was hers and only hers, so to speak. "What do you expect me to do? Just open up my neck for you to take a drink?"

Okay, that was weird.

He stiffened. The sad in his gaze turned to hurt. "No."

Startled, the words popped out of her mouth. "Why not? You're a vampire, aren't you? Don't vampires take what they want?"

He drew himself up and turned cold. "Kind isn't something I'm used to."

Kind? Tori caught his gaze. Completely sincere. How was that possible? "All right. The sarcasm was uncalled for. Then again, maybe not. You haven't exactly been very nice. Kind is a two-way street."

"I'm beginning to realize."

"But you need to understand. I don't believe a word you've said. Not really."

"Very well. Point taken. So, I'll ask a favor in return."

"What?"

"Accept that I'm not used to dealing with humans nor am I used to dealing with human emotions. I appreciate your confusion," he replied, his head cocked as if he were listening to words she couldn't hear. "Sometimes truth isn't exactly truth. It becomes what we want the truth to be. However, I still need your blood and would appreciate your consent."

Tori gaped. "You mean, if I didn't say yes, you'd go away?"

He shook his head. "No. Think of your worst addiction, and then multiply by ten thousand. And you still wouldn't understand my need."

Addiction. Right. She was talking to a vampire who was telling her he needed her blood in the most terrible way but acting wounded because she didn't believe a word he said.

"Right now you're trying to convince yourself of a fact you feel shouldn't exist. I assure you. I do exist. I am still flesh and, well, not as much blood as I'd like. I need your help."

Seemed as though, Tori didn't have much choice. The oath was clear. "Very well. You have your duty. I have mine. I'm a doctor. Even though I deal with the dead, my oath is to heal the sick, which I suppose includes feeding wayward vampires."

There. In the furthest recesses of his gaze, behind the hurt. Anger. And yet you reap what you sow, don't you?

He lifted his chin. "I expected no less."

Okay. Now she felt guilty. After all, according to him, he'd just saved her life. Tori held out her wrist. "Here."

He didn't say no.

Tori's townhouse opened directly into her living room, where they were standing. A set of stairs on the left went up to the second floor and the bedrooms. She wondered if she shouldn't start running up them, then bolt the door.

"Perhaps you should," he murmured.

Not giving her a chance to answer he reached out, grabbed her arm, and led her to the couch, pulling her down next to him as he sat. His finger traced the inside of her arm. Tori shivered. Even if her mind didn't quite remember his touch, her body sure did. She could feel her cells expanding, opening, inviting him to drink. And that wasn't the only thing opening. Heat invaded her belly. Desire seared through her. Her legs fell open. Was she really so cheaply bought?

"What are you doing to me?" she choked out.

"Giving you what you want. In exchange for what I want."

Oh my. That was...arctic.

And yet all she could feel was heat, the need to grab his hand and shove it between her legs. Was this possible? Then she realized. He'd said he'd drunk her blood before, and the same thing had happened.

She'd gone nova. And yet she didn't know anything about him except his name. And he was about to bite her flesh.

Bite her flesh. *Seriously?*

He skimmed his lips across the underside of her wrist. Her veins answered the call, and a particularly large one popped up. How did he do that?

The clinical side of her watched in absolute fascination as his incisors grew. Then there was a pinch, and whoa! Instantaneous high. Her head began to spin. She sank back into the couch and realized he could do whatever he wanted to her and she wouldn't care. Actually, she wanted him to do anything and everything—and more than once.

He stopped drinking and lifted his gaze. "No, you don't. You're already angry with me for taking advantage of you the last time."

With her nipples like tiny pebbles, her bones filled with jelly, and her insides a mass of yearning, Tori didn't even question how he knew. She needed release, a hot, hard, mind-blowing release. She whispered breathlessly, "You can't leave me like this."

"True. Not taking care of your need would be cruel. And, despite your feelings for me, I won't."

Her feelings? What did that mean?

He pulled her up onto his lap, and all logic flew out the window. He continued to drink but not as fast or hard as before. Her head rested against his shoulder. Between the euphoria and the lightheadedness, Tori had lost all her inhibitions. She leaned in and nibbled on his ear lobe. He sucked in his breath, and Tori felt immense satisfaction. Two could play this game.

Only it wasn't a game. Since a gown wasn't fun to drive in, Tori'd changed into an oxford and jeans for the ride home. First her shirt buttons. Then the button on her jeans. She slipped her tongue out to taste him. Cool to the touch, not salty like normal skin. But as he sipped, as his cells flushed with the warmth of her blood, his skin heated.

Once he finished, he lifted up and his head bent. He nipped and sucked down the line of her neck, but he didn't bite. Tiny shivers raced down her chest. Her nipples steeled as his palm, coarse and rough, kneaded her breast.

Both swelled. Her chest expanded. Yearning. And then she realized. Beneath her leg. Something else was growing, expanding. Hard. Demanding.

Tori wanted him inside her. Pounding. Like the beat of her heart. Like the flow of her blood.

His hand slid down to cup her mound. She twisted and turned completely out of control. She sought his mouth. He turned away.

Trying not to be hurt by his rebuff, Tori sprang up off his lap. Maybe vampires didn't kiss.

She shucked her jeans in seconds flat. She bent over and unsnapped his pants. And then she looked up.

Storm clouds swirled in his gaze. Behind them lightning fired. Thunder rumbled. Heat and longing, the likes of which she'd never felt before, seared through her. She freed his cock and pushed his pants down before drawing him into her mouth. He tasted so damned good. Just as a man should. Slightly musky with a hint of testosterone. Damn. It'd been so long since she'd been with a man. *Really* been with a man.

He moaned and pulled her up by her shoulders. Desire could either soften a man's face or strengthen it. His features steeled.

She scrambled up onto his lap, centered his cock, and took him inside her body one excruciating inch at a time. Full. Huge. So incredibly delicious. Her muscles wrapped around his entire length and squeezed.

"Not yet," he choked out. Strain tightened his cheeks. Cords stood out on his neck.

Fat chance. Tori lifted up onto her knees and slammed down onto his lap. His breath hissed through clenched teeth. Again. Even harder than before. He moaned. Pulling her close, he lathed her nipple with his tongue. Then he bit down on it with his front teeth.

Tori moaned until he was almost out of her body, then slammed into her. "Yes," she cried out. "That's it."

Pressure built. She lost contact with all reality except the joining of their bodies. All she wanted, all she could think of was reaching the top of the mountain and jumping off. And then she did with a familiar banshee cry.

He moaned. She did the same, only louder. The world exploded in pleasure. Again. And again. And again. He stilled and slammed her hips down one last time. He cried out, thrusting deep inside. Then she collapsed on top of him. The world spun. And dimmed. And she drifted off into darkness, her body sated yet her psyche unfulfilled. But not before she saw satisfaction suffuse his features and a hint of warmth fill his gaze.

Chapter Five

HUNTER LIFTED TORI OFF HIS BODY CAREFULLY, AS IF SHE WAS made of the finest glass. Fragile yet strong. To be protected yet not needing protection. Because she was fearless. Because she cared. Because she rushed to help a ruthless vampire leader, not knowing who he was but knowing her life was in danger.

Her fortitude tugged at him. *She* tugged at him. Although he'd been careful, she'd matched him movement for movement. Most women couldn't take all of his length inside their bodies. Tori could.

How fascinating. How wonderful. How perilous.

Hunter placed her on the couch and fixed his clothes, regretting taking advantage of her. Yet from the moment he'd first seen her at the wedding, he'd known she was different. Something inside her pulled him to her as no one had before, and his attraction to her frightened him. He was a vampire and she a human; the two should never mix. And yet he couldn't help himself.

Was it simply the call of her blood or something more? He had no right to ask, and he should never have indulged his fantasies. With a darkness from the past menacing him, with a member of The Council making it very plain Hunter wasn't trustworthy and rogues threatening his cell, he'd placed an innocent in grave danger.

Hunter dressed her quickly, marveling at his response to her yet again. His blood quickened, pulse pounding. He stopped to admire her long, tanned legs; the sweeping curve of her hip; and the dark nest that had brought him so much pleasure this evening.

He shook his head. Desire was a necessary evil, one satisfied quickly and forgotten. But with this woman? He shuddered. Victoria Roberts could prove to be more dangerous than a rogue. From the moment he'd seen her, he'd wanted her. He still wanted her.

Hunter took a second to remember. She'd put all the women at the wedding to shame as her gown had seemed to glide over every muscle. She'd carried herself with effortless bearing. And those damned legs of hers, showing through the gap in her dress every time she'd moved.

She'd taken his breath away.

His head lifted as he buttoned the last button of her shirt. Mercedes had returned and nearly reached the house. A light knock at the door brought him back into the present. He walked over to the doorway and opened it. "Enter."

"Sir." He nodded. "No sign of any other rogues. The two vampires we're following have headed north toward the mountains and the woods. If there was anyone else with them, we're not picking up any sign. I would never doubt your word, of course, but if there is a third vampire, he is not with them."

"Prudent. A worthy adversary." And, if the man behind these attacks was who he thought it was, just the beginning of the game. So be it. "Some instincts never die."

Mercy frowned. "Sir?"

"Self-preservation." Her frown deepened, still not understanding. "Animals are easier to feed off of. Fewer humans means fewer witnesses."

"Yes, sir," she nodded. "I'll remember that."

He watched his lieutenant draw in a deep breath and hide a smile. The room reeked of lovemaking. "Comment?" he challenged.

"Umm." She coughed, and her gaze skittered away. "No, sir. Sorry."

She looked down to see the staining on his shirt, then up to search his face, alarm filling her gaze. "I'm all right, Mercy." His mouth quirked. "And now you understand the, um…?"

She grinned. Hunter allowed a slight smile in return. "You and your men are released from duty tonight. Go feed and take your pleasure. I'll drive the doctor to the compound by myself."

"Are you sure you should go alone, sir?" she asked with a quick frown. "My men and I are more than happy to accompany you."

"I know. I'll be all right, Mercy. I don't believe there will be any further danger. My guess is this bunch won't want to double back tonight. We'll have trackers out in case they do?"

"Of course." Mercedes seemed affronted by the question. "The Lady Samira texted me.

She says she will be waiting for you at the compound."

Texting. Internet. Instant gratification. Hunter wondered if he'd ever get used to this modern era. "Excellent."

He walked back over to the couch, bent down, and lifted Tori into his arms. Mercy opened the front door for him.

Tori's head curled into his chest, her cheek resting right over his heart. A sear of tenderness ran through him. He stiffened and shook his head. Tenderness had no place in his life and never had. Life equaled survival and nothing more. Period.

He placed her in the car like a valued treasure. Once on the highway, he was able to think.

Casperian.

Master. Tormentor. Breaker of spirit. Destroyer of soul.

Hunter thought back to his human existence. He'd killed without remorse, without regret. The taking of a life in the arena had simply meant another day of survival. It was the nights that had killed him. Slowly. Moon by moon. Sold to the highest bidder. Male or female. He'd meant no more to them than a cow or pig. He'd been there to satisfy a hunger. His body had been given away so his master could watch. No, not for the sex, although he'd often thought that was part of it. No, for the power over another human life. They could do anything they wanted to him. And Casperian had controlled it all.

Hunter glanced over at the woman sitting in his car, remembering her soft, brown gaze and the steel in her spine. "Don't make me feel," he begged.

Strength and honor. From one so fragile. She had no idea who or what he was.

The miles sped by. The highways were mostly deserted this time of night. Still, he knew to be prudent. So much easier than getting caught. Although the idea of a chase, drinking from the officer to fill his reserves, then making him or her forget had a great deal of merit.

He reached the Palisades and glanced down at her again. Soft wisps of hair curled about her face. He sighed. No good was going to come from this night. None at all.

Once he reached his home the gates of the compound opened, and he pulled the car inside. Sam was there to greet him when he reached the house. She opened the car door, took in the sight of his shirt, and asked, "Hunter? What happened?"

Loath to expose his past, Hunter hesitated as he got out. "Someone I long thought dead seems to be very much alive and very much a vampire."

Shock filled Sam's face followed by complete dismissal. "Impossible. I know every vampire created. No one else from your time exists."

"I'm afraid you're mistaken, Sam. This vampire knows things from my past no one knows. Not even you."

"Not possible," she reiterated. Although this time she frowned.

Hunter didn't want a debate. What he needed was answers. "I don't have time to argue, Sam. A rogue—the same kind we've been seeing more of lately—attacked Dr. Roberts."

Sam always moved. She was like a bee around a hive. Always making sure the hive was safe. She stopped pacing. "Why would a rogue attack her?"

He wanted to pace with Sam, be in the middle of a movie that allowed time to reverse, not have this strong, beautiful woman lie in the passenger seat of his car. "Because I took your advice and enjoyed the doctor's company. I put her at risk, although at the time I had no idea how much risk. This…person…wants nothing more than to make me suffer."

He watched Sam draw in a deep breath of worry and yet exhale with a smile. "You care about her. Fascinating."

They knew each other well, but vampires were born loners, so not as well as each one thought. Which was, no, had been acceptable until now.

"She's a weakness, Sam. And whoever's playing with me knows this and is using my weakness to their advantage. As I would."

Sam crossed her arms and began to pace again. She was thinking. Yet Hunter couldn't hear her thoughts. She was the only one who could close her mind to him, an ability that was most aggravating at the moment.

"Yes," she finally answered. "You may be right. But caring isn't always a weakness, Hunter."

"Right now it is. A dangerous weakness. We're under attack. And have been ever since Mikhail was turned into a rogue."

Hunter glanced over to see Sam agreed. Her hand cupped her chin, her forefinger tapping lightly on her lips. He turned to look at the woman sleeping in his car. "She makes me vulnerable. My people have sworn to protect Stacy, now they'll have to protect Tori, so she makes all of us much more open to attack. They're human."

Sam shook her head at him. "Tori?" she asked, repeating the doctor's shortened first name. Hunter continued to watch her try hard not to smile. Sam seemed to have an Achilles' heel for humans, but she was not weak. He'd been the recipient of her ire and watched her discipline others of their kind with a fierce sense of justice.

"What you refuse to understand is that their humanity gives them a strength you'll never comprehend." Her face filled with worry. "I don't think the orchestrator of this insanity is playing with just you, Hunter. I think you're being baited. As am I."

Who could possibly bait Sam? And, more importantly, why would someone do that? Sam was the most powerful vampire alive. "If you have any idea what's going on right now, I'd like to know."

She shook her head but didn't quite meet his gaze. "I don't."

"All right," he answered, accepting her word for now. "But remember this. Anyone seeking my territory will have a fight on their hands, I guarantee you," Hunter vowed. "And I will protect my people to my dying breath."

Sam reached up and squeezed his shoulder. "That's what I'm afraid of, Hunter. That's exactly what I'm afraid of."

Chapter Six

Tori woke to unfamiliar surroundings the next morning. Dream or reality?

The room seemed simple enough with beige walls and white crown molding. A single dresser sans television set stood across from her. A chair sat in the corner next to a window. A man—no, a vampire sat in the chair. Hunter Pierce.

Tori swung her legs over the bed and lifted her hands to rub her face. Then she realized. Naked. Bare-assed naked. *Who the hell took off my….?*

Mortified, she groaned.

"I assure you," came a deep baritone she knew all too well, "the pleasure was all mine."

Really? There were two ways to play this at this point, and Tori chose to brazen it out. She lifted her chin and rose, shoulders back, chin held high. His gaze raked her from head to toe, darkening, banked with unleashed desire.

"My clothes?"

He bowed his head and indicated the closet. "Freshly laundered and pressed."

"Thank you."

She pulled the door open, yanked her shirt off its hanger, and bundled the rest against her chest before she turned to face him. Was that a smile? Was he laughing at her?

"No," he answered as if he'd read her mind. "Simply admiring perfection."

His answer deserved a tirade or no retort at all. Tori clamped her lips together and stormed into the bathroom. "I don't like being played with," she shouted through the door.

"Not my intention," he answered loud enough for her to hear.

Right.

She showered and cleaned up in record time. With a deep breath, Tori readied herself for battle and stepped out. Instead, she found him gone and the most incredibly beautiful woman sitting in the chair he'd vacated. She'd seen her at the wedding, hadn't she? Straight, midnight-black hair; almond eyes, golden yellow—she reminded Tori of a panther. Was she as dangerous?

"Good morning, Dr. Roberts. Yes, we met briefly at the wedding. I am Samira Anai Se-Bat. And no, not normally."

Tori'd been right. She did remember her from the wedding. Then she realized. The woman had just read her mind. Tori felt every muscle in her body constrict. No, reading minds was impossible. As impossible as being in a house full of vampires? Tori didn't know. But one thing she did know. First Hunter, now this woman—and she absolutely hated the invasion of her privacy. "Damn, I wish you people would stop doing that."

"I imagine it's terribly invasive. And we do block out as much as we can. But we're only vampires." Samira grinned. "Please call me Sam."

The woman held out her hand as she rose. The word *regal* pounded in Tori's brain. As did a suggestion to relax. Tori shook her head in stunned surprise as her muscles listened and she clasped the proffered hand. "Where am I? And how did you do make me loosen up?"

Sam rolled her eyes and walked over to open the door. "Men," the woman denigrated.

"So inconsiderate. I'll explain everything on the way to the dining room. You must be starving."

At the words *dining room* a picture of her lying on a table being bitten by a horde of vampires raced through her brain.

"Oh my goodness," Sam answered. "No. We're not monsters, Doctor. We're not vultures, simply beings trying to survive. As are you."

Tori snorted in disbelief. "Forgive me if I don't quite believe you. Hunter took advantage of me."

Sam shook her head, a slight smile still curving her lips. "Hunter took advantage of a situation," she corrected. "And I agree. They're men. They don't appreciate the subtlety of life." The smile widened into a full grin. "Or death."

Was that a vampire joke?

Sam's grin broadened. "I imagine it was."

Affronted Tori asked, "Are you reading my mind again?"

"Only because you're shouting your thoughts," the vampiress replied, her grin fading. "Not consciously, I assure you."

Shouting her thoughts. *Surreal* just took on a whole new meaning. "And the picture of me on the table? That wasn't words."

Sam shrugged. "I'm a bit different than the rest."

They walked into a formal dining room with steaming chafing dishes on a sideboard. There were tables and chairs, urns of what she thought was coffee, cups, utensils, just like a cafeteria.

"We have a full-time blood donation center on the premises, and humans run it."

Tori didn't know how to answer. A blood donation center? What irony. And yet, how brilliant.

"We have places all over the city," Sam continued to explain. "You'd be surprised at how many people are so down on their luck they need to sell one of the few things that is truly theirs to sell."

"Actually, I'm not surprised at all," Tori muttered.

"We give out hot meals as well. Especially in the city. Some of the homeless, the addicts, we can't use their blood. But we feed them anyway. Services pick up the unused or leftover food from restaurants, and delis bring whatever they can to us. We also pick up unused

produce and dairy from farmers upstate. The blood and food donation centers are a way of employing people as well."

"Why can't you use their blood? I would imagine you should be
able to drink any kind of blood."

"The taste. Some of the homeless are too sick to drink from. They
taste the same way you would know something was tainted, I
suppose?"

Tori shook her head, having a hard time reconciling the idea of
vampire charity with their need for blood, which they took without
asking. Restitution, perhaps? Or maybe a way of keeping their blood
supply going?

"It is. But I'm not sure if growing crops and breeding animals for
food is any different than what we're doing." The woman seemed to
be angry at first, but then she shrugged. "And one of our first rules is
we don't kill when we drink."

"You're right. I apologize. I'm—I'm having a hard time taking all
of this in."

"I understand." Sam paused, and Tori watched her brows
straighten and her posture soften. "You seem to be having the same
problem Stacy had in the beginning."

Suddenly it hit Tori. "Wait a minute. I'm not having a problem.
You are. Stacy told me."

"She talked to you?" Sam asked, her jaw tightening.

"Only in generalities," she replied, remembering Stacy's remark
about a nondisclosure agreement. Some agreement, huh? "But I
understand now."

Sam nodded and relaxed, seeming to accept Tori would follow her
promise of doctor-patient confidentiality. "Stacy says we have a
unique morphology."

Oh. My. God. "Hunter wasn't kidding. That means Chaz is a
vampire too," she breathed. "And Stacy knows?"

"Of course," Sam answered, her face filled with worry. "And I'd
appreciate your discretion. The people who work here don't know the
truth."

Stunned, Tori gasped. "Whoa! Wait a minute. How do you keep it
a secret?"

"Well, to answer, I'd have to say some of the myths that have been created about us are over-exaggerated. Because we lack pigment in our skin, we do burn but more like a sunburn, not in flames. And being nocturnal simply makes sense since sunlight does create a problem. We also sleep during the day. We call it a vampiric sleep. Kind of stops us from going out, but seems to be necessary as it restores us."

"Sleep? Really? Do you dream?" Tori asked, intensely curious now.

Sam stared at her, lifting a brow. "No. Not normally."

"And this sleep restores you?" she asked, eager to know more.

Sam nodded. "As we age, we require less and less sleep. And our abilities increase. Which is why I was able to grasp the picture in your mind."

"Wow."

Tori took a moment to process. Then she looked around. A few tables were filled with people talking to one another. Obviously they were workers. A couple tables were occupied by only one or two people. One woman was even reading a book, much like any office cafeteria, except nicer. The mansion carried an air of sophistication.

Then she realized. "Aren't you playing with their lives?" she blurted. "What if one of your people decides they're tired of not having the real thing?"

Sam waved her arm at a table and pulled back a chair. "Come. Why don't you go grab something to eat?"

Tori found she was starving and piled her plate with eggs and fruit and toast. And coffee. Hot, steaming, fragrant coffee. She walked back over and placed her plate on the table.

"Let's sit down, and I'll try to explain." Tori watched Sam breathe in deeply and exhale with a smile. "I don't eat. Doesn't mean I can't appreciate the smell of food."

Fascinating.

Sam smiled as she sat down. "I suppose you'd have to try to understand what it's like to live as long as some of us have. Living alone for hundreds upon hundreds of years, constantly moving so people don't know you exist. Small groups of people, villages hundreds of miles apart. It was…lonely. And trying. Sometimes just to stay alive."

Tori stopped chewing and swallowed. "Exactly how old are you?"

"Five thousand years, give or take." Incredible. No, impossible. Tori stopped her hand midflight from taking another bite and stared. "I was the high priestess of our race and revered as a goddess once." Sam laughed softly. "Too much to take in, Doctor?"

"I'm not sure," Tori replied, her mind a whirl.

"Look. As a scientist, you appreciate logic, right?"

She nodded, wondering what Sam was driving at. "I do."

"And you understand the fight-or-flight instinct, right?" Tori nodded again. "What do you think happens when people are threatened?"

"They run or they fight back."

She watched Sam's gaze darken. "Exactly. Secrecy has been our way of staying alive. Humans don't always run."

"All right." Tori dug in to another bite of eggs and chewed, her mind running wild with thoughts. "But I saw Hunter in action. You're more powerful, faster, and stronger. What could you possibly be afraid of? At least from a human being like me?"

Sam smiled sadly. "In the past? Knives, swords, axes, arrows. Now? A semiautomatic weapon will do just as much harm. We do bleed, as you remember after seeing what happened to Hunter."

"I know." She must've seen the picture in Tori's mind. "But your skin knits almost instantly."

"Which causes a slew of problems when humans are suspicious of everything they don't understand. You know, waking up staked to a cross because of superstition isn't a good way to die," Sam threw back at her. "Neither is waking up buried beneath the ground."

"That really happened to you?" she blurted.

Sam nodded, her gaze darkening. "I was able to get away. Not all of us have been as lucky."

Tori wasn't sure how to react. She kind of wanted to apologize. But then she thought of Hunter's behavior and didn't.

"Compound fear and superstition with demographics and a lack of a steady food supply. How do you think all of this adds up?" Sam finished.

Tori swallowed and dug her fork in to her eggs. She began to understand. "Secrecy. I get it. Much safer."

"Exactly," Sam agreed. "The last thing any of us would want is to call attention to our existence by initiating a blood bath. Certainly not in this modern world. Not with videos and cell phones and texts."

Tori thought of several social media venues and watched Sam shudder. "Gotcha."

"As it is, with the rogue that went crazy on us and nearly killed Stacy, we had quite a bit of covering up to do."

The eggs inside her throat formed a cold lump, and she swallowed heavily. "'Nearly killed Stacy'?"

Sam continued to gauge her reactions. "I see she didn't tell you about this particular event." Tori wondered why. To spare her? Then again, Stacy hadn't told her about vampires either. Because she couldn't. Secrecy. "We destroyed it," Sam continued. "But there seem to be others. Like the rogue that attacked Hunter last night."

"You all keep using the same term over and over. A rogue vampire? All Hunter told me was it was powerful and dangerous. Which I got firsthand when it attacked him."

"May I see?"

Tori shivered and rolled up her sleeve. "I was lucky. He missed me for the most part. But he didn't miss Hunter."

She watched Sam pause. Was Sam seeing the pictures in her head? Tori hoped so. "Unfortunate," the vampire queen murmured.

"Yeah. But I'm still here. And I'd like to understand. What's a rogue vampire?"

She watched as Sam seemed to be debating with herself about what to say and what not to say. "I'm not quite sure how to explain. I guess we'd need to begin at the beginning. Vampires, contrary to those myths again, aren't immortal. We do age. At the last stage of a vampire's life, we become a *Sinsir*. There's no set time, but eventually the craving for blood becomes too strong to withstand. It begins to consume us. When that happens, our minds and bodies begin to deteriorate. We can feel the change coming on. We call it going 'rogue.'

Once it begins, the deterioration cannot be stopped. The *Sinsir* must be killed, or it will kill and drink and kill and drink every human and animal with blood in it."

Tori shivered. She thought back to some of the gory horror movies she'd seen as a kid. She watched Sam flinch as she saw the same pictures. Then more pictures of what had happened in the parking lot filled her mind. A sad smile grew on Sam's face as she nodded in understanding.

"So, you're telling me a compound full of vampires is the least of my worries, is that it?"

"Yes. We issue what we call orders of protection. The vampires here take a solemn oath not to drink from humans on these premises. It is strictly enforced."

"How strictly?" A sick feeling invaded Tori's insides.

"They forfeit their lives."

"Oh." The sick feeling tried to grow, and she swallowed hard.

Sam's gaze warmed again. "We're not inhuman, Doctor."

"I'm not sure I would like to be responsible for another life," Tori interrupted. On top of the reality irritating her insides, Sam's formality was starting to grate. "Could you do me a favor and hang the 'Doctor' thing. 'Tori' is fine."

"Sure. Tori." The high priestess rose and pushed her chair under the table. "As I was saying. We're not inhuman. Every member of this —I'd like to use the term *family*, but *society* is closer—gets nights off and vacation days."

"Makes sense."

"Doctor," Sam paused. "Tori. We need your help. You need our protection. Right now, you're in grave danger."

"From what? The boogeyman? Hunter killed whatever it was that attacked us—"

"Not exactly," Sam said, cutting her off.

"What do you mean?"

"Actually, Hunter only wounded the rogue. Mercedes and her men eventually killed it."

All of them? For one rogue? Not good. "Hunter also said it was a young vampire. How's this possible?"

Sam's brows drew together, and she bit her lip. "We're not quite certain yet."

"All right," Tori replied. "You want to call that thing that attacked me a rogue, go ahead. But it's dead. Which means I have no worries."

She watched with disbelief as Sam's features turn grave. "Again, I understand all of this is a bit much to comprehend. But I assure you, the danger is real. Two other vampires who we suspect are about to go rogue have your scent. When they turn, they'll come back for your blood. Their last meal."

Vampires, *Sinsir,* and rogues. Oh my!

"You do realize how this sounds, don't you?" Sam didn't answer. But she'd heard and stood there, trying to be patient. "Okay. Fine. You've made your point. But I can't simply drop everything," Tori replied. "I have a life. I have my work. People counting on me."

"I understand completely. However, arrangements can be made." Tori stared. "Arrangements can always be made."

Really. "And if I don't want arrangements to be made?"

"A decision of this nature would be unwise." She watched Sam sigh. The vampire queen cocked her head as if listening, then stepped back. "I must go. I'm needed elsewhere. Finish your breakfast, and I'll ask Mercedes to bring you down to the lab. Perhaps I can convince you to at least take a…let's call it an emergency vacation."

Tori had no intention of upending her life simply because they said she was in danger. "Go and do what you have to. Just understand I'll do the same," she told Sam.

"Understood."

She smiled. But researching their biology? Now there was a tantalizing thought. "I still have a ton of questions to ask." Especially of Hunter.

"By all means." Sam relaxed and winked. "And no, Hunter won't be there. Maybe later."

Tori laughed. "I'm really going to have to learn how to stop thinking, aren't I?"

"Yes," Sam laughed. "You are."

Chapter Seven

HUNTER WATCHED TORI LOPE TOWARD HIM. SHE HAD THE ROLLING gait of a cheetah, long legs that ate up ground. That ate him up.

Focus!

Turned out focusing would be hard. No, extremely hard. He'd allowed her some freedom and exercise to explore the grounds and watched her walk through the extensive gardens. Hunter wasn't used to beauty, dismissed external splendor as an extravagance he couldn't afford. Now he wondered. Perhaps the time had come to simply enjoy what had been placed in front of him.

Dr. Victoria Roberts had no idea how beautiful she was. Hunter had seen enough women throughout his existence on this earth to know. And while external beauty was always pleasing, her inner strength and fortitude attracted him to no end.

Hunter shook his head, surprised with himself for sending Mercy away. His attraction to Tori made her dangerous, incredibly dangerous.

While giving her some time to digest who and what he was, he realized another danger. The gardens might've been meaningless, but she was not, and her importance concerned him. Humans and vampires were, at best, a bad blend. Although Charles and Stacy were together, they were an anomaly, the exception to the rule. But a human placed right in the middle of a personal vampire dispute? *Dispute*, he snorted to himself. All-out war was more like it. Either he or Casperian was bound to end up dead by the other's hand. Damn! All of this was his fault. He'd put Tori in this danger and could find no way to get her out.

"Apologies. Mercy had business elsewhere, and I wanted to explain there was no insult meant when you woke up."

The muscles in her cheek tightened. He could see a tiny vibration below the corner of her eye. "You could've thrown some of my things in a bag."

"I didn't think of it. Your safety was uppermost in my mind."

"Really," she drawled. "And you couldn't have borrowed something from Mercy? Or Sam?"

"Again, I didn't think of it. I'm sorry." Hunter paused, a hint of trepidation mixed with guilt in his gut. "You asked me for the truth, so I shall give it to you. I wanted to admire your beauty as you slept. Nothing more."

"Some people might call that perverted."

"Is art perverted, then?"

She didn't answer, and Hunter escorted her downstairs. He watched awe fill her face as she glanced around the laboratory, her previous ire forgotten. "Whoa. This is some place."

"We can make it better. What would you suggest?"

She didn't even hesitate. "A chemistry analyzer. Preferably one that can also run immunoassays. A hematology analyzer for cell counts. An electrophoresis system for protein determination. Coag analyzer. Microplate readers, washers, and scanners. A really, really good microscope. Like molecular. Benchtop centrifuges."

Had she said this to shake him? "It can be arranged."

Her eyes widened. "Sam kinda said the same thing. You do realize how expensive this is going to be, don't you?"

"Resources aren't a problem." Her brow raised. "We have certain artifacts saved over time that are worth a great deal." Hunter decided not to elaborate. Certain aspects of vampire existence didn't really need to be explained further.

"Imagine what you could do at a high stakes poker game," she murmured. "You'd know everyone's hand in advance."

"Using my abilities would be cheating," he replied. But Hunter already knew he wasn't above such an act. Survival was and always would be the name of the game. But now was not the time to delve into this topic. He brought the subject of their conversation back where it belonged. "You've made me curious. Why didn't Stacy ask for these things?"

She laughed softly. "Although Stacy was blood banker, she's a forensic chemist now. I'm a clinical pathologist. She deals more with investigating outside the body, so she went for the mass spec and the chromatograph. I investigate inside the body. I went for the analyzers."

"Interesting."

"Are you going to kidnap me?" she asked. Was she trying to catch him off guard?

Was she thinking she could? "I can still hear your thoughts," he answered, explaining how futile that possibility really was.

"Yeah. I know. Doesn't make me very happy either," she bit out.

"Apologies," he added sincerely. She bowed her head, acknowledging he couldn't help it.

"The one rule we prize above all others is free will. There aren't any chains on any doors." Hunter reached into his pocket and gave her cell phone back. He'd even charged it for her. "You're free to leave."

Surprise filled her face. She stared at him hard, as if trying to read his mind. "You'll be harder to guard in this way. But make no mistake, I will guard you. The person responsible for the first attack is trying to get at me through you. You're a target he'd like nothing better than to use."

Venatorius.

Even now his voice echoed in his mind, causing a slight shudder.

"Person?"

Her tone stung. And helped him collect his thoughts. "A long-standing disagreement," Hunter answered, deciding to continue as if she hadn't asked.

Yet the past wouldn't leave him be. It would never leave him be. And so once again, the past invaded is his mind.

"Where have you been, Venatorius? I sent for you hours ago."

Had he cared, he would have said his master's voice irked him to no end, high-pitched, petulant, and demanding as it was. "I have been training, my lord. Was it not your wish for me to win the games tomorrow?"

"Indeed. However, I required your attendance."

He bowed. "I came as soon as your summons arrived." Not exactly true. He'd taken his time on purpose. Because it was one thing he could do. "I am here now."

"Are you, Venatorius? Are you?"

You will never know. For that is my weapon against you. *"I am your slave, Dominus," came his bland reply.*

He put just enough puzzlement into his tone to make sure his master believed him. He knew he'd succeeded when his master sighed. A servant brought a vase filled with oil and scented water. His master dipped his hands in the water first, dried them off, and then poured the oil into his palm. His master's hand, the hand covered in oil, caressed his biceps. Venatorius sought refuge in a place no one could reach him. When he found it, the hand meant no more to him than the wind or the sun.

"What do you think of, I wonder? I have performed this ritual with you every day since I purchased you."

His master's hand caressed his chest, rolling over his huge muscles, fingers splayed to cover as much of his skin as possible. He knew what his master craved and refused to give in. "You retreat when I touch you. Why?"

"Retreat, lord?" A vast expanse of emptiness spread out before his psyche. He didn't retreat, would never retreat. As a gladiator, he was expected to fight and live, or fight and die. The word retreat *was as foreign to him as the word* freedom. *"I stand here before you exactly as you require."*

His master used two hands to work over his skin. They kneaded the aches out of his tired muscles. He supposed he should be grateful.

Grateful. For being allowed to live.

He preferred the silence and allowed his master to work on his body without thought. "Do you dislike my touch?"

"I do not think about it."

His master snorted. "You wound with the subtlety of an elephant, Venatorius."

"Wound, lord? Again, I do not understand. I am a slave. I am not allowed to like or dislike."

The hand caressing his chest now worked lower over his abdomen. "Every day. Every day." And lower. His master's fingers cupped his balls, massaging gently. "You never respond." The words were almost an accusation. "Where do you go?" his master asked again. "Where do you hide?"

Where you can't find me.

Hunter returned to the present, bitterness filling his mouth. There was something very wrong with the thought of being grateful to be alive. And when he'd protested the constant killing? No reason to be grateful for the punishment that should have killed him.

"A disagreement I'd prefer you not be involved in," he told Tori, trying to keep his resentment out of his tone. "This isn't your fault. But neither of us has a choice. Either we do this the easy way or the hard way."

"For you, you mean."

He smiled. But his gut had already begun a slow burn. She still refused to see the magnitude of his predicament. And hers. "Of course."

His smile faded, anger burning deep. "Perhaps you could arrange to take a small amount of time off?" he asked Tori. "Surely you'd like to perform some of your experiments on us? After all, not only are we not human, we're not even animals, are we? Another kind of lab rat, right?"

Her eyes widened. "Damn you! Get out of my head!"

How was she able to get under his skin? Where was the cold indifference he managed so well? "I wish I could. Believe me."

"Look. I'm sorry," she apologized, seeming sincere. "What I was thinking wasn't nice. And I don't normally go out of my way to be nasty. But you haven't exactly been all warm and fuzzy with me either. Let's call a truce."

"What kind of truce?" he asked, more suspicion in his tone than he wanted.

"You're right. I would like to investigate. Your...race...offers an unprecedented opportunity to study a different type of biology." Her chin lifted, her next words filled with righteous pride. "But you need to come down off your perch too. Just because I'm human doesn't make me lower than the dirt you walk on either."

"Agreed," he retorted, knowing deep inside she was right. "You'll have to forgive my prejudice, I'm afraid. You see, when I was human, I was exactly that."

"Exactly what?" she asked, confused.

"Lower than the dirt you walk on," he replied using her exact phraseology.

Hunter couldn't believe he was telling her this. Only Sam and Charles knew. "I'm nearly two thousand years old, Tori. And when I was human, I was a gladiator and a slave."

Chapter Eight

Was it true? Two thousand years old? A gladiator and a slave?

If so, Hunter would be fiercely protective of the right to be free.

Tori couldn't help wondering as they crawled along with Saturday-afternoon shore traffic going down the parkway. July weather in September brought out the beachgoers trying to bolster the last of their summer tans. She tapped her fingers against the steering wheel in frustration. Tori hated traffic.

She glanced over for about the ninetieth time. Hunter had given her a car, a very tripped-out luxury car. With one caveat. He had to come along for the ride.

Shaking her head, Tori wasn't sure of anything anymore. Why had she agreed to this madness? Because of one thing and one thing only. The vulnerability in his gaze as he'd told her what he'd been. Which, for the record, she still wasn't quite sure she believed.

Vampire. Gladiator. Self-appointed protector. Lover?

He shifted in his seat. In repose he looked younger, softer, and more approachable. And he probably knew every thought flying around inside her head. So she turned on the radio, low, and, without even realizing as they inched along, began to sing.

"You have a beautiful voice," he murmured.

Startled, Tori threw him a look. His eyes were closed and face seemed content. "I thought you were sleeping."

"I was. Your singing woke me."

"That bad, huh?" she asked.

"On the contrary. I haven't heard such a pure sound in a very long time." He settled in his seat. "Why do you hide something so beautiful?"

About to deny, Tori answered with the truth instead. "Stage fright. I guess I'm afraid people will judge me. That's the one thing you can always count on from the dead. They don't judge." She bit her lip, a hint of the devil riding her. "Present company excluded."

She looked over to catch his mouth quirk. Yet his eyes didn't open. "I promise not to judge, then. Would you continue?" He paused. As if he didn't make requests of others very often. "Would you sing some more for me? Please?"

A man like Hunter commanded. He didn't ask. Softly at first, she sang. Then with more gusto until she finished by belting out the last verse. He clapped gently when she was done. "Thank you."

Not sure how she felt about what she'd done, she murmured, "You're welcome."

How long had it been before she'd been able to warble even a note? Music came from the heart, but she'd lost hers a long time ago. She was told time healed all wounds. Not exactly.

"Are you all right? I sense a terrible sadness in you. As I did the night of the wedding."

Both hands clenched the steering wheel. She thought of a spring day and an empty field to stem the rise of her emotions. If she shouted out her feelings, she wasn't going to let him hear these particular thoughts. Her past was none of Hunter's business.

"I'm fine," she answered, loosening her fingers from around the plastic. Driving helped, as she had to concentrate on the road now that the traffic was moving faster.

They continued until Tori was finally able to get off the parkway. She drove down a main artery and pulled into the hospital parking lot for staff only. "Do me a favor, please? Stay in the car. I'll be as quick as I can."

"No, I won't be hard to explain," he protested, reading her thoughts again.

Tori rolled her eyes. But she was glad he hadn't yet seen the hurt she kept buried deep inside. "Okay, you won't. But I'll never hear the end of it, and you might not get out unscathed. I work with a lot of single women."

She watched him shudder at her words and wondered if he could see the picture she created in her mind. A smile grew on his face. "No need for the picture, I assure you. I promise not to move."

Tori got out of the car, walked into the school for medical laboratory science where she taught a couple of classes and helped direct the clinical chemistry department. She walked in to find her boss in his office. "Frank. You're still here."

Frank looked up, obviously wondering why she was there on a Saturday afternoon. "In the flesh."

Tori bit her lip. What was it, lately, with everything everyone said ending up like a vampire joke? "I have to ask for a favor."

Her boss frowned, leaning back in his chair, the springs creaking badly—like most of their equipment, held together with spit and rubber bands. "What's wrong? Are you okay? You look a little pale."

Pale? Flesh? Ugh!

Tori shook her head to get the vampire humor out of her head. She let go of a deep breath, wondering how good an actress she could be, although the pain of it never left her. Ever. "I hired a private detective." While this was true, the rest would be a lie. She lied, hating to do so, but there was no other way Frank would let her go. "I got a call from him last night. He's up in Minnesota." Minnesota was far enough away not to warrant being followed. "He has a lead on one of the perps."

"Bastards," Frank muttered, bringing her to the present with a jolt. "Freaking goddamned bastards." He grimaced. "At least one of them paid the price."

How could she answer? That she was glad one had been a drug

addict and had OD'd shortly after he'd murdered her family? She wasn't anymore. She just wanted the pain to stop. "Yes."

"God, Tori." Frank's gaze hurt with her.

Tori did what she did best. She stopped breaking. She denied the emptiness. She surrounded the hole inside with a wall so it wouldn't destroy her. She shared the moment all over again with her boss.

"I'm so sorry," Frank continued. "It must be hell having all of this dredged up every time someone thinks they've found something."

Hell? Frank would never understand. You had to lose a child, a beautiful blonde, blue-eyed pixie to understand.

"For the record," he continued, "I remember every second of that flight."

Tori swallowed hard. She pictured a single brick. Then another. And another, slapping mortar in between until she could breathe again.

"I know. And I can't thank you enough, Frank. You know I can't. But you also know I don't have much of a choice." One tortured inhale. An exhale. Another brick. "Lately I've been wondering if it's even worth continuing the search. It won't bring Kelly or my folks back."

Tori struggled. Sometimes the construction didn't go so well. Sometimes pieces of the wall fell down. Sometimes entire pieces of her fell into the heap. And yet no matter how badly she shattered, she kept trying to put the pieces back together.

They'd found Kelly slumped against the wall. Her neck snapped like a matchstick. When Tori had found out, she'd thought the world ended. But there was more, so much more.

Tori's eyes fluttered open to a semi-sterile hotel room. She wondered for a moment what she was doing in one. Weak light filtered through two not-quite-closed curtains. She stared at the ceiling, trying to swallow past a tongue two sizes too large.

Hotel food. Ugh. Too much salt.

She reached for the half-empty water bottle on the nightstand and drained it. She sat up, feeling odd and a bit woozy, thanking her common sense for not going with everyone for a last nightcap.

Swinging her legs over the bed, she reached for her phone. Five missed calls?

Her stomach hollowed. She shook her head to concentrate. She didn't recognize the number. Then she asked the most important question. Why hadn't she heard her phone go off? She hit the Volume button. Damn. That last meeting. She'd turned it down and forgotten to turn it up.

Her heart pounded. The hollow in her belly became a pit, ready to sink her at a moment's notice. She scrolled through her received calls. Pain shot through her brain. She ignored it. No voicemails, no calls from her father. She drew in a pure sigh of relief. All quiet on the Tuckerton front.

Tori leaned back and rubbed at her face. She waited for the pounding in her brain and the trembling to subside. Then she looked at her phone again. Just the same number. Breathing carefully to keep her head from exploding, she trudged into the bathroom, took a couple of pain relievers, downed more water, walked back by the bed, and then she called.

"Hello? You called me?"

"Dr. Roberts?"

"Speaking."

"This is Detective Whitlock."

Whitlock? Her brain drew up a picture of a stern, serious-looking young man with a buzz cut. "You called several times. A little early to be working on a Sunday morning, isn't it?" Then she realized. CST. She was an hour ahead.

"Where are you, Doctor?"

"Chicago. At a conference. Why?"

He drew in a deep breath. Her fingers tightened on her phone. "I'm sorry to have to inform you, but there was an attempted robbery at your parents' house last night."

Her hand shook in earnest. Her heart pounded in her ears. The water in her stomach flipped over, sloshing like a rough sea. A little bile rose up her throat. She swallowed the sour taste back down. "A robbery? Is everyone all right? Was anyone hurt?"

"I'm afraid your father was badly injured. Your mother was knocked unconscious."

Tori shook her head no. Her dad? *Images of her father broken and bleeding flashed through her mind. Her knees gave way, and she fell onto the edge of the bed, mind racing. She needed to hold him. Tell him she was there. He'd be okay. No, she needed to call Frank and tell him to get them on the next flight home. Then her brain fired on all eight cylinders. If her father and mother were in the hospital...*

"Detective, who has my daughter? Where is she? Did she see any of it? Please tell me you have her and she's safe."

A long silence. Why? What was going on? "We have her."

Thank God. But something was still off. "Detective, you're scaring me. What's going on? Where's my daughter? Where's Kelly?"

A very deep breath. "Your daughter is dead, Doctor. I'm sorry."

NO, NO, NO, NO, NO. Impossible.

"You need to get back to New Jersey as soon as possible. We're doing every-thing in our power to find the men who did this." Her turn not to answer. "I'm sorry for your loss."

Frank! Pick up, dammit! *"Hello?"*

"Frank. It's Tori. I don't even know where to begin. I just got a call from the Tuckerton police. Kelly is...Kelly is..." If she said the words, they'd be true. But they couldn't be true. No. Not possible. This was all a mistake. A terrible mistake. She didn't believe it. She wasn't going to. "Something about a robbery."

"Oh my God, Tori." Silence. Did he understand? Could he? They were wrong. That's all. Kelly was fine. She was sleeping in her bed. With Teddy. "Listen. I'll call the airline," Frank said. "Just get dressed and pack. We're out of here as soon as possible."

How did a person know when they were truly broken? Did the pieces all fall together in a heap, or did one section slough off at a time?

Tori walked into the morgue, more than familiar with the room. The bubble that had surrounded her through the flight and the drive home kept reality out. She walked over to the table. They lifted the sheet. Her hand lifted to tuck it back in. Just as if she was home.

"She needs Teddy, Frank. She always has Teddy with her when she sleeps."

Next to her, Frank drew in a ragged breath. "C'mon, Tori. We need to get you home."

"Yes," she mumbled. "Home. Kelly is home."

There was a reason why she worked with the dead. It was easier to live this way.

"I'll need a couple weeks' emergency vacation," she continued, finally halting the torture inside her brain.

"A couple of weeks?" Frank echoed with chagrin. "Really?"

She nodded. "I know my request puts you on the spot." God, she hated lying and hoped her face didn't reveal her deception. "But it's not like I take vacations."

He looked away but not before she caught the commiseration. "I know."

"Listen, Frank. You lived with this too. First Kelly, then my dad going a couple weeks later and then my mom. I know the police have tried," she sighed. "But I'm warning you. If this isn't settled for good, I might just end up in a not-so-expensive rest stop. So be prepared. The vacation might end up permanent."

Frank shook his head and tsked. "You do realize I can't let you do that, don't you? I really need you? I need you alive and working? Here? Sane? Not in an institution? Yes?"

"Thanks for the genuine note of caring," Tori muttered back. "You're a real treasure."

Frank laughed gently. "I know."

Was she really tired of the pain or tired of fighting? When had she changed? In the beginning, the fire of hatred kept her body functioning, kept her mind filled so she hadn't had to feel. And she had every right. Now? Funny, for the first time Tori wasn't so sure.

But then she thought of Hunter. Was it right to be like him? So cold and unfeeling? Hating humans? And, it seemed, even hating existence? Tori shook her head. So much effort. And where would all that expended energy get her?

Her boss, friend, and confidant drew in a deep breath and let out the air slowly. "All right. Two weeks. Not a day more. That's all I can cover." His brows drew together almost into a straight line. "And I'm not bailing you out of anything you get yourself into, do you read me?"

Would she trade her life for a taste of revenge? Tori mock-saluted. No. There was still a part of her deep inside that believed in the oath. And a part of her was bone weary from asking why all the time. She swallowed her feelings. It was either bury her pain or break down completely. "Yes, sir." She turned to leave.

"Hey, Tori?"

She swung her head around. "Yeah?"

"I'm sorry. Deeply sorry."

As if he hadn't told her those very same words already about a thousand times. "I know. Thanks."

Tori hated using Kelly and her folks as an excuse. Talking about them only dredged up the pain. Kind of like whip marks on your back that never healed, then got whipped again. Stinging and biting and ending with an ache deep inside. But it was the only plausible excuse she could come up with. Frank knew her too well to believe she would just up and go on a trip to Greece or something.

Tori walked back to the car, filled with those old wounds and a new wave of heartache. She tried to control her thoughts and failed. Hunter's seat was upright, and there was compassion in his gaze as she got in. She didn't want to explain, but he already knew her pain. She put it into words for the first time in a long time.

"Peter and I were engaged to be married. We were searching for places where we could do our residencies together. He was going to be a surgeon. I was sticking with pathology. My birth control failed, and I got pregnant. He left. Decided he didn't want kids. But I had Kelly."

He didn't answer right away. Then he asked, "How did they die?"

Tori choked out the words. "I went to a conference out of town. My first 'vacation' in I can't tell you how long. While I was partying and having a good time, my parents were murdered and my daughter discarded like a piece of garbage. Home invasion. The police said my folks were easy targets." She drew in a deep breath. "My dad. He—he kept a baseball bat by the bed. The police think he tried to go after the robbers, and that's when everything went south."

Tori pictured another brick and another, slapping down mortar with a vengeance. It didn't help. For a moment she wanted to double over and start screaming, never to stop. The cold in his tone had the same effect as a bucket of ice water. "I'm sorry."

"Really," she drawled.

Was she being unfair? Perhaps he wasn't just cold and unfeeling. Maybe he was trying to get her to buck up by not playing into pity. At least the question helped her get back on track.

She tightened her fingers around the steering wheel before letting go. "So am I." Rather than let him see her confusion, her weakness,

Tori filled her mind with an evil picture. "I'm sure what I'm thinking right now isn't exactly legal."

His mouth quirked. Yet his gaze told her he knew pain. This kind of pain. "I've done worse."

Tori swallowed hard. "My mother and father were old fashioned, normal, regular grandparents. I was told they went shopping in the afternoon to buy Kelly a present. That was how the thieves marked them." Tears filled her eyes. "I can't help thinking if they hadn't gone shopping that day. If they'd stayed home. If *I'd* stayed home. If my father hadn't tried to go after them. So many ifs."

Tori shuddered, locking down on the breach. "They loved her so much."

"And you?"

She didn't answer. How could she put into words the hole he was trying to find? Love? Such a paltry word. Kelly had been her everything.

And they still couldn't find the other men who'd done it. Maybe this was why she couldn't speak. Some kind of closure, any kind of closure would help fill the hole in her heart. Wouldn't it?

His hand reached out and covered one of hers for a moment. "Again, you have my sympathies, Tori. Your justice system is complex. And perhaps rather lacking. Should you wish, I can look into the matter for you?"

With a bitterness that would never heal her she shot back, "Lacking? Right." Tori shook her head. "No thanks. You might bite first and ask questions later. I wouldn't want the wrong person hurt."

He snorted. "We don't make those kinds of mistakes."

Horrified, Tori shot back, "I don't profess to be prescient. Why do you?" She paused. "Or maybe the question should be how can you? What—or should I ask—who gave you that right?"

The answer to her questions was because he could. All of the above. Which made her mad.

She started the car and drove to her house using the need to focus to calm down. His singularity frightened her. He constantly cut to the chase, centered on a purpose without deviating. So did his arrogance.

She couldn't understand what it was like to be that sure of something. Then she did. He could read minds.

"I come from a simple place, a simple time," she began, doubting very much if he'd understand. "A community where people don't lock cars or doors. Where neighbors watch out for everyone's kid, not only their own. We all belong to one another. I wouldn't have the temerity to become judge and jury."

Because his eyes were closed, she couldn't read his exact meaning when he murmured, "Maybe you should."

Wouldn't feeling entitled to those judgments become revenge and not justice? She almost posed the question out loud. Then she thought better of the idea. Hunter wouldn't understand. Then she realized once again he probably heard it anyway. Yet he didn't answer, and she appreciated his discretion. ·

As they pulled into her parking lot she said, "I have to clean, close up, do laundry, and pack. Not exactly exciting."

"Not a problem. I shouldn't go outside until late afternoon or so. I'll just doze."

They went in, his coat and a broad-brimmed hat protecting him. He hung up both in her closet, unlike most of the men she knew who would just throw them on or over the back of a chair. Then he sat down and made himself comfortable on her couch. Just once, she wished she could know what was going on in that head of his. Way better than what was going on in hers, she imagined.

But she did have a question. "You know, if you can't go outside and I get attacked…?"

He laughed softly. "I have sworn to protect you. Do you really think a little sunburn would stop me from saving you?"

"Just curious," she answered, although the tiny sear of warmth at his words made her next statement a lie. "Wondering how far your allegiance would go."

"I made you a promise," he insisted.

"You didn't have to."

"No, I didn't. But I did so enough. Trust me."

Yeah. The little word that meant so much. "Right."

Chapter Nine

HUNTER WATCHED HER WORK THROUGH HALF-CLOSED EYES. THE house seemed spotless to him, but she wiped and scoured and dusted until the place sparkled. Humans called it obsessive-compulsive behavior, but Hunter called it coping.

Pain. He understood his own but had never really considered another's before, or that there could be such varying degrees from so many different causes. Did different causes make one type of pain less than another? No, he decided, simply different and no less hard to bear.

A load of laundry went into the washer, then she went into her bedroom. He listened to the shower run. He rose, knowing what was going to happen. In Tori, he found a kindred spirit. They both knew loss. They even shared a common pain, the loss of a loved one, though she didn't know that yet. He knew of only one way to ease such incredible pain.

He opened the bathroom door quietly, watching steam surround her body. His heart stopped. Just that fraction-of-a-second missed beat, that jolt of awareness. All too familiar but in a different context. Always with the need, with the blood. Never with a woman, until now.

So brave to continue, to go on despite the devastation. He tried to imagine. Was it better to be so far away and not know the actual events, or was it better to have the horror happen before your very eyes? Hunter decided the best thing for both of them was to block out the pain by seeking succor. He opened the shower door and stepped inside. Droplets of hot water snaked down his skin. Every cell the fluid touched woke up, took notice, and drank in the water as he did the blood.

"Do you know how beautiful you are?"

Hunter hated painted faces. He hated the smell of makeup, cloying and stifling. Both sight and smell reminded him of the rich wives who'd paid his master for his services. Women with their fawning fingers and men with their furtive glances, they'd owned him, therefore what had been wrong had become right. But with her hair slicked back, Tori looked fresh, alive, and real. She looked right. And she smelled clean, of citrus and herbs.

Her gaze met his, searching. Her eyes were so soft, so round, they seemed infinite, yet they were filled with disbelief. Tori was intelligent enough to understand the consequences of his actions. They both knew she should push open the door and demand he step back out to drip onto the rug and shiver as the water turned cold on his skin. But all she did was acknowledge the danger. "You shouldn't be in here."

Even as she said the words she was working at the buttons on his shirt. He helped undo his trousers, letting them fall. She splayed her fingers across his chest, exploring, learning every muscle. He shucked his shirt and stood naked before her.

"I've done many things in my existence I shouldn't have done," he replied, deciding they were both wrong. He pulled her into his embrace. "This isn't one of them."

She stared up at him with the innocence of a doe and the strength of a lioness. He bent to one knee to pay homage. Not just to her body but to her.

Hunter started at her breasts, lathing each nipple into a tiny rock and then nipping just enough to make her jump. He kissed his way down her belly and over the soft curve of her hip, never touching her core, simply licking the outside of her folds until she was so aroused she'd come if he but breathed on her.

Somewhat satisfied, Hunter rose. She nearly jumped on him to get him inside her, clawing and begging. But he had other plans. He turned off the water and sluiced the droplets from their bodies with his hands. She lifted onto her toes to kiss him. He held back. She cocked her head, fingers caressing his cheeks, thumbs grazing his lips. By sheer will, she pulled his head closer and closer until their tongues began to mate. Each time she grazed one of his incisors, he jumped, a shiver of pleasure racing through him.

Leaning back, she broke the kiss. "That is so fascinating."

"Mood killer," he groused.

She laughed softly. "Never," she whispered as she brought his head back down again. She kissed the hell out of him, and Hunter realized he didn't want it to end. Then it did as she jerked back, fell to her knees, and paid homage to him.

Uh-oh.

Oh, he'd been the recipient of talented tongues. And sucked off more times than he cared to remember, especially by other men. But never worshiped. No one had taken the time, not the painted patrons, the whores, not even the one-night stands. Yet each time she nibbled, each time she teased, each time her tongue snaked out to tantalize, he knew. She was taking the time to learn his body. No one had ever cared what he wanted or what he felt.

Not even the blood. Until now.

The revelation rocked him right down to his toes. She cared.

Hunter's teeth clicked shut, and his breath hissed inward between them. He pulled her head away, lifted her to her feet, slid open the shower door, dried them both off with a quick swipe of a towel, and pulled her into the bedroom.

He could hear her heart racing—indeed, his was too. Her blood called to him, but this moment was about lovemaking. He pushed the urge deep down where it couldn't get out and flipped her over. She held on to her bed as he plunged into her warm cavern from behind, licking at her back with his tongue.

She cried out, and he filled her until he could go no farther. Then he slid out and slammed into her again.

Hunter sank into sensation. Her warmth enveloped him. Her inner muscles clenched and let go, drawing out every ounce of feeling. He pulled out and thrust again, finding a rhythm between their bodies. She reached the brink, and he stilled until she shuddered, waiting until she cooled off enough for him to begin again.

He reached up to caress her breasts and play with her nipples. She growled. He thrust deep inside and growled with her. Sometimes the build was slow. Sometimes hard and fast sated the body but not the mind. But this? Together they were lightning. Together they were thunder. Together they outshone even the gods and made a mockery of them. Together they came.

The explosion emanated from everywhere. Light flashed before closed eyelids. She shouted. He cried out. They shattered together.

Another first in a night of firsts. Hunter found release. Never pleasure. But at this moment, collapsed on top of her back, his own blood pounding in his ears, Hunter found all that had been missing in his bleak and terrifying existence.

Peace.

Chapter Ten

TORI CAME TO AWARENESS IN STAGES. HER HEAT WARMED HIS SKIN, which in turn warmed her as he lay wrapped around her, one arm about her waist, curved to meet her entire length. She settled into the mattress completely content. His arm tightened, and Tori decided she didn't really want to turn over. Instead, she relaxed and sank back down into his protective embrace.

Tori didn't normally sleep with men. Okay, such a statement wasn't exactly right. Tori didn't invite men to sleep in her bed overnight. Even afterward. She never wanted to get close to another human being again. Close meant opening. Close meant joy. Tori had no right to that emotion ever again. Close meant laughter, not tears. Close meant trying to live. And how could she try to live when all she felt was the constant pain of loss?

She'd been through every stage of blame. First, last, and always herself for not being home when they'd tried to rob the house. Second, her father for doing what had come so naturally to him, protecting his family. Third, her mother for suggesting the outing in the first place.

What good did blaming everyone do? Did it bring them back?

So much better to simply exist in the world and let the wall take care of the emptiness. Only she wasn't alone, now was she? And Hunter simply felt right beside her. How was that? Rather than answer, Tori dozed, flagrantly dismissing the rest of the things she needed to do. And when she awoke a second time, she was alone on the bed, covered by a blanket against the chill of the early autumn air coming through an open window and sated beyond belief.

She threw on a T-shirt and slacks and stepped out of the bedroom. The dishes she'd left on the counter from the dishwasher had been put away. The laundry she'd left in the washing machine had been dried and now sat neatly folded in the laundry basket. He'd even washed and dried his own clothes. And the garbage she'd left to throw in the outdoor trash was gone.

Hunter sat in her recliner, regarding her carefully. Tori decided to keep things neutral. "You're handy to have around."

She tried to read him, but he sat behind his stoic demeanor like it was a shield. "I don't like being idle."

Bemused, Tori simply stared. If she couldn't read him, she left herself open to all sorts of thoughts which, of course, led to all sorts of chaos inside as her gaze drank in every detail of his chiseled features. "Umm, thank you."

So hard to comprehend. Every time she thought she understood him, even a piece of him, he retreated. He became the ice man, taking what was around him inside but never letting anything out.

And yet she knew the river of fire flowing just beneath his cold hard exterior. She'd drowned in it. Which begged the question, who was Hunter? Why the on-off switch all the time? Tori wondered if she'd ever know as she walked over and lifted the laundry basket to put her clothes away. "If I'm going to move in for a couple of weeks, I need to pack some clothes and things."

"Anything you need can be provided. All of the equipment you requested will be delivered tomorrow."

"Tomorrow? On a Sunday? Impossible," she blurted.

He smiled. "Nothing is impossible. Arrangements can always be made."

Laughter bubbled, but she held it down. Sam'd said the same thing to her. "I'm beginning to get that."

Was his an offer she wasn't supposed to refuse? Not that she would after what they'd just shared. Then it hit her. Was this all one sided? Had they shared?

He stared at her, his gaze guarded. He'd heard the question loud and clear and wasn't giving her a hint of his true feelings. So here was another one. Did she even want him to share? Then she realized. She was playing with him. Stepping forward. Stepping back. Tori hated those kinds of games.

Her gaze fell to the floor. There was safety in the wood. From his thoughts. From hers. From what was going on between them.

"I've taken the liberty of ordering in." Talk about banal. "I hope you don't mind."

Don't think right now. It's easier not to think. Picture the ocean. "I could've cooked. Just for one, and all."

"Not necessary," he replied, studying her. "Food delivery services are very convenient."

Am I too? The words popped into her mind before she could stop them.

He frowned to hide—what? Was that? Could that actually be hurt in his gaze? Because she thought him capable of being beyond callous?

"Of course, you would know this being a two-thousand-year-old vampire," she added to keep a rein on her thoughts.

"Nineteen hundred and seventy-eight, to be exact."

Tori wasn't sure how to feel. One minute he was pulling her close, trying to make her feel better, and the next? God he could be cold.

"And for that very reason," he replied, still showing little to no emotion.

Tori wondered if she'd ever get under that thick skin of his. Did she even want to? "What reason?"

"Knowledge is power. Knowledge is survival."

Her first thought was their complete lack of understanding about their own physiology. What could be more important? They had absolutely no idea what constituted their own biology. Then she thought of basic instincts. Animals didn't question what they were. Was this closer to the point? About to ask, Tori changed her mind. "You say those words as if you think it's an 'us' against 'them' world. Sam doesn't."

His face tightened. "I'm not as good at looking at the 'big' picture."

If what he'd told her was true, then he had just cause. "I guess I'll have to remember that."

"Nor am I capable of caring." Had he just issued a warning? Sure sounded like one.

Okay. Neither was she. "I guess I'll have to remember that too."

Tori turned and stormed into her bedroom. She started slamming the clothes from the basket into her drawers, then realized he could hear. Was everything a battle to him? Did he always have to be the victor?

She went into the shower, rinsed off, fixed her hair, and packed. It became a matter of pride. Because Sam was right. Humans were as good as vampires. And she was a whole lot tougher than she looked.

Her food arrived. Lobster mac and cheese. Tori opened a bottle of light rosé and sat down. "I'd prefer it, next time, if you'd stay out of my head. I'm capable of telling you what I'd like to eat. Humans talk with each other. They communicate. I'd have thought you'd remember."

He shrugged off her barb, went over to her bar, and picked out a cabernet. Pouring a small amount, he sat down next to her. "I'll try."

Stunned, Tori stared at the glass in his hand. "You can drink?"

"Small amounts," he answered with a slight grimace. "More, and we get violently ill."

Damn. Despite everything, despite this insane need to one-up each other, he fascinated her. "Liver and kidneys probably don't function well. If at all."

Tori swallowed a couple of bites. The dish was her fave. And really good. After another couple bites, she asked the question that needed asking. "Am I just an object, then? A thing to be used and discarded when you don't want me anymore?"

Strange, how he seemed to crawl inside himself. Why? He couldn't possibly feel guilty. He used every opportunity to push her away and to make sure she knew her place. "I tried to warn you.

What happened with Charles and Stacy should never have happened."

Confused Tori asked, "Why?"

"It is forbidden. Humans must not know we exist."

She stared at him hard. "And the real reason?"

He didn't answer at first, and she got her first glimpse of the wall. Only pain, the kind of pain she knew, made that kind of wall. "Because their union will only bring sorrow. She will live, what? Another sixty or seventy years? And then what?"

Suddenly Tori realized. "Who hurt you, Hunter?"

"Everyone."

Unable to truly comprehend his human life, Tori could only guess. But he knew. He understood. They shared common ground.

Still, because Tori was human, she defended. "I feel sorry for you because you'll never understand. No, correction: you'll never let yourself understand. Charles is willing to accept that agony. He loves her."

She took a sip of her wine and continued in earnest. Because these were the moments that enabled her to get out of bed in the morning and allowed her to trudge on through another day. "Look. I'm happy for them. Stacy is my friend. She's my best friend. If she's happy, nothing else matters," she continued. "She helped me live through a part of my life that was unlivable. I'll root for both of them."

But I carry the pain of a loss no one will understand. "But I already know where this ends up," she continued. "At least I have that. Chaz doesn't, and he'll have to learn this lesson the hard way. While I'm happy for both of them, I'm also really, really sad. Sometimes it's better to have lived and loved, isn't it?"

"Is it?" he barked at her. Bitterness surrounded his next words, spat out as if they were made from acid. "I wouldn't know."

"You didn't let me finish. Sometimes it isn't."

And then she saw it. The agony. So much deeper and so, so much more than she could ever have understood. "I loved once. As much as I was able."

"What happened?" she asked in the same earnest tone as before.

He seemed about to change his mind and not answer. Then in a low monotone he said, "My master found out I cared about her. Groped her in front of me. Forced me to watch. He made sure I knew what would happen next."

Tori's stomach turned over. She pushed her plate away and swallowed a quick sip of wine to remove the sour taste in her mouth. "I'm sorry."

Without raising his voice yet making the sound as cold as a winter's day he asked, "Are you? Because she was carrying my child. He made sure I knew exactly what would happen to the baby, what kind of slave it would become. Life became too much for her. Do you want to know why?"

Tori nodded because she needed to know.

"Because after my child was born, she knew he would force himself to use her again and again until she got pregnant. With his child this time. Because a child with patrician blood would make a truly good slave. Good stock. A better breed."

Bile rose in her throat. "Force himself?"

"Yes. He preferred men."

She sighed, hating the cruelty humans were capable of. "I guess you do know."

He nodded. They shared the pain of losing a loved one. Now the shower made sense. She reached out to cover his hand with hers. He pulled back. "I don't want your pity," he hissed.

Tori retreated and rose. Now Hunter made sense too. The push and pull. The warm and the cold. The take and no give. She emptied her plate in the garbage.

"We were things. Animals. Cows. Pigs. Slaves. Do you know what being a slave was like? To be painted and dressed and sold to the highest bidder every night? To fight in an arena and kill and kill and kill?" She watched him stare at his hands, and she knew he was seeing the blood on them.

"I tried to warn you," he shuddered, drawing in a deep breath to collect himself. "Don't care about me. I'm incapable of those kinds of feelings."

Hurt. Hurting for him, Tori rose. She picked up her wineglass and walked out onto her balcony to watch the night deepen. In the distance she could just about hear the ocean against the shore. A song entered her mind. An old Barry Manilow song whose words talked about the wonder of sharing and letting a person inside. She hoped he was listening as she sang it inside her head.

Because Hunter was wrong. Every fiber of her being told her she was right. The human race? Not known for its stellar moments. And God knew she'd been the victim of one of those moments. But Hunter's problem wasn't that he was incapable of feeling. They were kindred spirits in this sense, for his problem was he felt too much, and when the dam broke, those feelings would drown him. Destroy him.

Someday it would happen. She almost felt sorry for him. For when it did, he'd realize circumstances didn't make a man a man. Or a vampire a vampire.

What was inside did.

Chapter Eleven

TORI DRANK TOO MUCH. FINISHED THE BOTTLE. HUNTER DIDN'T stop her, hoping it would ease her pain. He wished for a moment he could join her and try to erase the memories haunting him.

He also knew nothing would.

Hunter tucked his past deep inside where it belonged and got down to the present. While Tori slept, he could use this time. So, Hunter hunted, with some unexpected help. As he scoured Tori's parking lot for any sign of Casperian or Casperian's miniors, a sleek, black sedan pulled into a space near Tori's townhouse.

Hunter knew his opponent all too well, making the extra help very welcome. Still, he'd given no order, so he flashed Mercedes a questioning glance as three of her soldiers slipped out of sight to guard Tori.

"I'm off duty, sir. As are my men."

Highly commendable. Mercy was the consummate soldier. "You should be enjoying your time off, then."

She paused, her mouth quirking as she picked up on the scent of his recent lovemaking. "As you've been doing, sir?"

Was she needling him? "Yes."

She seemed to hide a smile as she answered, "We all took care of that before we left the compound."

He frowned. "That still doesn't answer my question."

She shrugged. "I like her. This human. She's different."

"She's food," he reminded her.

Mercy surprised him with a sigh. "She wants to help us."

"She's dangerous. Emotional bonds are dangerous. They make us vulnerable."

"They make us"—she stared at him hard—"human."

Hunter didn't answer. He rubbed the back of his neck with his hand. Sam had said the same thing. His hand fell, fingers closing into a fist. He wasn't wrong. Invisibility was the key to survival.

"We need to accept change, sir. I was thinking of talking to Tori and asking... I've been wondering ever since I met her, and then, when I saw you take her down to the lab, the question came to me again." Mercy hesitated, and he wondered why.

"What question?"

"I keep wondering why we don't work on finding a blood substitute, something with the ability to sustain us, something that would make us free to blend into this world."

"This isn't a television show!" he shot back.

Mercy gave as good as she got. "I know." She surprised them both with her vehemence. "I also know time dictates change. At the very least, we need to know more about ourselves so we can survive."

"Perhaps," he sighed. "Though right now, we have a duty to fulfill." He held up his hand to stop Mercy's next tirade. "And we need to protect her so we can find out how these rogues are being created."

"My men are perfectly capable," Mercy shot back, her tone filled with frustration.

"No, they aren't," he insisted, knowing he was right. "Even all four of you. Even as well trained as you are. You're still working against the odds."

"Not when I'm around."

Hunter whirled. How the hell hadn't he sensed her? Damn, the woman was like a cat. And the absolute last person on earth he wanted to see now. "Vanessa. It's been a long time."

Flaming-red hair, emerald-green eyes. Tall. Almost as muscular as a man. Yet stunningly beautiful. Another Paladin who called herself Vanessa because one definition of the name was "being overlooked by others, taken for granted." He wasn't sure how that was possible. She was hard to miss.

"Hunter," she acknowledged.

Hunter couldn't help noticing as Mercy paled for a moment. He stiffened. "Let's agree to not like one another and be done with it," Vanessa added, her gaze not on him but on his lieutenant.

"All right. Let's also agree that I didn't ask for your help. This is a private matter."

She smiled. "Not so private anymore." She turned to look at him. "Mercy doesn't hold a grudge; why should you?"

Mercy swallowed hard, her tone like ice. "Don't put words in my mouth."

Vanessa smiled. "Perhaps I was a bit hasty in this part of my assessment." She slid her fingers over the side of the well-polished car in what looked like a caress. "Oh well."

"Serena was part of my cell," he growled. "She was unique. She had a way of—of bringing light into our darkness."

He could see the pain swirling in Vanessa's gaze. But not so much in her thoughts. Seemed Vanessa had grown over the years. She'd used to be much more transparent. "I don't normally admit this, but I actually loved her, you know."

Hunter's heart constricted. Every time he let his guard down and cared. Every time. "She was my daughter."

"As much as anyone can be these days. But I get it. It's easier to pin her death on me than on yourself. Just remember, Serena was like trying to cup water in your hand. There for a moment, then gone through your fingers. She was damaged way before she became a vampire." Vanessa let go of pretense, her voice turning to steel. "You should never have changed her."

Hunter thought of Tori, so strong, so steady. Then he thought of Serena, so mercurial, so flighty. Whimsical. But so beautiful. A beauty that shouldn't have gone to waste. "You're right. I should never have changed her."

Dead silence. Funny, Hunter never thought he'd ever surprise Vanessa.

"Did I just hear you correctly? Did you just admit making a mistake?" She laughed. How bitter she sounded. "Wait a minute. Why isn't the sky falling?"

"I think that's quite enough," he shot back. He lifted a single brow to make his point. "Trust me, it won't happen again."

"The mistake, or the admission?" she asked, enjoying his discomfort way too much for his liking.

"Both."

She leaned in. "Well, all right, then." She reared back. "Wait a minute. Is that—is that human perfume I smell?" Laughter swelled through the damp night air.

Hunter ignored her even though his guts burned. Serena wasn't a subject he wanted to focus on. "Mercy, get Vanessa situated and bring her up to speed before I kill her. Then both of you come and join me at the far end of the parking lot. There's no telling where or when these rogues will attack again. We have work to do."

Hunter walked away, but he could still hear.

"Ness. Stop. He admitted he made a mistake," Mercy admonished.

"Won't bring her back," Vanessa sighed. Hunter understood pain. He understood Vanessa's pain all too well.

"If he hadn't turned her, she would have died from her human wounds," Mercy continued. "You can't fault him for trying to save her. He thought he was doing the right thing."

"I know." Ah, there was the bitter overcoat, the taste that still lingered.

"There was no way to know she'd been trying to commit suicide."Hunter found he appreciated Mercy's defense of his actions, even though they didn't need defending. "Maybe she ran out of the house thinking better of it. Point is, human or vampire, she wanted to die. Eventually, she did."

"I know, damn it!" Poor Vanessa. They'd both loved the wrong woman for the right reasons. "I couldn't stop her." Then he asked himself the true question. Had his actions stemmed from love, or had they grown out of pity?

Silence. Long, drawn out, and telling. "You do realize," Mercy continued, "your pain tears me apart, don't you?"

Now Hunter could hear the misery in Vanessa's tone. The past did carry the sting of a viper at times. "I'm sorry. You know I never meant to hurt you."

"And I told you I'd take any piece of you I could get. Still will. But you need to get rid of her ghost. Or you'll never truly be free."

Ghosts. Letting go of them could be a difficult proposition, Hunter thought. Especially when they wanted to remove you from existence. He thought of Casperian, and his insides steeled. There would be a reckoning after all. Part of him rejoiced. The other part wondered.

The longer one lived, the more ghosts one seemed to compile.

Not a great place to be.

INTERLUDE

ANTONIUS FLAVIUS PROCULUS CASPERIAN DESPISED FAILURE. HE despised these "modern" men even more. Not one of them had an ounce of strength in them. Not one of them would withstand the intricacies of an emperor's court. Why, he'd had slaves tending pigs with more brains. And to return empty handed? So very, very unacceptable.

"Such a simple task, gentlemen. Such a simple task. Kidnap one human female and bring her to me unharmed."

Neither vampire spoke. Thank the gods! At least they understood the peril in such an act.

"I even allowed you to taste the Nirvana," he chided. "To enhance your powers."

"We only did what you said sir," the one called Peter answered. "Honest."

"Did you?" Casperian asked, ignoring the man. "You know the rules. Nirvana is not to be trifled with. When I gave my consent, when I allowed you all to taste, my order was to be carried out with moderation. With restraint. Did you think there'd be no consequences?"

"Sir?" the one called Harry squeaked. Such a pity, a name like Harry. Short. Dismal. Without honor. Much like the vampire trembling before him. "Sir?" he asked again. Casperian watched his Adam's apple bob up and down as the idiot swallowed hard. At least this one knew enough to be frightened. "Donnie couldn't help himself, sir. It was like he was, well, addicted. Kept talking about it. All the time. Never stopped. Got to be annoying after a while. Nirvana this, Nirvana that. I wanted to shut him up, I did."

"Yes, yes," he waved the answer away. "I'm beginning to understand."

An unforeseen side effect. Instant addiction. And from there? Continue to feed. And go rogue anyway, it seemed. "How much did he take?"

"Only what you said," Harry reiterated. "One drop. No more. At least, as much as we knew. He could've taken more, but we didn't see him try."

An army of rogues. Completely unstoppable. Such a delightful thought. Almost as sweet as the end result of his plan. A shiver ran through his body.

"Gotta tell you," Peter chimed in. "This stuff. Crazier than any shit I've ever taken. Man, what a rush."

He already knew. The idea was simple. The plan brilliant. Create an army of rogue vampires who would listen to one voice. His and only his. They would kill on his command. Then they would die a few weeks later, only to be replaced by new soldiers whenever he needed them.

The execution of the plan? Now that was disappointing. And the addiction? Very disturbing, but at most a temporary setback. The uncontrollable thirst was the true problem. An army of vampires with uncontrolled thirst would decimate their food supply, possibly to the point of extinction. He shuddered at the thought.

No. They could be managed. He had to make this work. *Think, man. Think.* Why was the addiction random? Why one vampire but not another? Was it as simple as an IQ of ten? He snorted. Not bloody likely. No, he had to find the trigger. He had to figure out how to control the vampires before they went rogue.

As he stared at the two idiots before him, Casperian's mind whirled. Could a rogue be trained like an animal or a pet? Given blood for a good deed, starved for a mistake until the rogue knew who his master was?

At first, the idea titillated so much the consequences became over-shadowed. Now, not only did his one failure haunt him, that witch Samira knew of his existence. A secret he'd managed to preserve for nearly two thousand years with the help of his maker.

"I didn't call you here to discuss your personal enjoyment," he bit out, his tone colder than the Arctic. "I need answers."

Neither of them dared.

He was Antonius Flavius Proculus Casperian of the Equestrian Order of Rome. Direct kinsman to the line of the Caesars. To think he was now forced to deal with such inadequate beings. How low would he really have to go?

Casperian shuddered. This modern world was becoming a major disappointment. However, if this was indeed a setback, stupid had its uses.

"Go and rest," he told them, softening his tone. "When you awaken, find the woman. You know her scent."

"Yes, sir," Harry replied, backing away and leaving as soon as possible.

But the other one lingered. Peter. That was his name. Casperian lifted a brow and stared down at the vampire, who cleared his throat to hide his fear. "We tracked her to her home. Big dude was with her. Black hair. Really cold eyes."

He'd already surmised. "And?"

"His people tracked us back to the helicopter. Thought you should know."

He nodded and dismissed Peter with a wave of his hand. Amaz-ing, the objects man had learned to create. Airplanes and cars, build-ings reaching the sky. And yet man had also lost the ability to delve into the devious, to circumnavigate intricate plots, to wend his way through mortal—no, moral—combat.

The helicopter had been a flash of brilliance if he did say so himself. But Venatorius was no fool. Thank the gods. The thought of an adversary of lesser nature was unworthy. However, the element of surprise had been lost. Very well. Giving away part of his plan could be dealt with. And, he was quite certain, so could the problem with his drug. On the surface, his plan might look more like a sieve. But the game was far from over. Far from over.

Chapter Twelve

TORI LOOKED UP FROM FINISHING UP LEFTOVER PAPERWORK AS Hunter returned to the townhouse. She wished he could feel the pain in her head from the wine, eased now by taking some pills and drinking a full bottle of water.

Still, wanting him to commiserate didn't help the empty feeling inside.

True to his word, he stayed right next to her. Closing up the house was easy, and she gave what was left of her perishables to Mrs. Cantone, her neighbor. The elder woman always enjoyed her free gifts. Tori took a great deal of pleasure in cooking and always made too much for one person.

They drove back to the mansion late Sunday night after the bulk of the shore traffic had made its way north. Neither one spoke much, and Tori tried to keep her thoughts under control. So much better for both of them this way, to let the wall surround her mind and her heart. Better to think about working, use their medical problems as a way not to think about anything else, and, above all, not let him know what she was feeling.

Now she stood in the lab staring, unable to believe he'd done exactly as he'd said. Tori walked around gazing at all the shiny new equipment feeling like a kid in an FAO Schwarz Christmas commercial. "Who set all this up?"

"Distributors. We deal with several in the medical device field because of the donation services." He paused, and she turned, catching a rare smile on his face. "They were only too happy to comply."

Tori still gaped. She knew the drill. A sale like this meant field service engineers to install the equipment and tech service reps to run them and make sure they were functioning properly.

"And each company had strict instructions to make sure their equipment was running perfectly before they left."

Hunter wasn't one to mess around. Still, she couldn't help but drool over her new domain. And no regulations. How lucky could she get?

"If I'd known these things were going to be such an aphrodisiac," he teased, "I'd have purchased more."

"Very funny."

"I'm not sure I was kidding."

Tori pulled back her gaze to stare at him. Every damned time. Every single goddamn time. Heat sizzled in her belly. His gaze darkened. The room began to fade. "Oh no you don't," she muttered. "I have work to do."

He smiled. He didn't need to say anything. Simply standing there looking gorgeous was enough. He knew it too.

"I need samples," she replied, ignoring the embers waiting to spark. "Lots and lots of samples."

"You wish is my command," he replied with a mock bow.

She shook her head. "I highly doubt that."

His mouth quirked. "I'll have my people come down after their shifts are complete."

"Excellent." His head cocked, daring her to acknowledge their connection. Damn him. "All right. Enough. You need to leave. Now. You're a distraction I can't afford."

"Am I?" a feminine voice asked.

Tori whirled. "Stace!" They both half ran to hug each other. Then they leaned back, laughed, and hugged again. "Oh my God, I can't believe you're here." When Tori let go, she found Chaz standing right next to Stacy. She could almost see the bands that knit them together. "It is *so* good to see you."

"Ditto."

Her gaze flicked over to Hunter. A slight smile played about his lips. "I thought you'd enjoy the surprise."

"Yes. Thank you." Stacy smiled at Tori, and Tori found she no longer felt completely outnumbered. "God, it's good to be with someone who understands."

"Another human?" Chaz asked gently.

A bit ashamed, Tori said, "Look, that didn't quite come out right. That's not what I meant."

"No," he countered. "It came out exactly as it was meant. What you're implying doesn't mean you're wrong. We are two different races." Despite his words, Tori thought she heard an edge in his voice.

"Mea culpa. But you also must understand that a few days ago, I didn't know you existed. I thought you were human. That's not a lot of time to process. Or accept."

"You're right," Chaz agreed, his features softening as he stared at his wife. "Stacy didn't quite believe me either."

Tori watched them gaze at each other, feeling like she was a voyeur. Such intimacy belonged in a bedroom. Or did it?

To cover her discomfort she added, "The second thing you need to do is understand every now and then I get stared at like I should be on a plate. Feeling like I'm someone's dinner is hard to reconcile."

Chaz sighed, turning towards her. "I'm sorry to hear you feel this way, but I'm not surprised. Although you *are* aware of the consequences?" Tori nodded. "I guess this means we all have work to do to trust one another."

There went that little word again. So small and yet so big.

Stacy turned and gave Hunter a quick hug. They both seemed a bit awkward after they let go, and Tori wondered what had happened to cause their discomfort with each other.

"Very true," Stacy agreed, her tone getting down to business. "Now why don't you gentlemen go disappear for a while? Tori and I need to catch up, then we have some serious work to do here. Okay?"

Hunter turned to leave, but Chaz took his time saying goodbye. Tori almost felt she was intruding. The moment was so...intimate. But then Stace grinned and pushed him away.

Once the men were gone, Tori stared at Stacy. She looked tanned and fit, such a deep contrast to Chaz with his pale skin. "Sam contacted us," she added. Stace looked beyond happy. She looked soul happy.

Filled with chagrin, Tori apologized. "I'm sorry."

"For what?" Stace asked. "Hell, I can only take so much beach, you know."

"Alone?" she asked, hating herself for the question.

She watched Stacy's face fall a little. "You take the good with the bad, sweetie. You know that." She brightened. "Hey. Any worse than the internal combustion engine Harold? You do remember the night I'm talking about, don't you? The Mexican food? God! You were lucky. I was sitting in the back seat. I think I washed my clothes three times to get rid of the smell."

Tori burst out laughing. She'd forgotten. Leave it to her best friend to remind her. "Stace, c'mon. You know me. I just can't wrap my head around all of this. I mean, hell. I deal with the dead daily. It's really weird when they walk and talk, you know?"

Stacy nodded. "They are, but they aren't. I don't know how else to explain it." She kind of half grinned. "At least, this is my theory anyway. We'll have to see if we can find out."

Tori agreed but with reservations. "What if we find out something they don't like?"

Stacy paused, her fingers trailing over the edge of the chemistry analyzer. "We give them the truth—nothing more, nothing less."

The doors opened, and Hunter and Chaz walked back in. Tori watched both, noting Chaz was softer in manner and feature, where Hunter was all sharp lines and edges. Yet both carried themselves with grace and an undeniable strength. "We're going to plan a defense, so I'm having food brought down for both of you," Hunter told them. "The rogues that have been created may be able to find you, Tori. They may try to attack the compound. If they do, we need to be ready for them."

Tori still felt unsure about needing to be defended, so she didn't answer. "Your donors should be arriving shortly," he added.

She acknowledged Hunter was doing what he thought best. "Thank you."

Both men seemed ready to leave, when Tori realized something didn't add up. "Chaz? May I ask a question?"

"Sure."

"Stacy said you were in security. I always assumed this meant you were or you'd been a human cop. Why do you need vampire cops?"

He shot a quick glance over at Hunter, then sighed. "Going rogue used to only happen when a vampire began dying. As you know, now it's much more common." He frowned. Was he uncomfortable because he didn't want to explain or because he didn't like what he did? "Anyway, sometimes vampires can't face ending their own lives. They let the change happen, and I have to hunt them down."

"You kill them?"

He nodded, his features grim. Obviously both.

"I know this is indelicate. But I need answers. Every piece of information I get will help my investigation." Tori paused. "How?"

He pulled a vial out of his pocket. "Rosary pea extract. It's a strong mixture."

She glanced at Hunter. "But you——"

He held up his hand to stop her from speaking. "Since you must know, Mercy staked the rogue that attacked you and cut off its head. Both methods are effective. We usually use both when we can. Then we burn the body. Most vampires don't have the strength to fight a rogue alone. Because I'm older, I do. And as you witnessed, even then, I found the fight a...challenge."

Tori shivered. Why did killing always seem so much easier than keeping people alive?

"Rosary pea extract," she repeated. "Stace?" she asked, turning to her friend. "Any idea how it works?"

Stacy nodded. "Abrin. It's a poison. A protein synthesis inhibitor. And in a very concentrated form. My assumption is once the poison is ingested it causes a total internal bleed out."

The wheels inside Tori's brain were spinning and didn't want to quit. A bleed out would take time, hence the rest of their method. Chaz seemed sad for some reason. Hunter simply stoic. No one liked killing. Then she thought about it. This was the death they all faced. Not pleasant. "Thank you."

"I can see we're intruding," Hunter said after the silence began to fill the room.

"We'll leave while you two get your geek on," Chaz added, trying to lighten the mood.

He walked up to Stacy and kissed her again for a full minute before letting go. Maybe he felt he had to stake a claim. Maybe he felt he had to show Tori love could conquer any difference. Maybe he simply wanted to wash the taste of death out of his mouth. Tori wasn't sure.

Hunter walked up to her. He reached out to cup her cheek and smooth the skin with his thumb. Killing didn't bother him. Not the way it bothered Chaz. And yet she knew the gesture was deliberate. Why? And then it hit her. Hunter was proclaiming the slave was worthy of the prize.

He turned without a word and walked away. As she stared at Hunter's retreating back Stacy laughed softly. "Did I just see what I just saw?"

Tori nodded. There was no other way to explain.

"Oh. My. God. The vampire made out of stone? The man with an ice block instead of a heart?"

"Yeah."

Stacy stared at the empty doorway and shook her head. "I never thought I'd live to see the day." Then she turned. "You go, girl."

Tori frowned. "I'm not so sure."

"I get that," Stacy answered, her voice filled with wonder.

"You know, it's not fair. I mean, they can be pretty damned arrogant when they want to. Hunter keeps thinking I'll ask how high when he tells me to jump."

"Chaz was kind of like that with me in the beginning too," Stacy agreed.

"He really needs to stay out of my head too."

She grinned. "I've got ways to get around the lack of privacy. I'll explain later."

Sounded interesting.

"And you were right that there are things they won't ever understand," her friend continued.

"Like kids?"

Stace nodded. "They close themselves off for protection."

"I know all about protection."

She reached out, her eyes filling. Tori shook her head. In a minute she'd start crying too. Time to steer clear of the subject. "They'd never understand a girl's night out."

Stacy laughed, wiping at her eyes. "Wine. Chocolate."

"A superhero with long, blond hair and a hammer."

"I've got my own now," Stacy murmured, her voice all kinds of warm and soft.

Tori smiled. "Yeah, you do." Was that a little stab of jealousy that hit her? After all, her luck with men rated below zero.

She breathed in deeply and let out the air slowly. "What do you say we start getting to work, then? This extract has me intrigued. I think we need to know the exact composition of the stuff, don't you?"

"Sure. But you're lead here."

Tori threw her a look. "Why? You have just as much expertise in your field as I have in mine."

"You're the doctor," Stace insisted. "The pathologist."

"All right, all right." Tori figured she had no choice, so she agreed. "Then let's talk this out for a sec. Oh and by the way, you just became phlebotomist number two."

Stacy laughed. "You're number one?"

"Hunter promised lots and lots of volunteers," Tori added with a nod.

She sat down at one of the counters marveling at how quickly they'd built the lab. "Good. Now, I'm trying to reconcile that they have no clotting factors but their skin knits almost immediately. I'm guessing it's a protein we've never ever seen before. And if it is, I'm guessing it's inherent in more than just their skin."

"And why the abrin works so well," Stacy replied. "Good thing you thought to get the gel electrophoresis system over there."

Amazed, Tori answered, "Who'd have thought it'd be that important. And what about the samples we collect? We're going to need serum if we want to find proteins. Only, I have no idea what their blood does."

"Talk about feeling a bit useless," her friend answered, shoulders slumping.

Tori frowned. "Why?"

"What good is an SBB here? Two master's degrees, and I don't have a clue."

"I could say the same," she retorted. "What good is a medical degree?"

They sat in silence for a long moment. Then Tori said, "We still have to start somewhere. So let's concentrate on the samples."

"What if the samples don't separate?"

She thought for a moment. "You mean serum and blood cells?" Stacy nodded. "We'll have to use donated platelets, I guess," she replied. "To get the blood to clot."

Neither one spoke for a while. But Tori was certain the wheels in Stacy's brain were turning just as fast, if not faster, than hers. "Blood types?" Stacy asked.

Tori shook her head. "Nonissue, I think. They're vampires. They drink from anyone."

"They?" Stacy asked, her tone pointed and filled with the question of what Tori meant by her words.

Suddenly Tori realized how her answer could be misconstrued. She reached out. Stacy had been one of the rocks she'd leaned on, and she wasn't trying to hurt her best friend. "Unintentional. Honest."

Stacy relaxed. Then her face diffused with love. "You know, Chaz is the most *human* being I've ever met."

"Funny," Tori answered, her tone wistful. "I was about to say the same about Hunter."

"Hunter?" she asked, her face a mask of disbelief.

"I know. Right? But it's true."

Stacy looked extremely skeptical. "I find him having feelings a bit hard to believe. When we first met, I had to convince him not to kill me."

Tori stared. "Really?" Stacy nodded. Now the awkward embrace made sense.

A shiver worked its way down her spine. Would he? Would he kill to protect his people? "Did you know he was a slave in his human life?"

Stacy shook her head. "No."

"Roman Empire, from what he told me."

Stace didn't reply for a long moment. "Certainly explains a lot."

Tori could almost imagine Stacy's disbelief. "I've looked deep inside, Stace. I can't imagine what he went through. All I see is pain. He's closed himself off."

"Haven't you closed yourself off too?"

Kindred spirits. Could it be this simple? She answered her own question. Nothing was that simple.

She lifted her chin. "Yes."

"Sorry, Tori," Stacy told her. "Accusing you of trying not to feel was unfair."

Was it? "No, you're right. You have no idea how I wish I could simply wake up one morning and find the pain bearable. God, how I wish time healed."

"It does. I know I've told you this a hundred times, but you simply have to accept."

She shook her head. "Nothing's that simple, and you know it. I've been living with this kind of pain for over two years. Hunter's been living with it for two thousand. I'm not sure there's a way to go beyond."

Stacy's features filled with a serenity Tori truly envied. "Yes, there is. It's called love."

Chapter Thirteen

LATER THAT NIGHT, HUNTER STOOD IN FRONT OF THE WINDOW OF his office. It was easier up here on the higher floors of the mansion. Away from the call of her blood. Away from *her*.

"I'm glad Sam contacted us," Charles told him as he walked in. "Even though I was enjoying the hell out of my honeymoon."

He nodded but didn't turn, feeling a bit sorry for the Paladin, the vampire cop who might one day end Hunter's life, and yet he still couldn't find it in him to let Charles see inside. Instead, he continued to look out the window, surveying everything he'd built. This home. This cell. This family. In unity, there was strength. He'd learned that lesson the hard way.

"I suppose Sam felt she had no choice."

"My job," Charles answered. "It's why I was made, why I'm a Paladin."

"I know." Was he wrong to want to protect? "But the playing field has changed, Charles. Someone is creating rogues. We're not talking one or two here any longer. There could be hundreds, for all we know."

He watched Charles shrug. "Still have to destroy them."

"Yes. But you know the extract is extremely hard to craft. We'll never have sufficient quantities if there are that many. And it doesn't completely kill them unless it has a long time to work."

"Maybe Stacy can help us with this particular problem. A synthetic form might be even more potent."

"I'm sure she'll try. As will Tori. But until then, we must go with what we have. Very few of us are old enough to take on a rogue by ourselves, and there aren't that many soldiers trained well enough to stay alive fighting them. Your people included."

"Vanessa can handle herself. You and I both know she can." Hunter listened as Charles sucked in a deep breath and felt his pain. "Could've used Pitch for this one."

Hunter agreed. "Yes. He should never have tried to go it alone."

"It's what we were created to do, you know."

"But not against one such as Mikhail." In unity there was strength. "The others?"

"Ozzie knows the deal. Creighton's young. So's Alex. Mick hand-picked both for further training. They'll deal. They have no choice."

No choice. Why was that?

"What about your wife?" Normally asking the question wouldn't have bothered him. He wondered why it did now. "Will she be a distraction?"

"No," Charles answered as if he'd been expecting Hunter to ask. "She can't be. We both know that."

"Do we?"

Charles turned to stare. "Bottom line, eh? Well then, let's get down to it. And the answer is yes, I know the consequences of going rogue."

"I'll take your head if I have to," Hunter replied without a hint of feeling.

He watched Charles bite back a laugh. "As will I."

"Good. Then we understand each other." Hunter reached into his jacket and pulled out an envelope. "This arrived by courier yesterday. I think Mikhail knew he was in trouble and his investigation was bearing fruit."

"Consequences," Charles murmured, taking the envelope from him. "Something tells me this should be a private fight, but it isn't."

"No," Hunter agreed. "And I can't keep others from getting in the middle of it. His name is Casperian. Kin to the royal order of the house of Caesar. He was my...master."

Surprise filled Charles's gaze, then faltered. "I see. But not your maker."

"No." Hunter shuddered ever so slightly. "No one knows this, and I'd rather you keep it a secret."

Charles nodded and said in a solemn tone, "Anything you say to me is privileged information. Although I can't swear I won't use it if I have to."

Hunter's mouth quirked, and he inclined his head. "My maker was Antu, Antu-Si-Tiyat."

"I always wondered." He watched Charles release a deep breath. "He certainly puts a different light on things, doesn't he?" Charles rubbed the back of his neck with his hand. "Then it's a good thing I contacted Vanessa."

"We—ran into each other," Hunter bit out. Damned redhead always managed to get under his skin. "She was at Tori's home."

This time Charles did laugh. "Already digging, I see."

"With all the subtlety of a bull in a proverbial china shop," he bit out.

"She does get results," Charles added, and Hunter waited for the vampire's laughter to abate.

As he did, for the first time in his life *as* a vampire, Hunter wondered if the end justified the means. "Results."

Hunter felt Charles grip his shoulder and started. "Serena wasn't your fault. I'm sure Sam's told you you're not to blame a hundred times."

"Not your business." They used to be called his private affairs. Now? "Or hers."

Charles let go. "True. Casperian isn't either. But it will be if you walk into a rogue battle with your head up your ass."

Offended, Hunter turned. "Indeed."

Charles grinned. "You know, your bark is much worse than your bite. Wish I'd known it sooner."

A warm feeling filled him. He stiffened. Emotion was not allowed.

Friendship was forbidden. The arena allowed no sentiment. No friends. A mistake meant death. Pity meant death. Caring meant death.

"I think Tori's gotten under that thick hide of yours," Charles continued. "Not the worst thing in the world, you know."

"She's dinner," Hunter declared, trying to hold on to the place deep inside where feelings didn't matter. And yet?

"Keep lying to yourself." Charles laughed softly.

Hunter realized the conversation reached an impasse. Either he told Charles the entire story or he told him to leave. "I have a cell to run. Keep me informed of your progress."

Charles nodded, his gaze still curious, and left.

Was he lying to himself? About Tori? Hunter turned from the window. Even worse, was he lying to himself about dying? Hadn't he thought about it? Night after night? A clean death in the arena and an end to the abyss he'd called his human life?

One fraction of an inch, one slip of the blade, one wrong placement of the foot or the shield arm. Strange. He could never give up his life in such a fashion. There was no honor in letting Casperian win, and if nothing else, Hunter was not a coward.

He looked around at his office as if seeing the room for the first time. Simple. Austere. His one concession the huge mahogany desk he now sat behind. Perhaps he should have indulged himself more and placed some works of art on the walls or put a rug on the floor to cushion his feet.

No, decorating would have made him just like the rich patrons who'd bought his body night after night. He could still hear their whispered words of encouragement. He could still feel their fawning caresses as if they'd cared about him; he'd still shuddered inside at their touch. Cared about him? Only one person on this earth had ever cared about him. Antonia.

Hunter rose and looked out the window which made up the wall behind his desk. Had he loved her? Soft, sweet, shy, fragile Antonia? No. He'd let his guard down though. He'd broken the cardinal rule about emotions and feeling. He'd smiled. Why, he'd even laughed.

With a well-rehearsed detachment, Hunter remembered.

How Antonia had suffered. How the stark reality that his child would be a gladiator just like him had knifed at his guts. How his first master had laughed at his pain. How his second hadn't cared.

Venatorius wondered at the sight of the whipping post in the middle of the atrium, thinking idly how many men it must have taken to bring such a heavy object into the house. Five guards surrounded him, when two would have sufficed. And three spears pointed at his belly as the other two soldiers chained him. What was going on?

"Ahh. You've decided to join us, good Venatorius."

He didn't answer.

"You've done something quite remarkable, Venatorius. You...surprised me."

With a slight frown, he wondered out loud. "How?"

Two guards pushed and pulled a woman into the room. A hollow formed in the pit of his belly. Antonia.

"She bears your child, I'm told."

He lifted his head in shock.

His master chortled. "You didn't know? Excellent." Then the man turned to his guards. "Hold her."

His master trailed his fingers all over her body. She tried to jerk away from the man's touch, but the guards held her even tighter. "Have I moved you yet, dear Venatorius?"

Rage filled his being, but he only clenched his hands. By the gods. Why are you making her suffer?

He loosened his fingers and shuddered, pulling down the mask he always wore. He drew in a ragged breath.

His master became even more flagrant with his caresses, outlining the curves of Antonia's breasts and the V of her legs. Then he cupped the small protrusion of her belly with his palm. "You don't deserve to have a child, Venatorius. You're a cold-blooded murderer. A child of yours could never be trusted, except in the arena. A child of yours would be just like you, a cold-blooded killer." His master tsked. "And so, the child, if it is strong and a boy, will become a gladiator just like his father."

Icy fog filled him, the kind of detachment of one already dead. He closed his eyes so his master wouldn't see the fire of hate inside. He searched for the place of nothing and searched and searched, until finally he opened his eyes.

"I see my words had little effect. I marvel at your capacity not to care, Venato-

rius. And so, I swear, if the child is a girl, she will join her mother in my service. I've decided to make Antonia my personal servant."

Hunter remembered being thrown back into his cell. He remembered the agony. He'd known exactly what his master had meant and felt each and every caress as a blow, over and over, until what had been left of his heart had drawn out of his body too. Then and only then, in the deepest darkness of the night, had he asked the moon the ever-eternal question. *Why?* And when there had been no answer, he could only beg those unseen gods to spare her agony.

Yeah, they'd helped all right.

The hardest had been seeing the light fade from her eyes, knowing she'd lost the will to live.

"You will not be going to the arena today, Venatorius."

Surprise filled his gaze.

"Finally. An emotion," his master chortled with glee.

He stilled, hiding his feelings carefully. "Anyone would find this action surprising, Master. You have been promising my match to the people for weeks. I do not understand."

"Nor is it your place to do so," his master snapped. Then he changed his tactic and softened, cupping Venatorius' cheek with his hand. "I have been asked to stage a private fight instead. A very...profitable fight. Outside the city."

Venatorius frowned. But curiosity got the better of him. "By whom?"

His master seemed taken aback. "Venatorius? Have I finally clawed my way beneath that skin of yours? Are you curious?"

Forcing himself into his neutral place again, he bowed. "I fight where you tell me to fight, Master. I kill what you tell me to kill. It matters not where or for whom."

"Good. Then you will go to the baths. This evening's entertainment must be perfect. Do you understand? Perfect."

"Yes, Master."

He turned on his heel and walked away. But his mind flew in a thousand different directions. Something was terribly wrong. No one had the power to disappoint the patrons of the arena and get away with it.

Whoever controlled the games controlled Rome. Even he knew this truth.

All afternoon and all evening, foreboding sat on his heart like a stone. He followed his rituals, but tonight they were edged with an unexpected emotion: fear.

Not of death—a slave never feared death—but of the unknown. And when a single litter arrived to take him to his destination, he became even more uneasy. Slaves didn't ride in litters. They walked.

And his master was nowhere to be seen.

They arrived at an estate several hours outside the city. Venatorius was taken to a small arena built into the ground. To one side of the arena, carved out of the hillside, stood a resting place for the dead. How apt.

A voice entered his head, bidding him enter. Before he even had time to question, his feet moved. Once inside, he found his master submitting to a very pale man, his master's face a mixture of fear and ecstasy. Blood dripped down his master's neck, twin rivulets winding down his skin.

At his entry, the man looked up. He licked his lips, then sharp fangs pierced his master's flesh once again. Horror seared his soul.

The man pushed his master away, and a sharp stab of fear pierced his gut. Only years of training kept Venatorius from allowing this man to see. He put himself in the neutral place and stared back at the man with a faint hint of distaste. Man?

"You wonder about me, but you control your fear. Excellent."

His heart raced, faster as the man drew closer. "My master said you wished a private fight."

"He is no longer your master. I am."

The pulse in his neck skittered. He swallowed hard. "As you wish, Dominus."

The pale man stepped closer. Venatorius read many years upon his face and a certain kind of boredom that went with those years. He knew the sign well, for he had read the lack of emotion many times on the faces of the rich patrons who purchased his services.

"Come. Follow me."

They walked into the building he assumed housed the dead. The atrium looked like any rich patron's atrium, with flowers and couches and a small pool filled with golden fish.

Suddenly, he heard screams. Antonia? Fear shivered down his spine. Still, he lowered his head to acknowledge the change in his status and, more importantly, to hide his emotions. His new master seemed pleased.

"Venatorius. Greatest of all the fighters." The man lifted his chin with a finger. A cold finger, the kind that sent chills down to the toes. "You know you are going to die, do you not?"

He stared into black eyes showing no warmth, no life. "Death has no hold over a slave, Master. It is a welcome release from bondage."

"Indeed," his new master sighed. "Perhaps not as welcome as you might think."

"Dominus?"

That same cold fingertip trailed along his cheek. He shivered. "You've made me curious, slave. Tell me. What do you fear, then?"

"Nothing."

His answer seemed to surprise the man. "Are you sure of this?"

Venatorius cocked his head, wondering. What game did this new master play? "I am."

"Why?" he asked, his tone genuinely curious.

"Because I do not care."

"Very well."

His new master snapped his fingers. Two soldiers stepped forward in the torch-light. Then they brought in Antonia. She stared at Venatorius, begging for his help. He had none to give.

His new master threw her down onto a couch, where the soldiers held her, then his master leaned over and he bit her neck, blood trickling down to stain the cloth of her shift.

Venatorius hesitated. He didn't understand. What was this new master? Why was he able to drink blood?

"Can you feel her warmth fade, great warrior? Do you not understand that I take her life inside me?

This time, Venatorius didn't hesitate. With a roar, he ripped the monster away from the only person who'd ever cared for him. He lifted Antonia in his arms. She opened her eyes. But he was too late. Her gaze forgave him. Then the light dimmed from her eyes.

His cry echoed across the walls of his new prison. Not just a woman who'd given him caring when no one else had, but now there would be no child born of his loins. He set her down onto the marble floor as if she were a treasure. His heart beat faster and faster. His body shook. All the years of holding in his emotions exploded. His hands fisted. His legs coiled. With a great cry, he charged. He didn't remember the rest. Only the sound of mocking laughter. Seemed he'd pleased his new master after all.

Chapter Fourteen

SEVERAL DAYS LATER WHEN TORI WAS JUST FINISHING HER LAST phlebotomy, when her hands started shaking. Her heart started pounding. A picture filled her head. Mrs. Cantone. Such a sweet, innocent old lady but now with twin puncture wounds and blood dripping down her neck. A man—no, a vampire—with stark features. A thin nose; a long chin; and close-cropped, black hair like Hunter's. A faint cock to his head which reeked arrogance.

As if he knew she could see him, he grinned.

Tori put the tube into a rack, ripped off her gloves, and bolted. Stacy ran after her. "Tori! What is it?"

No time to explain. He'd put the picture inside her head. Of that, she had no doubt even as she pounded on the elevator button. The doors opened, and she ran through them. They closed as Stacy ran toward her and Tori mouthed, *I'm sorry*.

He called himself Casperian.

Down to the garage. Running out before the elevator doors stopped moving. The car keys were still in her pocket. The engine growling to life, and tires squealing on concrete. Fingers drumming on the steering wheel, waiting for the main gates to open.

Hunter shouting inside her head. *Tori, stop!*

Fat chance.

Palisades Interstate. Route 80. Turnpike. Garden State Parkway. Complete focus because she'd never driven this fast in her life before. *Tori. Stop. Please.*

"Get out of my head!"

Waiting. Holding her breath each time she looked in the rearview mirror. Expecting to see a line of state troopers, lights flashing, sirens blasting. Knowing brave men would be in danger but, coward that she was, wanting the protection. Could a bullet stop a vampire?

Professional opinion? No. Slow one down? Absolutely. Stop a rogue?

Tori opened her mind. *Who are you?*

Venatorius and I go back an exceptionally long way.

Venatorius?

You call him Hunter.

Adrenaline rushed through her veins. *How are you able to communicate with me?*

Let's just say I'm different from the rest.

She trembled, then gripped the steering wheel even tighter. If this vampire could put pictures and words into her head from a distance, did it make him more powerful than even Sam?

For a second, fear became the number one hit on her playlist as she decided to play NASCAR. Then a deeper emotion took over. Anger. Red-hot, burning anger. Because the end could never justify the means. Not ever.

Tori hated people who played with other people. She hated people who said one thing but did another. She hated people with ulterior motives who used others for their own benefit. She'd suffered from a man like that. His name was Peter. The other sorrow in her life. The bastard who'd walked out on her right when she'd needed him the most. What an imbecile she'd been —so starry-eyed and in love, she hadn't seen the real Peter. Then she'd realized it was her car, her money, and her apartment. Because of her second job in a lab.

Funny. Or was it? How had she never seen that in certain ways she'd been just like Hunter? A puppet. A thing. A slave.

Peter. Proposing on the beach during a vacation she'd paid for.

Then getting back home and counting the days after her period. Realizing what being pregnant meant and how overjoyed she'd been, only to become confused when Peter hadn't shared her joy. The complete and utter shock of his reaction creating such emptiness when he'd gotten so angry. He'd started screaming at the top of his lungs, then he'd stared at her in complete disgust. He'd wanted her to take care of the problem right away. He'd wanted her to get rid of the baby.

And that was when she'd realized. No symbiotic relationship here. Peter was and had always been a total and complete parasite. He'd used her to get what he wanted. A free ride. With the side dish of free sex.

What an incredible actor! How had she not known? Then again, as she examined the past, she realized just how he'd trained her. When she'd done something for him, when their world had been about him he'd heaped praise and affection. When she'd contradicted him, when she'd defied him? He'd showed such cold disdain, such drawn out indifference that she'd be forced to give in just to feel warm again.

How could she have been so stupidly innocent? He'd used her and taken everything he'd wanted and discarded her like the piece of garbage he'd thought she was. God, it still hurt, adding to an already unbearable agony. And yet he'd given her the greatest joy she'd ever known, her daughter, Kelly.

Tori glanced in her rearview again. Still no cavalry. Which made her grateful and disappointed, all at the same time. However, by now, Hunter had to be following.

Hunter. Tori thought about how he must have felt, without choice and without hope, simply accepting the unacceptable.

Masters. They were nothing more than overblown bullies believing they held the power. Had Casperian been Hunter's master? Was this what the vampire had meant by "going back a long way"?

Slaves. Hunter living the unlivable. Fighting back the only way he knew how.

Obviously, this Casperian wanted to hurt Hunter, even after two thousand years. A long time to hold a grudge. Which meant this Casperian was one pissed-off vampire.

And yet, she asked herself, shouldn't Hunter be the one holding the grudge?

Tori pulled off the parkway, raced through the toll, took corners way too fast, and continued to gun the engine. She ran two red lights and sped down Main Street, turning onto the street for her development. Tires screamed as she pulled into the parking lot for her townhouse. And then it hit her.

Trap!

Of course.

She slammed on the brakes and hit the high beams. He didn't even try to shade his eyes. Tall, thin, his bearing aristocratic, this was same person as she'd seen in her mind. Casperian had his arm draped casually over Mrs. Cantone's shoulders.

"Don't hurt her."

Whatever are you going to do to stop me, my dear?

All the way down the parkway Tori had believed she was right. She had to believe she was right now. "Power only exists as long as the threat exists."

He reared back. In surprise, for sure, but Tori almost thought he was going to laugh. No, guffaw. He didn't. Instead, he stared. *Really.*

Tori threw the car into Reverse. She began to back up slowly, never taking her gaze off the pair in front of her. Casperian finally let go, and Mrs. Cantone fell to the pavement. Tori prayed she didn't break anything.

Dense fog rolled in from the ocean, a typical fall night at the shore. She thought about driving toward the marsh, wondering if the sea could hide her.

Thud.

Right on the top of the car. In the time it took to form one thought. Whoever was on the top of her car, he had to be one of Casperian's men. Tori hit the accelerator really hard.

Thud.

Another vampire. Obviously they were playing with her.

She put the car in Drive and hit the accelerator again. Her tires squealed and rubber burned, then she slammed on the brakes and threw the car back into Reverse. One soldier lost his balance and rolled backward down the hood.

She nearly smiled. "It's called inertia, fellas."

The other punched down on the roof, metal screeching as indented. "Uh-oh. Not a bright move, guys. Hunter really likes this car."

She threw the car into Drive again, swerved and pulled a one-eighty. Defensive driving school—something they wouldn't know about—and then nothing. She wasn't moving. They were holding the car. Fine. She let up on the accelerator. Again, they'd forgotten their science. As soon as they let the car down and it touched ground, Tori hit the gas. Tires squealed once more as rubber hit the pavement, and the car shot forward. One of them must've realized she might get away and ran in front of the car.

God, they could move fast.

Tori didn't stop. Wasn't going to.

The soldier jumped out of the way at the last second. The car bumper caught his leg as she sped by. Tori could almost feel the crack as his leg shattered. He cried out, then he was shouting curses.

One down. For a minute anyway.

She punched it, tires continuing to scream as she pulled back onto Main Street. The diner. The police station. Innocent lives. But she had no choice.

Do you really think human guns will stop me?

She tore into the lot, slammed on the brakes, threw the car in Park, jumped out, and ran into the police station.

"Jeez, Doc. Where's the fire? You okay?" Sergeant Wilkes asked, frowning, his features filled with concern.

"Someone's following me. They were in my parking lot. Three men. My neighbor…she's over seventy."

Those words were all she had to say. Sergeant Wilkes got on dispatch. Pronto. "Dispatch. Seargeant Wilkes. Ten-ten in progress. Oceanview Estates. Herbask. You copy?"

"Herbask is en route. ETA two minutes."

"Three men," Tori gasped, her heart hammering. She closed her fingers into fists to stop them from shaking.

"Elderly female versus three males," the sergeant continued. "In the parking lot. Dispatch, send EMS."

"Got it." The sergeant repeated what she'd said, then let go of the radio. "Who are they, and are you hurt?"

"I'm fine, but Mrs. Cantone… I had to draw them off. Some kind of gang. I had to get them away from her. Once you see my car, you'll understand."

He nodded. And then it hit her. "Shit!"

Sergeant Wilkes stared. "What's wrong, Doc? Sounds like you did the right thing."

Hunter. Stay away! He's using me as bait.

Did you think I didn't know? Do I look like a fool?

Where are you?

"Here."

Tori looked up, never more grateful to see anyone in her entire life. But Hunter ignored her. "Sergeant Wilkes? My name is Hunter Pierce."

Tori couldn't help herself. She ran into his arms. They banded around her, and her whole body shook. His cheek rested on top of her head for a moment, then he gently pushed her away. "My car is outside. Here's my license and registration. My people have already contacted Mrs. Cantone. She's fine and resting comfortably in her home."

"Your people?"

"I'm in private security, Sergeant. Elena DeArenas from the governor's office asked me to look into gang-related incidents in this area. I'm afraid I, uh, ruffled a few feathers, so to speak. The leader of this gang knew the doctor and I are dating, and they seem to have sent me a warning."

The dispatch radio barked. "This is Herbask. We're at Oceanview. Bunch of suits and SUVs all over the place. No gang members in the area. You want us to stay?"

The sergeant handed Hunter back his identification. "Seems you have things under control." Then he sighed and said to the officer, "Herbask. Wilkes. Make a few extra rounds tonight. Make sure they don't come back."

"My people will still be there."

"Appreciate the help. Would've been nice if someone had let me know you guys were down here though. You know?"

"Indeed, Sergeant. But you must understand, the fewer people who knew, the less chance someone would have finding out the truth. And you've already seen the consequences."

Tori watched Sergeant Wilkes nod. "However," Hunter continued, "now that you know, I trust you'll forget about our visit? After all, I'm supposed to be undercover."

"Not sure how you're gonna be incognito now with all the ruckus," the police officer muttered. Then, he seemed to pause and agreed. "Gotcha. Sure. No problem." Sergeant Wilkes looked over at her. "You sure you're okay, Doc?"

Tori wondered. Did vampires have the ability to plant suggestions too? "I'm fine now, Sarge. Thanks."

"Thank you for all of your help," Hunter echoed. "I'll be sure to mention your cooperation."

Wilkes preened. "No problem. Thanks. 'Night."

Hunter grabbed her arm and pulled. He squeezed until he nearly cut off the blood flow, not to mention the pain. "You're hurting me."

He didn't answer. He didn't let go. Not while they walked out of the station. Not while they stormed down the steps over to his car. He opened the passenger door and held out his hand for the keys. She dropped them into his waiting palm. He practically threw her into the seat. As he shut the door, his other hand ran over the dent in the roof.

Uh-oh. Not good. Um, make that very not good.

They drove back to her townhouse in silence. Thankfully, the ride was less than two minutes. Hunter pulled into a parking space, got out, and slammed his door so the car shook. Then he opened her door, grabbed her arm, yanked her out, and didn't let go. This time she was sure she'd end up with a bruise.

Tori opened her mouth to defend herself.

"Don't!" he cried.

He nodded to Mercy and her men as they climbed the few steps onto her small porch, then he shoved the front door open. "Wait a minute," she protested, wondering how that could be.

"It was already open."

Casperian.

Hunter slammed the door shut and threw the dead bolt. The next thing she knew, he had her pinned up against the wood. His mouth didn't just engulf hers, he inhaled her.

Anger. Frustration. Ah, there it was. Fear for her. All in his kiss. Sometimes there weren't words. There couldn't be. Sometimes there was no softness. There couldn't be. Only need.

Tori ripped at his shirt buttons. He was already unsnapping her slacks and pushing them down. She stepped out of them.

His fist wrapped in her hair, pulling her head back. Fire. Heat. Lightning. All in his gaze. Hunger. Not just for her body. For more.

His hand clawed at his belt. He unsnapped his pants and unzipped his fly. "You." He shoved his clothes down to his knees. "Disobeyed." One arm lifted her against the door. "My." The other spread her legs. "Direct. Order."

He positioned himself at her core and paused; she nodded and waited with bated breath until he slammed into her. God, she wanted him. He pulled out and slammed into her again, filling her body. He felt so good inside. So right. Tori moaned as he pulled out. And opened her eyes in surprise when he didn't thrust again.

He let her slide down his body and captured her mouth with his. His gaze promised torture. Every touch of his tongue promised ecstasy. He broke away, and she watched his flesh grow even larger, making her want a piece of this bad boy.

Instead, Hunter pushed the clothes off his legs and grabbed her arm with the same fierce grip as before. He threw her at the couch, bending her over the armrest. There would be no gentleness between them, no give and take, only animal mating on the most primal of levels.

Tori already knew Hunter wasn't simply communicating about disobeying orders.

She grunted as he entered her, balancing her weight on the couch. He didn't just fill her, he tried to shove his entire body inside her.

Pushing her blouse up her back to her shoulders, he unsnapped her bra, while grinding and twisting and turning his hips into her core.

"More," she gasped. "I want more."

He gave her exactly that.

Her breasts fell into his waiting palms. He pulled on her nipples, just this side of causing pain. Tori moaned louder.

He leaned down against her back, his breath hot and moist against her ear. Then he withdrew until he was just at the edge of her core and pushed inside until his body ground against her mound again, with her fingers fisted in the couch cushions to hold on.

"You," he bit out between rapid breaths.

All the way out and all the way in. Tori's insides twisted and tumbled all over themselves.

"Will," he continued.

His incisors grew. They scraped against her back as he licked her skin. And he tweaked her nipples, shooting fire through her body.

"Never."

He slipped his fingers lower, brushing against her nub.

"Do that."

He pulled out and pushed in, pistoning in and out with a force just this side of brutal. Faster. In. Out. In. Out.

"Again."

Fat chance.

Tori screamed. She orgasmed so quickly she almost missed the build.

He brushed her nub again, and she thought she'd never stop coming. And in the next moment, his breath hitched. He pumped once. Twice. And then he came with her.

Hunter kept up the pressure, and Tori simply kept coming. Until finally, with one last scream, a huge explosion melted her bones.

He fell onto her back, both drawing in huge gulps of air. He didn't kiss her. Didn't drink from her. Simply pulled out, put on his clothes, straightened them, and walked out of the front door.

Tori lifted. Her legs shook. She glanced down at her arm to see a red mark where he'd grabbed her. There was a soreness between her legs which wouldn't be gone by tomorrow morning. Not once had she ever thought he would hurt her.

Bemused, she picked up her slacks and thong, threw them onto the bed, and went into the bathroom. She undressed and stepped into the shower. Suddenly, Tori realized he was mad at her. Damned mad. Vampire mad.

Then she grinned. If this was angry sex, she couldn't wait for makeup sex.

Chapter Fifteen

HUNTER STOOD IN THE MIDDLE OF THE PARKING LOT OF HER townhouse, wondering how he'd gotten there. His insides churned, digging and clawing. With what? What did he want so badly that he'd be this physical with a human being?

"I'd have strung her up by her thumbs, but she might've liked that."

There was a voice he really wanted to hear. "Vanessa," Hunter growled.

"No. Really. I enjoyed the show. Would've been better in person, but…"

This time Hunter really let his ire be known. "*Vanessa.*"

She threw back her head and laughed, making Hunter feel about two feet tall. "Instead of standing there mocking me, you should be out there doing your job tracking his soldiers."

"Mercy beat me to it," she replied, her tone amused. "Besides, this was much more fascinating. Still is, I think."

Hunter turned back toward Tori's place to give her a piece of his mind. Again, she beat him to it. Damn that long-legged lope of hers. He inhaled deeply. She smelled like bodywash. Not floral or tropical. Crisp and clean. "You don't own me."

Vanessa stilled beside him and sucked in her breath. When he didn't explode right away, really wishing for some privacy now, he listened to Vanessa guffaw. "I am so loving this."

He watched Tori turn. "Who are you?"

"Vanessa," she answered, trying to hide her mirth—and failing. "Charles and I work together."

"Another vampire cop," Tori deduced.

Vanessa shrugged. "You seem to need extra protection. I'm the cavalry."

"I do, do I?"

Vanessa smiled. "You don't seem happy about my being here. Oh well. Ta-ta, darlings. I'll just leave you two lovebirds alone to figure it out."

"It," Tori repeated.

As cryptic as ever, Vanessa simply waved goodbye and got into her car and left. Hunter braced himself for the storm he knew was coming.

"Alone at last," Tori said, her gaze blazing.

"Look. I know I was a little rough, and it was my fault. I lost control. But you do have to admit it wasn't all me."

"We'll get to that part in a moment," she told him, her voice rising. "First and foremost, I don't take orders from you. Do you understand?"

"You'll do what I want you to do when I tell you so you don't get yourself killed," he bit out.

"No."

Did he just hear her right? "Excuse me?"

"I said no. I'm not one of your soldiers. I'm not one of your people. You don't own me. And you certainly don't control me."

Hunter's jaw snapped shut. His hands fisted. He could feel tiny tremors in his fingertips. "You'll do what I say when I say it."

She stared at him. Was there amusement in her gaze? "No."

His blood boiled. Was she crazy? Did she want to die? For as sure as he was standing in front of her, death was what Casperian wanted.

"What are you going to do, Hunter?" she goaded. "Lock me up? Throw away the key? Make me your prisoner?"

"For starters."

"Go ahead," she dared.

He reached out to do exactly as she said, when he stopped. Perplexed, he realized he didn't understand what was happening between them. "What?"

"I said go ahead." She smiled, this time with all the certainty of the universe. "You see? You have no real power over me unless I give it to you."

Wait a minute. Why were things all backward? She should've been following his orders. She should've been scared. All right, at least concerned. If for no other reason than her own safety.

"Of course I have power over you. I can pick you up, carry you over to the car, knock you out, and take you back to New York."

She nodded, her features serene. "Yes. You can. And hold me there against my will. Even keep me there until I hate you. You can physically kill me with a snap of your fingers."

So why did everything feel so wrong?

"But you only have power over me," she continued, "if I give you that power. You can do anything you like to me, physically. But you don't own my soul. And you never will."

"I don't want to own you. I want to protect you."

She stared at him, pity filling her gaze. "When I want your protection, I'll ask for it." She sighed.

"How dare you," he hissed.

"Dare? I don't think you understand. By refusing your offer I'm not trying to insult you. I'm trying to make you understand I can take care of myself."

"You can?" he asked, drawing himself up to his full height, his tone filled with scorn.

Tori scowled. "I believe in myself, Hunter. No one handed anything to me during my life." She drew in a deep breath and squared her shoulders. "I fought and scraped for it all, especially my medical degree. The father of my child walked out on me, never acknowledged she existed. I had a choice: get strong or die."

He knew that choice well.

"I got strong, Hunter. And it's why I believe I would be able to hold onto the tiny kernel that makes me...me."

Hunter couldn't help the next words that shot out of his mouth. "Are you sure that tiny kernel is you and not the wall you've built to protect yourself?"

She grimaced. "I'm not. I don't think it matters."

"Oh, but it does."

"Why?" she asked. "Strong is strong. If we're going to talk about building walls, why didn't you? Why haven't you?"

"You don't understand," Hunter roared, all the pain and anguish of centuries a knot in his belly which became a hot poker, burning and twisting inside. "I did. I have. And it doesn't make any difference. Walls can always be broken."

"And they can be rebuilt."

Chapter Sixteen

TORI SAT ON HER COUCH, UNSURE IF SHE'D DONE THE RIGHT thing. After all, he was two thousand years old. You'd think he'd know better. Humans could defend themselves. Humans could be just as strong as vampires. Maybe just not physically.

A knock sounded on the door. "It's open," she groused.

Another reason to drink. She took a large sip from her wineglass before looking up. "Oh. Hello, Sam."

Sam stared down at her with a bemused smile. "May I sit down?"

Bitterly Tori answered, "Why do you even bother asking? You know you can, and I wouldn't be able to stop you. You're stronger than I am physically, but physical strength doesn't mean I can't protect myself."

"Which becomes a problem for Hunter, doesn't it?" Sam sat, back perfectly straight yet completely at ease. "I'm not sure if it's part chivalry or honor or pride. Maybe it's duty. Or all the above. He doesn't understand."

"He doesn't *want* to understand. There's a difference."

Sam nodded. "Yes. He's stubborn. Just one of the many ways he's protected himself throughout the centuries."

"I know how to be stubborn too."

"Yes. But inside you, you carry a spark of defiance, the spark that says *this is still my home no matter what you do to me or it,* and you always will. "

"I do." She rose to refill her glass. "Would you like some? Nothing special. Just a simple red."

"Yes, I would. Thank you."

Tori poured another glass and handed it to Sam before sitting again. "Allow me," Sam said. "To life."

She inclined her head to the words and all the implications that went with them. "Yes. To life." The touched glasses and drank.

"I told Hunter to go away," Sam added. "Mercy and her men and Vanessa were already gone by the time I arrived."

"Thank you."

She paused, unable to stop the question from filling her mind. Sam answered with a picture of him walking along the beach. Solitary and alone. "Forgive me. The invasion was probably unfair. I can leave if you wish."

Tori laughed. "First, I just invited you to share a drink so that would be rude. Second, I'm independent, not stupid."

Sam smiled. "I'm beginning to like you more and more, Tori. You remind me of myself in some ways. And yes, my statement is a little narcissistic, so I hope you'll forgive my arrogance." She studied Tori, and Tori gave back as good as she got. "You are indeed independent. You've also gotten Hunter to think for the first time in his existence."

Tori could feel the heat creeping up into her cheeks. "At the cost of my privacy. I mean, closed doors are meant to keep things in, aren't they?"

"Yes. And I'm sorry about the lack of privacy. We really do try to be discreet." She hesitated. "I'm not trying to pry. I can't help but hear. Your family. Their destruction is true?"

Tori nodded. "Yes." More words were unnecessary. Sam's darkened gaze told her Sam could feel her pain.

"I'm sorry."

She sighed. And took a few minutes to regroup.

"Hunter can be...trying at times," Sam continued.

"Umm," Tori muttered, a bit abashed. "Yeah. And shouting in the middle of a parking lot made my privacy go out the window, didn't it?" Sam started to answer, and Tori held up her hand. "Rhetorical question, and mostly my fault." She gulped the wine this time. "For the record, I may be impulsive but I'm not stupid. I knew it was a trap. I didn't realize I was the bait until it was too late. I thought this was strictly Hunter's gig."

"I know." Sam sipped and turned the wineglass a couple of times, swirling the liquid inside. "You're right. Nothing fancy. Just a simple wine."

"So am I."

Sam stared, then beamed. "Oh, I don't know." She watched Sam's gaze travel over her home but found no judgment when that gaze returned to hers. "We still need your help Tori."

"I know. I'm not going to back out now."

"Thank you." Sam leaned back and relaxed into the sofa, and Tori realized some of her importance to these people. She found she liked being needed. The dead didn't need.

"Actually, while you and Hunter have been creating a commotion here, I've been able to dig elsewhere."

She watched in amusement as Sam rummaged around in a Coach backpack-purse. Who'd have thought?

"Why not?" Sam asked. "I'm not allowed to enjoy Coach or Dior?"

Tori shook her head. "No offense meant. But given most of you are soldiers, well, Stacy and I were wondering if any of you would understand a girl's night out."

Sam's face lit up. "Show me." She stilled, then her mouth quirked, became a grin, then a full-blown smile. "I think I would like this thing every much. Although I'm not sure about the chocolate, this actor is very enticing."

Sam reached into her bag and pulled out a vial filled halfway with a pale-pink fluid. "Anyway, I managed to collect this from one of the vampires who attacked you a few days ago. He'd begun turning rogue. By my estimate, he was only a few months old."

She handed Tori the tube. Tori rose, got a biohazard bag out of her medical kit, put it in, and put the specimen in the refrigerator.

"Obviously impossible. Right?" Sam continued. "So I probed his mind. One word. *Nirvana*. The name of the drug this Casperian is using to create the rogues. And a thought. One that scares me to the marrow not in my bones. Thousands like him."

"Are you sure? I mean, Casperian's got to understand. If he destroys every human, he destroys his own food supply."

"That would be logical. However, this is about power, not logic. For Hitler, soldiers and armies were just a means to an end. Complete control of the earth was his objective."

"Well, gee, total destruction makes a ton of sense," she mocked. "What's the good of ruling rocks and sand? Without humans? Vampires won't exist. I don't get it."

"Neither do I," Sam sighed. "Anyway, this Nirvana also seems to be addicting. More than one drop, I was able to ascertain, and it starts the onset of going rogue. But the process seems to be slow as if the Nirvana is fighting with the youth of the vampire."

Tori bolted upright. Could it be this simple?

"You've thought of something."

Tori started bouncing, she was so excited. "Yes. Of course. I don't know why I didn't think of it before. Cell aging."

"Cell aging?" Sam echoed.

"Mitochondria. Out-of-control pistons. An engine that won't stop firing."

"I understand the analogy, but I'm not quite sure I understand the context."

"The only cells that don't have mitochondria are red blood cells. They don't need them. Their main function is to transport oxygen— oxygen mitochondria gives to other cells that need it. The cells that do have mitochondria convert ADP into ATP and back again. And every time it cycles, energy is given off. It's how the body keeps going."

Tori jumped up and began to pace. She gulped some wine, coughed as it went down the wrong way, and set the glass aside. She needed her wits about her now.

"You drink red blood cells. Which means you don't have bone marrow and don't produce them. Some of your organs function, and others don't because you don't need them. But no matter what, your cells need to create energy, and the more energy you need to create, the more red blood cells you need to consume."

"All right. Your words make sense. But going rogue usually happens to older vampires."

"Okay. But what if this Nirvana is a trigger of some sort? What if it acts like a spark? And the spark sets off a chain reaction that can't be stopped inside the cell. Without enough blood to supply the ever-increasing need for oxygen, the cells will burn themselves up. Do rogues ever die? Naturally?"

"We don't know, Tori," Sam answered, frowning. "Because we kill them. Or else they'll destroy an entire city of humans in their need to feed."

Tori's stomach hollowed. "Sam. You have to get me back to the compound. I need to talk to Stacy. I need to get back to the lab and start testing the sample you gave me."

Sam finished her wine and rose as well. She put a hand on Tori's arm to still her. "No, Tori. Hunter needs to take you. Not me. It's his home, not mine."

"But—"

Sam shook her head. "No. You need to settle things between you first."

Stunned, Tori simply stared. "You'd put my needs before your own? And your entire race?"

"I would."

She wanted to ask why, but the question seemed to be rhetorical. "Where is he?"

Sam inclined her head toward the door. "He'll be arriving shortly."

"Thank you."

Tori reached out and hugged Sam. Startled at first, Sam didn't react. Then she wrapped her arms around Tori and squeezed. "No, Tori. Thank you. What you're trying to do for us can never be repaid."

Chapter Seventeen

FOR THE FIRST TIME IN HIS LIFE, HUNTER HAD NO IDEA WHAT HE was doing. He'd run to the ocean to drown her out of his head, letting the incessant roar of the waves fill his brain. There were things even the strength of a vampire couldn't conquer. One was the might of Mother Nature. Another was the stubborn resolve of a woman named Victoria Roberts.

Damn it! He was a vampire leader. He had nearly a hundred vampires under his command. And yet he couldn't even keep a simple human female safe.

Simple human female?

What a question.

Hunter still couldn't figure out what had gone wrong, where he'd lost control. He could still feel the explosion of their bodies and the aftershocks that had rocked him to his toes. He could still feel the swell of admiration as she'd told him off, the bubble of pride as she'd held herself equal to his people and to him.

God, she was driving him crazy. He wanted to spank her, then pound his body deep inside her core.

You need to tone down your thoughts. They're terribly erotic.

Get out of my head, Sam.

I will, I believe Charles told you, when you get yours out of your ass. She's different, Hunter.

Yes. I'm beginning to understand your point.

He watched the waves roll in and out, beginning to understand the consistency of time. They hadn't changed in nearly two thousand years. Could he?

Good. I'm glad you're starting to think. Because we need her help, Sam continued. *And I need you to have a clear head. You're the one who knows this Casperian best. You're the one who can plan the best way to defeat him.*

Defeat him? Could he?

I'll wait for you to come back to the house before I leave—just to be safe—and then meet you at the compound later. I have some things to take care of.

Sam stepped out of Tori's front door when he finally got there. "She's smart, brave, and she has an incredibly huge heart, Hunter. You've waited nearly two thousand years to trust someone. Don't you think it's about time you did?"

"She's human," he muttered. And yet?

"Being human is not a plague," she shot back. "Or a condition."

"No. But we both know what it makes her."

"Do we? Certainly not less than we are."

Hunter sighed. What was happening to him? His world, his existence had been crystal clear until a few days ago. "So she told me."

"Was she wrong?" Sam asked gently and smiled as if she could see right through him. "Are you sure about that?" Confusion filled him again.

"I think some of your answers are in there," Sam told him, pointing at Tori's front door. "If you're brave enough to try to find them."

"Impossible. Ill advised. Just plain wrong," he insisted, falling back on his tried and true.

Sam simply smiled and clapped him on the shoulder. She walked to her car, got in, and drove away. How odd. And yet?

Suddenly, Hunter felt the need to shed some of the weight he carried. Unsettled, he walked to the door and knocked softly.

"It's open."

Not wise, but Sam had just left.

She was standing on her balcony against a background of stars. His heart turned over in his chest. God, she was beautiful.

She turned and walked toward him, her face filled with excitement, her gaze defiant. "I need to go back to the lab and talk with Stacy. I think I've figured something out."

"Very well." He drew in a deep breath and let the air out before continuing. "But not until we get a few things straight."

She made a face. "Are you going to go all 'Hunter' on me?"

His mouth quirked. "I was. I can see now it would do no good."

At least she had the grace to shrug. "Look. I'm not used to cat-and-mouse games. Especially vampire games. Seems like you have even fewer rules than humans."

Did they? Probably. And Casperian had even less. Something he wanted her to understand.

Her gaze found his. Her shoulders straightened. Her chin lifted. But she did seem at least a little contrite. "I'm sorry," she apologized.

"Apology accepted."

She stared. Waited. Then stared some more. "And?"

"I was wrong as well." Hunter would never apologize for his existence. Or his right to exist. She shouldn't have to either. But he'd made a mistake and knew when to admit he was wrong. "You're right. I don't own you. And so you know, the thought is truly abhorrent."

She stared at him. He read compassion in her gaze, not pity. "Given what you've told me, I don't doubt it."

"Perhaps we can find a compromise," he suggested.

"As long as you understand I'm not one of your soldiers and refuse to be treated like one," she answered, adamant in her stance.

He nodded. "And you understand my actions stem from concern for your well-being—a great deal of concern."

Her mouth quirked. "Roundabout way of saying you care," she groused.

"You still refuse to understand. I wouldn't be here if I didn't."

Without warning, Hunter felt the night catch up with him. He swayed. Her face fell, and she hurried toward him. "Are you all right?" She surmised rather quickly what was wrong. "You're hungry."

He waved her concern away. "I'll feed when we get back to the compound."

She shook her head and held out her wrist. "Least I can do." She sat down on the couch, and he sat next to her. Her warmth enveloped him. "Doctor's orders."

A touch of wonder filled him at her generosity. "*Gratus*," Hunter replied with a slight bow of his head.

"You're welcome."

Hunter steeped himself in the river of her life, need filling his belly. In his mind he could see her blood travel through her arteries, into her heart, and out into her veins in answer to his call. Her heart sped up, and the tiny pulse in her neck raced.

"Whatever you do, don't make me high like you did the last time. I need a clear head so I can work when we get back to the compound."

"Very well."

Hunter bit down gently so as not to hurt her. She winced, then shivered. Warmth filled him. She grew a little colder. Loss of blood did that to a human.

She started to babble a little. "The doctor in me finds this beyond fascinating. I can feel little pulls as you draw up my blood. You know, I'd always wondered about the mechanism. I'm way too clinical to ever take vampire movies or shows seriously."

Obviously, he didn't answer. She tasted *so* good. And he found her nervousness rather endearing.

She continued to blather. "But something incredibly interesting is happening. I mean, we just, umm, you know."

He did, indeed.

"Well, I'm, like, ready to jump your bones again. Right now."

Jump my bones?

Hunter looked up. The question in his gaze caused her to explain. "Slang. And dated, I admit. But appropriate considering what I do for a living. It means I really want to make love with you again. Like right here. Right now."

Hunter continued to feed. He found it strange. Not too many people wanted to "jump his bones" when he drank their blood. In fact, most of them wanted the exact opposite, to be as far away as possible. He, too, found her instantaneous attraction most interesting.

Hunter paused. He knew he should stop, but she tasted so sweet. After one last draw, he tore his mouth away. "Are you all right?" he asked, concerned he might've gone too far.

She looked pale and cold. He rose and threw a small blanket from a chair around her shoulders. "I'll be fine. I just need some coffee and some sugar. I'm a little light headed."

Hunter rose and tucked her into a chair in the living room. A small gesture she seemed to appreciate. "I'll make some."

Not too long after, he brought her the cup he'd brewed and a breakfast bar from a box in the cabinet. She drank the coffee slowly and nibbled the bar. Color began to return to her face, and Hunter breathed a sigh of relief.

"I know I shouldn't ask this, but," she began, "would you be willing to share some of your memories?"

Taken aback, Hunter didn't answer right away. Sam had advised and he was willing to share some of his past, but no one had ever wanted to know about him. The real him. "Why would you want to see them?"

She hesitated, seeming to be fighting with herself. "I need to understand you. And Casperian. Your motivations. This…this relationship you have."

"Just our relationship?" he asked, a thread of hurt in his tone.

"No, not just the relationship," she seemed to backtrack. "I'd like to know about you too."

But the damage had already been done. "I would think it would be obvious," he answered. Not good enough. *Never good enough*, he thought, his hatred of what he was like lye to the tongue. "Master and slave."

"Yes, I get that part."

"Then what part don't you get?" he asked, using her own words against her.

She stilled, answering with care. "This Nirvana is a drug. Is Casperian the type of man to go to school and learn pharmacology?

Or is he dealing with a drug manufacturer or some facsimile thereof? Or perhaps both?"

Hunter sat back and realized all he could feel was a knife-like slash of hurt. Part of him had wanted to share with her. Part of him had hoped she wanted to know because she wanted to know, not because she felt she had to know. Still, she deserved an honest answer. "Your questions have merit. I suppose I can simply tell you."

"Very well," she replied. "As long as you don't think something will get lost in translation."

Meaning leave something out so as not to damage her frail sensibilities? Her sensibilities weren't the reason for his hesitation. "I survived," he answered as a prick of embarrassment filled his being.

"Hunter. Please. I'm not here to judge. You keep thinking all I want is to know about what drives Casperian to hate you so much. That's not true. I want to know more about you, Hunter. The real you. I'd like to be your—be your friend. If you'll have me. Friends listen to friends' secrets without blame. Don't you think it's about time you told someone the truth?"

Hunter breathed deeply and let go. Perhaps it was. Still, the words didn't come easily. "I was stolen from my family at the age of five. I'm Celtic. My people were known for their horses and their abilities to train them. Roman soldiers slaughtered my village and everyone in it and stole our horses for their army."

Hunter slipped into memory. "I served the legions first. Doing whatever the soldiers ordered when they weren't kicking me or backhanding me. But because of my abilities and my knowledge even at so young an age, they let me work with the stable masters. Those were the best times, the times alone with the horses. I would brush their coats with a rough cloth until they gleamed in the sunlight. I would bring them small apple treats and talk with them. I cared for them, and they cared for me."

He smiled, remembering their beauty, their gentle giving, his pain as the soldiers had abused them. "I had one, you know. My mother gave him to me."

"A horse?"

"Of course. But something even more special. A carving. Of a horse's head. He had red eyes. They gleamed in the firelight." His smile faded. "I wanted to work with the horses forever. But Fate had other plans. As I grew older, the soldiers began using me. I guess the term that comes closest would be 'combat dummy.' No one cared if I lived or died. But I did.

"Soon word got out about my fighting skills. I fought for the centurions first. Then the tribunes. Finally, the commanding general, Marcus Tiberius Corvus. General Corvus liked to gamble. He ended up losing me in a wager to Casperian. I always thought dying in the arena would be an honorable death in a place where I alone controlled my destiny. I soon learned."

Hunter tried to keep the despair out of his voice. He failed. "I was given matches which were complete routs, favors owed to Casperian to build my reputation."

"Fight fixing?"

He nodded. "I was forced to slaughter men far below my abilities; they forced me to fight without honor. They wouldn't even give me a fair fight." The old bitterness that never truly left filled him. "And I learned. I was a greyhound. I was a Thoroughbred. My only importance was to win my next match and make my master money. Winning was my only purpose."

"Show me," she whispered.

Hunter shook his head. "No. Not necessary. You need to understand Casperian, not the brutality of my time."

She sat back. He felt her mind open. When she did, he gave her images. Images of laughter, flickering lamps, tables laden with food, sweet strains of music in the background. And then he gave her his hunger. Gut-wrenching human hunger. Gnawing, stomach-eating hunger.

"How do you feel, Venatorius?"

"Tired." He tried to remain stoic, calm, blank. "Hungry."

His master beckoned him closer to the dais he rested on. "Yes. You worked hard in the games today."

Casperian bit into a huge, ripe grape, juice bursting inside his mouth as the flesh split open and leaked out onto his cheek for Venatorius to see. Next was a huge hunk of soft, chewy bread, followed by a bite of tangy cheese. Then Casperian tore off a pigeon leg, sauce dripping, sweet and succulent, and bit off a piece of tender flesh, his teeth gleaming white against the dark brown of the bird.

Hunter let her feel the heat of the saliva flooding his mouth. He let her feel the pain of his stomach as it had cramped and caved. He let her feel the torment as Casperian had said, "You may go to your quarters now."

And her next vision. *With Venatorius lying on a straw-covered ledge, the rough edges biting into his back. He sat up as the door opened. A tray was placed on the floor along with a single oil lamp. On the tray sat a hunk of hard, stale bread; a bowl of boiled beans; and the partially eaten pigeon leg.*

Statement made.

Was it enough for her to see that cruelty, for her to know a small part of what he had suffered? He certainly hoped so.

Chapter Eighteen

TORI WAS GLAD HUNTER WAS DRIVING. SHE NEEDED TIME TO process. She wasn't used to barbaric cruelty, even though there was nothing new about it. Humans simply weren't always kind, and she hated cruelty, fought against it with every word of the oath she'd taken. *Do no harm.*

And yet she refused to let evil get the best of her. Every breath she took, every memory of Kelly—the laughing and giggling, the thousand hugs, even more kisses. She missed her baby with every particle of her soul. She fought against malice and brutality with one word. *Love.*

"Casperian had power over every aspect of your life. Right down to the smallest detail."

"Yes."

Tucking her daughter back inside, she tried to imagine. She put herself in the hovel. She stared at the iron bars of a prison that allowed no escape. Her hand ran over the rough stone of the ledge which gave no comfort for sleep. She tasted the stale bread and bland beans. And she wanted more. A hollow ache carved her insides. She wanted the fruit, the sweet wine, and the whole pigeon.

Hunter likened himself to racing animals, but he had been less than an animal. Handled with care because of his bite, caged for his master's safekeeping, and kept because he was only as good as his next kill or...

"Say it," he whispered.

Tori refused. For it would demean everything that had gone on between them.

"Say it!"

Okay! You want it? You got it. "Or your next fuck."

Then again, Tori had to wonder. He'd never been given the chance to develop a "self." So she asked. *Were you hugged? Kissed? Loved?*

He answered with one profound moment. A glimmer. From way far back in the deepest recesses of his mind. *His mother. Creating a cocoon around his body. The security of a mother's embrace. The warmth. The love.*

He knew. Filled with remorse, Tori wondered how he'd been able to plant a picture in her mind. Then she realized she'd pressed him to the edge. Ever the investigative scientist. Always excavating, when a shovel would have sufficed. And now that she'd opened his shell, she wasn't sure she liked the meat inside. "I'm sorry. I had no right to dig."

"Well, well," he sneered, his tone raw and tart. "The righteous, crusading doctor. Ready to save the world. Ready to save me. But at the first sight of a little ugly, you run."

Ugly?

Tori filled her mind with the image of Kelly laughing and running to greet her after a thirty-six-hour shift. The warmth, the security, the love of their embraces. Then she showed him a picture of Kelly lying in her bed, curled up around Teddy, asleep and trusting in a toddler's world. A world Hunter never got the chance to know. "I just realized. And I'm deeply sorry. I've been pushing at you, and you've been pushing at me."

Silence. Deafening silence. And then a single word. "Accepted."

He sounded sincere, and Tori shuddered, reining in her emotions, rebuilding the hole in the wall. Because if the wall was all she had, then that was all she had. Didn't mean it would be forever. Mile markers came and went, until she sighed and asked, "What do you want from me, Hunter?"

"Nothing."

"Are you sure?"

"I am," he answered, certainty ringing in his tone.

Tori paused. She wanted all that was between them out in the open but had just apologized for the very digging she seemed unable to stop. "Aren't you looking for absolution?"

"From what?" he asked, sounding a touch confused.

"Your past, for starters."

"I could say the same about you, now couldn't I?"

Tori sucked in a deep breath. "Yes. Maybe this is why we keep pressing each other. We all carry our own guilt. But for some reason, you seem to want to wallow in it."

She watched his face very carefully. He frowned. "I do not," he retorted.

Another truth. "You don't like being told you're wrong, do you?"

He snorted. "I'm not."

"Well then, think about this," she told him. "When you're a slave to the past—and I do hate using that word, but it fits—the past dictates. And it will continue to dictate. I know it's not an easy fight to win, but you have to try."

"You know nothing," he bit out. "All you do is dare to presume."

"I know. Stupid of me, isn't it? But there you have it. I care."

"I told you not to."

"Why, Hunter?" He didn't answer. "Are you afraid I'll want more? Haven't you been pushing back at me to keep me at arm's length for that very reason?"

He didn't answer. Tori could feel the cold radiating off him in waves. She shivered. "Or maybe you don't want to wallow in your past, you want someone to jump into the pool with you."

"Why would I want you to wallow in my past?"

"Understanding? Aren't you looking for someone to understand exactly what you went through?"

"I. Do. Not. Want. Your. Pity."

"You don't?" she asked. "God. Pity is all you've been asking for since the moment we met. You want me to feel every pang of hunger, every bite of the lash." Sadness filled her. "You want me to tell you that you didn't deserve the treatment you received. Okay. I'm telling you. You didn't deserve the treatment you received."

The car jerked forward as his foot slammed down on the accelerator. She waited a minute, then advised, "I wouldn't speed if I were you. There are cops patrolling the highway, and you don't want to have to explain a speeding ticket in court. Unless, of course, you want to continue feeding and then give them the drug."

Tori didn't have to read minds to know her sarcasm hit its mark. The car slowed down. "Are you finished?"

Her flesh beaded at the chill as he said, "Yes."

"Good." She looked over and didn't like the slight smile on his face. "You say I didn't deserve the treatment I received. But I did."

"No. No one did."

"You're wrong. For every life I took, every thrust of a sword I didn't have to wield, I deserve worse. I should've died. Ended the farce. Instead, I chose to continue."

"And you think surviving makes you unworthy? Someone else would've taken your place. Maybe even enjoyed the killing and not had even a glimmer of a conscience."

"I knew exactly what I was doing. I killed out of hate. And I would do it all over again."

Tori realized Hunter had a long way to go to reach any kind of forgiveness and she was wrong to try to force the issue. He simply wasn't ready yet to hear any kind of truth. But that also meant she needed to protect herself.

"Gotcha. Like I said, I'm sorry. Seems we're both guilty."

"Both?" he asked. Now he sounded bewildered.

"Boy, for someone who can read minds, you can be really deaf, dumb, and blind when you want."

Dead silence.

Tori fought with herself all the way back to the compound, knowing he would hear the conversation going on inside her head. Had she gone too far? Had he?

Once they reached the gates she said, "I'm a doctor. I took an oath to save lives. The oath doesn't differentiate between bad or good, human or vampire. I'll help you. Because it's my duty. But also because your people need my help."

"My *people*?"

"Could you, for one possible instant, not be an ass?" she asked.

"Your words go both ways, you know," he sneered. "What you say and what I hear are two different things. I'm not even sure why you're bothering. I'm mean, we're a duty, right?"

Tori breathed in and out deeply to hold onto her temper. "For the very last time: stay out of my head."

"You have no idea how much I wish I could."

"Good. Then stay away from me. But before you do, read this loud and clear." She waited until she was certain he was listening. "For them. For your people. The people who deserve my help. Do you understand? Not for you. Because right now, you don't even rate the ground I walk on."

"Because I'm a vampire?" he roared.

"No! Because you're an idiot. You keep picking fights so I'll stay away, so I won't get close. Fine. I'll stay away. But remember one thing. You don't have to prove you're good enough to anyone but yourself."

"I don't have to prove my worth to anyone period," he raged. "Certainly not to you. The vampires in this compound know I've built a home for them; they know how long it took and how hard this feat was to accomplish. They have a safe haven here, a constant food source, and protection in numbers. They don't have to be alone anymore."

"Neither do you."

He didn't answer. They screeched to a stop in front of the house. "Fine," she fumed. "You hated being human, and now you just hate. I get the message. Do. Not. Come. Near. The. Lab. Are we clear?"

"Crystal."

Tori made it a point to slam the car door as hard as she could before going inside the house. She had no idea there were tears dripping down her cheeks until she reached the lab and Stacy faced her with alarm in her gaze.

"Oh my God, Tori. Are you all right? What happened?"

Her arms curled around her midsection, but she refused to give in to the pain. Or the anger. "You wouldn't happen to have a ten-by-ten, soundproof vault hanging around, would you?" she asked, wiping at her cheeks.

Stacy fished a tissue out of a box on the counter and handed it to her. "No. But Chaz can fly us to his home in Virginia if you need to get away."

Charles hurried in. Both stared at her with compassion. "I will never get used to this non-privacy thing." He walked over and got her a bottle of water and handed it to her. "Thanks."

Tori took a sip, swallowed, then sat down and buried her face in her hands. Despair filled her. Would he ever be able to see the truth? She rubbed her face, lifted, smoothed her hair back, and wrapped it into a ponytail.

"Hunter has…issues. I wasn't kind. Things kind of devolved from there."

"I always wondered when someone would crack that armor of his," Chaz replied softly. "You're not wrong, you know."

"Neither is he."

Chaz walked over to her and squeezed her shoulder. "There are nearly one hundred vampires living here. I believe, at last count, there were over eighty specimens taken. I think we all know your motives are far from selfish. Hunter may lead because we want him to, but we are an independent bunch when we want to be. Stubborn too. You have friends here."

Tori smiled up at him. She patted the hand resting on her. "Thanks." She rose and lifted her shoulders. "Best medicine right now is for me to get to work."

"I guess that's my cue to leave." He walked over to Stacy, kissed the hell out of her, and left.

Once he was gone Stacy asked, "You okay?"

"No."

"Gotcha. All right. Work first, and then wine. Lots and lots of wine."

Tori opened one of the large stainless-steel refrigerators and sure enough, there sitting on the shelf were racks and racks of tubes. She put on a pair of gloves, even though she didn't think there was anything to worry about, and took a specimen out of a rack. Then she picked up the bag with the specimen Sam had garnered.

"Sam got this one from one of the 'infected' vampires?" Stacy asked.

Tori nodded. "That's what she said."

"Jeez. Look at it. Barely a red cell left. Thin. Let's try to centrifuge it. See what happens." They put the tube in for ten minutes.

"No separation," Stacy confirmed.

"Okay. We do this by the book. Literally. We keep notes in lab notebooks. All observations. Each tube gets numbered and logged in. With all the donor data we have. Including this one."

Stacy nodded. "I've already started a database in the computer. We can continue adding information from there."

"Good. Anything else I need to know?" Tori asked.

"While you were gone, I tried to spin down random tubes. Just to see if they would. Some did, some didn't."

"Let's try correlating the amount of cells with age first."

Since Stacy had already logged the specimens into a computer database, the correlation was simple. Sure enough, the older a vampire got, the less they clotted. Adding platelets to each specimen helped, allowing Tori to run chemistries on the remaining serums.

While she was running those, Stacy took the specimen from the "infected" vampire and ran it on the mass spec and the gas chromatograph.

They'd been working for six straight hours when Chaz walked into the lab. He hugged Stacy and gave her a quick kiss. Then he turned to her. "You both need to eat and get some rest."

Tori nodded, fighting her need to continue. She wanted to see the next result. And the next. She loved being a scientific detective. But there was more. Something driving her.

Hunter, perhaps?

Chaz raised a brow. Tori smiled, a bit sheepish. He nodded to let her know he'd keep her thoughts to himself. Then, from behind his back, he produced a bag that had the seriously awesome aroma of smoked meat and garlic. Her mind went right to garlic and vampires, and she lifted her gaze to see Chaz smile.

"Where did you get this from?" Stacy cried, grabbing at the bag.

She looked down at her watch. "It's six o'clock in the morning. Where in God's name did you find a deli that was open?"

Chaz laughed, putting the bag on a desk away from the equipment and pulling out hot pastrami sandwiches, green pickles, and coleslaw. The works. They laid out the food, and Tori had a half a sandwich in her hands and a bite in her mouth before she could even think. "OMG, this tastes good. Really good," she said in between bites.

Then he pulled out a six-pack. At this exact moment, here couldn't be anything better in the world, Tori thought. "Hot pastrami sandwiches and ice-cold beer. Unbelievable."

"Nothing is impossible," he answered, popping a bottle for himself. He inhaled deeply. "I can almost taste them myself." He half-smiled. "In my day we called it ale."

Tori sat back and devoured most of her sandwich before the question popped into her head. "What's your story, Chaz? How'd you get to be a vampire?"

He hesitated a moment. "I don't normally tell people."

Again, Tori felt contrite. "Sorry. I wasn't trying to pry. Seems my curiosity keeps getting me into heaps of trouble."

"No. It's okay," he answered. "I was literally in the wrong place at the wrong time. I was a guard in the tower of London. Without knowing, we'd imprisoned a vampire. When we opened his cell to take him for execution, he drained all of us dry. There's a choice that remains. Accept death, or beg for eternal life. You get one split second to decide. My fellow guards died. I lived."

"You wanted to become a vampire?"

"I didn't even know the word until Mick found me."

"Mick?"

"Mikhail. My mentor. A vampire cop like me." Chaz paused and gulped some beer. "You see, I decided to accept my fate and die. When we drink to feed and give a human the drug, the Lethe, no one gets harmed. But when we drink to kill? Or when we drain a human to create a vampire? I don't want to call it venom. *Venom* would be too harsh. More like a vampire essence, I guess, gets transmitted. At the moment of my death, the essence decided not to let all of me die. Some of my humanity remained. When this happens, it's kind of different. Vampire cops are different. We're vampires, but we owe no allegiance to being a vampire. I guess that allows us to kill rogues when we have to."

"Do you wish sometimes he hadn't?" she asked, then wanted to bite her tongue for letting her mouth rule her head. "Created you, I mean."

His eyes widened, but he answered honestly. "Yes. Like I said, I didn't even know the word for a few centuries. I had no idea what I'd become. Only that I needed blood to survive. Along with my additional physical attributes." He sighed, and pain filled his gaze. "I went home after it happened. I drained my wife to the point where she got sick and died. I couldn't help myself."

"Damn. I'm so sorry, Chaz." Tori really wanted to kick herself. "You weren't to blame."

He smiled, sad and stoic. "I was and I wasn't. Depends on how you look at it."

Tori nodded. "Same's true for Hunter, is what you're telling me."

Chaz smiled and set his beer down. Stacy stared at him, love pouring from her gaze. Tori was almost jealous. Almost.

"He'll be a tough nut. But I've always found him to be fair. And he genuinely cares for the vampires who live here."

"And the humans?" she couldn't resist asking.

Chaz grinned. "Not for me to say. But he treats Stacy and the other humans who work here with the utmost respect." He nodded, and Stacy walked over to him. They clasped hands. "Now if you don't mind, I'm getting tired, and I'd like to take my wife upstairs so she can get some sleep too."

"No problem." Tori grinned back. "We'll meet back here around four?"

"You bet," Stacy replied, hiding a yawn.

Tori thought Stace might be a little delayed in getting her sleep.

But this was okay. Stacy's happiness came with a price, so she was entitled to every moment of happiness she could get.

They left, and Tori looked around the lab. Analyzers were purring, specimens were incubating, and she, at the moment, had nothing more she could do. She cleaned up the remnants of their meal, walked into the elevator, and went upstairs. After a couple of wrong turns, she finally found Hunter's office. She knocked.

"Come in." He was sitting behind this massive mahogany desk.

"Thank you for all the specimens. You got more than enough for me."

"You're welcome." He finally looked up from the papers he was reading. "Anything else?"

"I was going to apologize for losing my temper. But something tells me I shouldn't bother."

"No. Please. Go ahead," he answered, his features smug.

"You first." Dead silence. "I thought not."

"Exactly." He sat back. "But I will tell you one thing."

She couldn't wait to hear. "What?"

"I broke a cardinal rule."

Tori frowned. She couldn't figure out where he was going with this. "What rule?"

"Never play with your food."

Tori didn't think. She didn't hesitate. She marched up to the desk, leaned over, and cracked him across the cheek. Stunned, she reared back. He could've stopped her hand easily. Why didn't he?

"Because I deserved being slapped."

All of a sudden, she understood. "Trying to be the big, bad vampire, eh, Hunter?"

"No. Simply underscoring the difference between us."

Tori saluted. "Reading you loud and clear...boss."

She pivoted and stormed away, hoping he saw every image her mind created.

Chapter Nineteen

"WHY DID YOU DO THAT?"

Sam. Hunter decided not to look up from his desk. "I don't recall hearing you knock."

"Says the man who craves respect yet gives none," she retorted, obviously annoyed with him.

Hunter dropped the papers he'd been staring at yet trying to read so unsuccessfully. "You know why." When Sam didn't answer, he sighed and looked up. "Because it had to be done."

Her face scrunched up. "Why? Explain," she commanded.

He answered in earnest. "Vampires and humans should never mix. Anonymity has been our way and should continue to be our way."

Staring at him with disgust, Sam sat down in one of the chairs in front of his desk. "Liar. You're not talking about anonymity and you know it." She cocked her head, her accusation ringing in his ears. "For someone who knows every nuance of suffering injustice, every possible slight from prejudice, you're a complete and total ass."

Hunter rose. "I don't recall inviting you into my office either," he answered, his tone cold and clipped.

"Fine," she said, pulling no punches. "One way to keep me out would be to treat me just the way you did Tori."

"I'm not wrong," he insisted. *I'm not wrong.*

She shook her head at him as if he were a child. "Besides being consummately stupid, I never thought you could ever be that cruel."

Hunter, his emotions simmering because he hadn't really liked what he'd done either, let them boil over. "It had to be done!" he shouted.

"Coward!" Sam shouted back, drawing up out of her chair to her regal height.

He couldn't believe she was treating him this way. "I serve no one anymore."

"That you had to say those words scares me, Hunter. I'd like to believe we've been friends all these years as well as compatriots in a common cause."

Apologetic, he answered, "We are when you don't go all high priestess on me."

She smiled, having reached the place she'd been leading him. "Didn't you do exactly the same just now with Tori?"

Had he?

"For the record, I hate when you use your psychology on me," he groused. She didn't answer. Her smile simply deepened. "All right," he sighed, knowing he'd never get any peace until he asked the question. "What exactly am I afraid of?"

"Caring. Feeling. Commitment. All of the above."

Hunter stilled, hearing a word inside his head he thought long dead. One he never thought Sam would shout at him. "Go ahead. Say it."

"Love."

He digested the word. Yes, it was true. He was afraid. Feeling made you—

"No, Hunter," Sam answered in a gentle tone. "Feeling doesn't make you weak."

"Feeling makes you vulnerable," he retorted. "And in this case, that's downright dangerous."

"For whom?" she asked. "I've lived way longer than you, Hunter. So know this. Love doesn't make you weak. It makes you strong."

They could debate this point all night long and not get anywhere. "Casperian would like nothing better than to find out I care about her. He'll hurt, maim, and torture her to get at me. Some things simply should never be. I'm doing this to protect her."

"How very noble of you," she half sneered. "Did it ever occur to you that she has feelings?"

His gaze whipped up to snare Sam's. "She's way better off hating me."

Sam shook her head at him. "You really are a mess." A half-amused, half-revolted look filled her features. "I'm going to try to repair some of the damage you've caused."

He pushed his emotions and his hurt way down deep. "Repair away."

"Fool." Sam drew herself up to her full height, every inch the high queen and priestess of a nation far greater than his own. "I don't need your permission. Neither does she."

Sam turned on her heel and left. Hunter pivoted so he could look out the window. Years of secret toil. Careful manipulation of money. Building this compound. Creating a safe haven for his fellow—were they creatures? Just another life-form, right?

Hunter asked himself the million-dollar question. What had he really wanted? Above all else? What was the true purpose behind this home?

He'd wanted to belong. He'd wanted to be part of a family. A culture. A society. He'd wanted the fruit, the wine, and the entire pigeon.

And now?

Now Hunter wondered. Had he done the right thing?

Yes. Absolutely. There should never be a mingling of their species. All right, he argued with himself, their races. No matter what the moniker, they were different. For one day the blood would win. The blood always won.

Vampire. Human. Could they at least try to coexist? What would become of the kind of friendship Tori wanted? Humans didn't trust. And with good reason. They were food—and would know they were food as soon as they realized vampires were real.

The fight raged on even though Hunter was certain he was right. He had his place. She had hers. Charles and Stacy were doomed to failure.

Weren't they?

And then the words popped into his mind. *How does it feel to become all that you hate?*

Hunter rolled his tongue in his mouth, not liking the taste of what he'd done. Releasing the bitterness, he let out all of the words. Casperian would like nothing better than to hurt her to hurt him, but Hunter and his people needed her. To fight this insidious plot, this monster. Hunter needed to protect his family. And his family came first. Therefore, she needed to hate him.

Didn't she?

God, what had happened to him? When had he become everything he despised? The first backhand to the mouth? The first sting of the lash? The first night he'd suffered the true indignity of his station, bent over a couch, open and defenseless to anything the man had wanted?

No. He knew the exact moment. His first games. The resistance of muscle and flesh, then his blade slicing deep inside another man's gut. That had been the moment. Because by then, it hadn't mattered anymore. He'd stopped caring about anything.

Dead inside. Then dead outside. How strange to finally admit. How fitting.

All those years. Alone. Being hunted by terrified humans who hadn't stopped to ask, who'd shot their arrows and thrown their blades, their axes, making him the one thing he hated above all else.

Outcast.

Until Sam had found him. Until Sam had taught him. What he was. What he could be.

Guess you didn't count on me being an arrogant bastard, did you, Sam?

Hunter.

His name sent a chill down his spine. Her fear enveloped him. He stood stock still.

We have a problem.

Suddenly, the door to his office burst open. Sam looked seriously pissed. But what simmered in her gaze scared the hell out of him. "I've looked everywhere, and I can't find her. Tori's gone."

Chapter Twenty

TORI SHIVERED AS SHE CAME AWAKE. COLD, DAMP AIR FILTERED down beneath her collar. She tried to make out where she was. A small, shack-like building. Smelled like damp, rotting leaves and aged wood—her gaze traveled the small area—with a large object in the corner that looked like some kind of a pump.

"You're awake."

God, her head hurt. She closed her eyes and willed the pain into a small ball. *Think, Tori. Think.* She reached up to touch what felt like a huge baseball on the back of her head, only to find her hands tied. *Great.*

"Who are you?"

"Jonas."

Her heart sped up, causing a hollow to form inside her stomach. Her head pounded at the same speed. Tori swallowed hard to get her fear under control. "What do you want with me?"

No answer.

"Newly minted?" she asked.

It was shadowy and kind of dark, so she couldn't really see his face. "'Scuse me?"

Tori shrugged. Either he was ignoring the question or didn't understand. "Nothing." She shifted. Her hands were tied. But not her feet. "Where are we?"

"New York."

Again, just a lot of help. Tori breathed in again. This time she tried to make sense of the air. Smelled like forest. Pine. Musty. Definitely like woods. Could be Stokes State Park, could be Bear Mountain. She decided to try the latter. "Bear Mountain?"

He didn't answer.

With a groan, she rotated her neck, and pain shot up through the base of her skull. Better not to do that. "What do you want with me?"

Again, he ignored her question. "The discomfort won't last long."

Tori rotated her neck again. "How would you know?"

"Just a mild brain injury. Maybe a contusion. Nothing serious."

She frowned. "You sound like a third-year med student." With a slightly British accent.

"Just about to graduate. With honors."

"Why would you be dealing with the likes of Casperian?" Tori paused. "Oh. I get it. Money." He shrugged. "He doesn't care about anyone, least of all you."

He glanced over at her, brows drawn together. "Feeling's mutual."

Wait a minute. Something wasn't exactly right here. "Really," she drawled, trying to learn more. "You've stirred up a hornet's nest, you know. My disappearance isn't going to go over too well."

He smiled, seemingly unconcerned. "Just a lackey doing a lackey's job."

"Which pays very well," she surmised. "What with student loans coming due."

He didn't answer.

"So you're not a vampire."

"God, no!"

"But you know about them. How? You do realize there's a posse of vampires coming to get me as we speak?"

Tori screamed the words in her mind over and over again. *It's a trap. Stay away!*

"You're playing with fire, you know," she continued. "Your boss considers you nothing more than a loose end."

"Not 'boss.'" A thoughtful look filled his features. "I have a contingency plan."

Whatever that plan was, Tori knew it had better be good. The vampire wasn't one to trifle with anyone or anything that stood in his way.

"Oh?" The high-pitched question sounded as the door to the shack opened. Speak of the devil. "And what is that?"

Several soldiers followed by a man stepped into the small room. Tall, thin, terribly pale, Casperian moved as if he owned everyone and everything around him. His close-cropped, black hair only accentuated the severe lines of his face. Long, hawk-like nose. Longer chin. Pale, nearly translucent cold eyes. Patrician to the core, arrogant, and —she already knew—a bully.

"I believe the expression is 'cat got your tongue?'" Casperian commented.

Jonas eyed his potential business partner carefully as he rose to his feet. But he still didn't answer. Tori wondered why.

"All right," the vampire continued. "I'm intrigued. You set this up. Why?"

Jonas took his time answering. "I have the key to Nirvana."

The man laughed. "Of course you do." Jonas didn't flinch, and Casperian looked a bit startled. "Very well. I'll play along for the moment. And what might that be?"

Jonas smiled. "Do you really think I'd be stupid enough to tell you? Here? Now?"

"You don't have a choice," the vampire answered, his tone turning deadly. Then he took a deep breath, letting the air out slowly. "But don't worry. I won't kill you. Can't promise about her though."

Brazen little bastard just smirked and pointed to a corner of the shack. She hadn't seen the laptop sitting on a crate in the shadows. Stunned, Tori didn't know whether to applaud him for his balls or his stupidity.

"Fine. I'll tell you," Jonas continued. "It's right there in my computer. All of it."

Casperian flicked his hand, and one of his soldiers went to grab the computer. "I wouldn't if I were you," she warned, beginning to figure out the game.

The vampire eyed her with suspicion. "Why not?"

"He's probably programmed some sort of failsafe into the computer. Without the right name and password—because fingerprint identity is useless since he's here—I'd say all the data will be wiped clean."

"Did you do that?" Casperian asked, his brows drawing together. Damn, the vampire actually looked pissed. Tori flicked Jonas a quick glance, rather impressed.

Jonas's mouth quirked. "Maybe."

The vampire stilled. Then he started. His eyes widened. He paused as if he was trying again, then he frowned. "I can't read your mind."

Tori burst out laughing. Her head nearly exploded, but she couldn't help herself.

The vampire tried again. Obviously with the same result because his lips thinned and his gaze really narrowed. He reached out and lifted Jonas by the neck. Jonas's face turned beet red. Then it started turning purple. Jonas flailed and clawed at the hand that held him.

"Temper, temper," Tori mocked. "You don't really want to do that, do you? After all, you shouldn't kill the one person on this planet who might be able to help you."

Casperian let go. Jonas clutched his neck, gasping for air and writhing on the concrete floor.

"I can make you wish you'd never been born," the vampire said to Jonas, each word coated in sick anticipation.

Tori watched in amazement as Jonas started to breathe again, then turned his gaze toward his attacker. "Don't...waste..." he choked out, "your time." Jonas hacked and coughed. "I don't know the password. Or the formula."

Dead silence. Then the door opened again. "But I do."

What?

Flaming-red hair, emerald-green eyes, almost as pale as Casperian. She bent down and looked at the marks on Jonas's neck, her gaze narrowing. "You all right, sweetheart?"

Jonas nodded and smiled up at this new guest. What the hell?

Casperian looked put out. "You thought to trap me instead?" His head cocked. "Your name is Vanessa."

She nodded. "Trap?" she asked, tapping a perfectly manicured finger against her chin. "Let's see now. I wouldn't say 'trap.'"

"You don't have the strength to take me on," he goaded.

She laughed softly. "Hadn't planned on it."

"Really."

Casperian paused, and the redhead continued. "But I never underestimate an adversary. You've told me a great deal without saying a word."

"Indeed." Now the vampire looked thoughtful. "How does he shield his mind?"

"Ancient meditation techniques practiced his entire life at the foot of the Dalai Lama," she sassed back.

Casperian's chin lifted. Tori watched his fist clench. "I don't like being played with. And I don't like being the butt of a joke."

She simply laughed. This time right out loud. "Darling, you're way too serious. Besides, I can't help myself. You asked for that." Vanessa seemed to be debating. "Jonas? Do tell the man and appease his curiosity."

Jonas coughed, hawked, and spat. "I was born this way."

"Indeed."

"Now, sweetie pie," she continued, turning toward the vampire, a sneer threading her tone, "why don't you go crawl back under that rock you slimed yourself out of."

Casperian seemed about to answer, then changed his mind. He motioned to his soldiers to leave. "Moves and countermoves," he chortled with glee.

Only one soldier remained, and Vanessa started toward him. They eyed each other, each gauging the small space they had for fighting. They continued to circle. A minute later, Sam and Hunter rushed into the shack. Out of the corner of her eye, Tori watched the soldier stop and pull a gun out of his waistband. There was a click, a whoosh, and then something arched toward her. She tried to duck. The next thing she knew, Hunter threw himself in front of her. Whatever it was never reached her. Instead, it hit Hunter. He grunted and landed on the concrete just in front of her. Something seemed to be sticking out of his arm. Hunter automatically reached for it with his hand, but he never made it. He crumpled. Then he lay as still as the dead.

Mocking laughter filled the room as he left with his soldiers. Casperian finally got his revenge.

Chapter Twenty-One

"Damn it, Vanessa!" Sam shouted, falling to her knees next to Hunter. "What the hell were you thinking?"

Tori scrambled over to him too, heart pounding, pain forgotten. He seemed asleep. She knew better. What did Casperian want most of all? For Hunter to suffer and die. And what better way to do that?

"Nirvana," she whispered.

One word. One death sentence.

"Damn it! I told you not to come," Tori moaned, trying to gather her wits and assess him.

Panic filled Sam's voice. "I couldn't stop him. He was like a madman."

"All I wanted," Vanessa whispered in horror, "was to tease Casperian out. Just tease him out. Jonas is unique. I thought he might get that weasel to make a mistake."

"Instead," Tori bit out, "he turned the tables on us. On you." She looked up at Sam. "We have to get Hunter back to the lab."

A hand reached out to grip her arm. Emerald-green eyes were filled with remorse. Vanessa opened her other palm. Inside rested the dart that had pricked Hunter's arm. "Thank you." Tori wrapped the dart in a tissue and put it into her pocket.

Mercy stood in the doorway, her face made of stone. But Tori caught her gaze. With one glance, they shared their terror. Mercy motioned to three of her men to pick up Hunter. She didn't say anything. She didn't have to because Tori knew. Mercy cared.

"Be gentle," Tori begged.

"You," Sam commanded, pointing at Jonas. "Come with us." She turned to Vanessa. "I'll deal with *you* later."

Once they were in the car on their way back to the compound, Tori tried to think. Hunter lay draped across her lap. He looked so at peace. "Is it true, Jonas? Can you really shield your thoughts from them?"

"Yes," he answered, his accent thickening. "Ness found me roaming the streets in London after my mum OD'd. She took me in, then adopted me and brought me to the States. Kinda raised me." He grinned. "I kinda lied about needing the money."

"Then you really are a med student?" Tori asked. He nodded. "You do realize the oath means *do no harm*, don't you?"

He shrugged, but Tori could tell he hadn't wanted to hurt anyone. "You try telling Ness no."

Indeed.

"Vanessa may have shown her strategy too early," Tori murmured, torn between worry for Hunter's condition and worry whether or not Casperian would now have the upper hand.

"Perhaps," Sam answered. "But the dart was meant for you, not Hunter."

For her? "A win-win," Tori replied. "I have a feeling there's more than just Nirvana on the dart. Think about it. If something happens to me, Hunter gets hurt. If Hunter follows and something happens to him? Self-explanatory."

Sam sounded ready to tear concrete apart as she asked, "How does Casperian know about you?"

"I don't understand," Tori answered.

"Our telepathic powers—if you want to call them that—only work in close proximity. I'm the one exception. Hunter is sort of an exception."

The car sped up as Tori considered. "The night I was attacked. Maybe Casperian was there?"

Sam shook her head. "Then Hunter would've known."

"Maybe he did and didn't want to say. After all, he hasn't been happy about any of this."

Sam shrugged. She turned in her seat. "Perhaps."

Tori continued thinking. "You know, we did have a shouting match in my townhouse parking lot too. Casperian might not know Hunter cares for me, but he certainly knows Hunter was trying to protect me."

Sam nodded without answering. Finally, she asked, "Will you be able to help him?"

Instead of answering Sam right away, she looked over at Jonas. "You just became my number one med tech."

He nodded. "Glad to be of service."

Sam turned toward her again. "You sound worried," she told Tori, her gaze still filled with a mixture of serenity and fear. "Don't be."

How? "You're all a medical nightmare," Tori confessed. She understood human biology, not vampire biology. Half the time she guessed. The other half, clueless.

Sam laughed softly. "I have to admit I've never been called a medical nightmare before." She pulled up in front of the gates. "Whatever happens, Hunter came to terms with his fate a long time ago."

Determination filled Tori. Just because she didn't understand didn't mean she didn't know how to investigate or figure things out. She hadn't lost her brains. Yet. "Well, I haven't."

"Good because I have faith in you," Sam replied.

"Faith?" she asked as the gates opened. "That's just totally awesome," she added, snark filling the words. *Stop*, she told herself, trying to rein in her emotions. "You know I'll do everything in my power to fix Hunter. But Vanessa was right, I'm Hunter's weakest link. She saw that. So has Casperian."

Sam shook her head. "You're also his greatest strength."

Damn it! "Not if I can't heal him."

"Trust yourself, Tori. Trust yourself."

She didn't answer. A group of soldiers from the compound took Hunter out of the car almost before the vehicle came to a full stop. They had him on a medical bed and up the steps by the time she got out of the car.

Stacy ran out to meet her. "What happened?"

"Casperian." Stacy caught her gaze, confused. "Long story." Tori pulled the dart out of her pocket. "I need to know what's on this dart, Stace. You're the forensic chemist. Go for it."

Stacy's fingers closed gently around the dart in her hand. "Will do."

They both turned to go into the house, when Chaz ran up to them, his face filled with dread. "They're giving him blood."

"What?"

A flood of anger filled her veins. "I tried to stop them," he continued. "So did Mercy."

Tori flew toward the elevator. She ran inside, feet barely touching floor, pacing the small space, then jumping out before the doors even opened fully. She ran into the lab, skidding to a halt next to the hospital bed. "No! Stop!"

A vampire she'd never met looked up. His brows drew together as if to ask what was an insignificant human doing telling him what to do? "He needs blood."

"NO!"

"Blood helps us heal," the vampire insisted with the tone of an impatient parent.

"You don't understand. We don't know what he's been given. I believe it's Nirvana, and we don't know exactly what that is or how it works. You have to stop."

The vampire ignored her and checked the IV line.

Sam marched in, gaze blazing. "Hold!"

She stormed up to Hunter and ripped the IV out of his arm, where it dripped on the floor. A whole lot of gazes followed those drops. Sam lifted her chin and raised a brow. Tori couldn't hear what she was telling them, but she hoped they'd listen to reason.

"But we've always given blood to the sick and wounded," the vampire who'd been giving Hunter the blood protested.

Sam answered so she could hear. "Do you challenge my word?"

The vampire thought about it. She had to give him credit for that. But Tori also didn't want to be responsible for vampire fighting vampire. "Can we please take this down a notch? We all want what's best for Hunter."

"Do we?" the vampire shot back.

"Look. I don't have time right now to argue. And I don't have time to go into detail. You're all under attack by a vampire named Casperian. This vampire is Hunter's sworn enemy. He wants to kill me because he's afraid I can help you."

"Help us how?" the vampire with the attitude shot back.

"I believe," Sam began, "Casperian is using some kind of drug to create rogue vampires."

The ensuing silence deafened.

"Hunter thought so too," Tori added.

Charles stepped up to agree. "I would be here if I thought otherwise. My duty is to destroy rogues. So far we've tracked two more vampires we believe are going rogue as we speak."

"Hunter killed the one who tried to attack me. Now why would a rogue attack me? I mean, c'mon. What am I?" she asked, the sarcasm in her tone building. "Just a human, no?"

Sam flashed Tori a quick look.

"Instead, your leader brought me here when he could have simply left me to die. Because I'm special. Because I have a skill you all need. I'm a doctor. A pathologist. I save lives." She paused, drawing in a deep breath. "I'm trying to save all of yours. So is Stacy."

Tori wasn't privy to the rest of the conversation. As it ended, Chaz walked up to her, compassion in his gaze. "They may be stubborn, but they're not stupid. Give them a chance."

Sam focused on the group. Obviously one last message. Then they all bowed and melted away, except the one with the attitude. He stormed off.

"That was fun," Sam groused.

"I'm not sure I like your definition," Tori muttered in agreement.

Mercy stayed. She looked embarrassed. No, not quite. And Tori learned another vampire lesson. Although vampires wanted a society, deep inside they were loners and felt little or no responsibility for other's actions. Another piece to the Hunter puzzle.

Still, Mercy tried to apologize. And Tori wondered. Could they change?

"You must forgive them," Mercy began. "They're kind of set in their beliefs. Comes from being starved and hunted over the centuries."

"I know," she sighed, torn from being hurt and hurting for them.

Sam reached out. "I'm sorry."

"Not your fault," Tori replied.

Hunter moaned, and all thought fled as she rushed to his side. His eyes popped open. He clutched his midsection. "I don't feel very well."

"Crazy fool. The dart was meant for me. What were you thinking?" she admonished.

His head lolled. He swallowed hard and tried to smile. "Reflex."

There was the Hunter she needed to see. She bent down and caught a whiff of the same smell she'd nearly gagged on from the rogue Mercy had eventually destroyed. Her heart sank, and her stomach hollowed. But she pasted a smile on her face. "Right."

"Never wanted…you involved."

She lifted up and ran a gentle finger down his cheek. His mouth quirked. "Stuff happens."

He moaned again, and Tori reared back, fear flooding her insides. "I need to get to work."

"If I didn't know better," Stacy added, bringing over a large white bucket, "I'd say he wants to throw up."

"Can that be?" Sam stared, aghast.

Tori thought for a long moment. "Yeah. It can." Sam motioned for her to go on. "Think about it. You're not alive. At least not as I understand it. But you're still a carbon-based organism. And this means you still have to follow the laws of nature."

Stacy nodded. "Makes sense."

"All right. Instead of trying to figure out what you are or you aren't, let's trying stepping outside the box a moment. Let's think of you as a different form of life."

Confused, Sam replied, "All right. But to what end?"

With an exasperated frown Tori answered, "Because I don't want to think of Hunter or you as, well, a car. But I'm going to have to."

Bewildered, Sam exclaimed, "A car?"

Beside her, Stacy murmured, "Of course."

"Yeah. I know. It sounds weird. But just consider this. How does a car run? It uses fuel, which it combusts with air which gives off energy to make the wheels turn. Think of the body. It uses fuel, which it combusts with air which gives off energy to make the limbs move. Are you getting the picture now?"

"I think so," Sam replied slowly.

Stacy bounced with excitement. "I'll be damned. Why didn't I think of that?"

Tori shot her a quick grin. "Because you were too close to the problem. So was I."

Sam still looked bewildered, so Tori explained. "The only thing I've seen so far making you different from being human is you've bypassed the intake of fuel. By drinking oxygen-rich blood, you don't need to eat. It's superfluous. You don't need a liver or kidneys or a functioning stomach, although how you process dead cells is beyond me."

Stacy laughed softly. "They only have the phagocytes they take in. I've been wondering that myself."

"All right, the analogy isn't perfect," she sighed. "But your brain still functions. Your heart still functions. Your lungs."

Sam caught her gaze. She was listening intently now.

"You're sensitive to pain, so your nervous system still functions. I think one of the keys to the process is your cells still function as if they were human."

"Process?" Sam asked, a bit insulted, by her tone, but mostly intrigued.

Tori grinned. "I'm having trouble categorizing your state of—well, I can't call you alive, but I can't call you dead either. So perhaps *undead* is correct after all."

"Thanks," she replied, a bit miffed.

"I wasn't trying to insult you. Just stating the facts as I see them."

Facts? Right now, Tori surmised, along with a deep hunger gnawing at his guts, Hunter wanted to get violently ill. "The process by which you stay 'undead' is the key. Hunter's need to expel blood is because his body is rejecting it."

"Rejecting blood?" Sam cried. "Impossible," she continued, appalled by Tori's reasoning.

"That would never happen. Ever."

Tori raised a single brow to hammer home her point. "You can't deny logic, Sam. Something is happening to the blood he's taken in, rendering it useless to his body—unable to carry oxygen. So his body is trying to get rid of it." She nodded, her mind whirling but her logic crystal clear. "And you just proved my point."

"How?"

"By protesting loud enough to tell me none of you would ever waste a drop."

Chapter Twenty-Two

Hunter awoke to the music of soft snores. Human snores. For a moment he was a child again, caught in that sweet resting place between waking and dreaming. He dared not move, for this would bring pain and the pain would bring back reality. So, he stayed still and concentrated on the beauty of the sound.

Of course, reality intruded—but slowly. Hunter knew he was in pain when he shouldn't have been, knew he'd been sleeping when he shouldn't have been, and wasn't quite sure how he'd ended up in this bed. A terrible hunger clutched at his insides. He acknowledged it, then dismissed it. He'd been hungry before.

Searching his mind, Hunter knew something was wrong. He shouldn't be in this kind of state. Vampires, with fresh blood and a vampiric sleep, were able to heal themselves. So being sick didn't make sense.

With effort, he went over the events of Tori's abduction. Absolute terror filled his mind again once he remembered. Casperian. Losing his mind thinking Tori had been his prisoner and that she'd been in danger. God, even now the pictures in his mind made him shudder. Because Casperian would torture her with every demeaning act the bastard could think of before he decided to kill her.

Hunter came to full awareness in stages. He was in the lab, and Tori was curled up rather uncomfortably in a chair beside his bed. And he was in this bed because…?

Drugged. The pinprick in his arm. The fire ants under his skin. His whole body shook as they returned and marched up and down. He stared at his skin, watching it ripple. What was wrong with him?

Pain clawed at his belly. Liquid fire streaked through his veins. Hunter clenched his fists, fighting the overwhelming urge to double over in abject misery.

The room began to spin. He closed his eyes and swallowed hard to get it to stop.

Hunter was a gladiator. He'd been knifed, speared, cut hundreds of times. As a vampire, he'd known pain thousands of times worse than any he'd experienced in his human life. The only times in his life when he'd been afraid had been when he'd faced the unknown, the way he did right now.

The ants marched again and were eventually replaced by fire. The burn sizzled its way to his fingertips, and he stared at them. The sting disappeared, only to be replaced by tiny shards of ice. Fire and ice. Followed by another sear of pain, the likes of which he'd never felt before.

Hunter doubled over. Something was terribly wrong. Saliva filled his mouth. Suddenly he heard Tori jump up. She pulled him over the edge of the bed. A bucket rested on the floor.

He made it just in time.

Blood, dark and acrid, surged out of his incisors. He watched it stain the white plastic in total amazement. He shuddered violently, the next explosion more forceful than the first. Sweat shimmered on his brow. The stench made his stomach turn over. A stench he knew well.

Tori picked up a washcloth, wet it with cold water, and wiped his forehead. He gasped for breath as he fell back into the bed, his cheek resting against the cool fabric of a pillow, his gaze filling with helpless confusion.

This had never happened before. Ever.

She helped him shift his weight until he was sitting up against the back of the bed to keep himself upright. His lips were slightly parted, the only sign of his distress being the extension of his incisors and his chest heaving for air. But the smell. Sour and coppery. Old and dead. He watched her face fall. Tori knew that smell. He knew it too. It was the smell of dead blood. Rogue blood.

"I'm here, Hunter. So is Sam." She held a cup of cool water to his lips to rinse the taste out of his mouth. "You've been asleep for nearly two days and nights."

Why? he wondered, dismissing the passage of time. He deserved no quarter, no forgiveness. Certainly not any help or kindness. "I don't feel too well."

Although she frowned, she also tried to shrug off his statement. "Hey, this is good news."

Really? His brain was swimming. The marching became relentless. "Ants."

"Ants?" she echoed. He could hear a thread of excitement in Tori's voice. "Tell me more, Hunter. As much as you can."

"Fire. Crawling. Inside my veins."

"Where?" she demanded.

"All over. But mostly in my arms, legs, and fingers."

"Do you feel pain?"

Somewhere in the recesses of his disoriented mind, Hunter heard the question come from another voice—the voice of a priest, the same priest who tied him to a cross and left him to die with the dawning of the sun.

A searing shaft of agony gutted his insides. He clutched his midsection. He knew that for his past actions he would have to pay, and he accepted his fate. "Yes."

"Good. This is a good beginning. Can you tell me anything else?"

"My head. I feel dizzy."

"Keep going, Hunter," she urged. "Keep going."

"I feel…drained. Weak."

A telling silence followed.

"Hunter?"

Again his body turned into this massive roll of liquid. Kind of like a waterbed. He had no substance but didn't think he was leaking anywhere. Yet.

"Listen to me, Hunter. This is good. Very good. Thank you."

He closed his eyes. The sleep. The sleep cured. Maybe he just needed more. "That's it," she told him. "Go ahead. Relax."

Time became irrelevant. Then the fire turned to ice and the ice to ants. And cycled over and over again.

He opened his eyes to the most incredible beauty, knowing he didn't deserve a moment of gazing upon such treasure. But it was the concern on her face and the slither of fear for him which warmed his heart the most.

He swallowed to try to wet his throat, then asked, "Why are you here?"

"I'm not sure what you're asking," she replied.

"Why do you stand by my side?"

She looked thrown for a moment. "I told myself it was because I was a doctor and you were my patient."

"And now?"

"And now I know I was lying to myself. I'm afraid I didn't have much of a choice. I couldn't help but listen. You were having a nightmare and talking in your sleep. Casperian hurt you so badly, and then you hurt him. Don't you think it's time to stop the feud?"

Feud? What a mild way of putting the bitterness churning in his guts. "You didn't answer my question."

"Actually, I did." Hunter frowned, not understanding. "I care about you, Hunter. As flawed as you are, and as hard as you've had to become to survive. I care about you. As much as you've tried to push me away, hurt me so I hurt you, I keep coming back. Because underneath the name, underneath the leader, under all the centuries of pain and mistrust and abuse, there's an untainted soul inside you, the soul of a man who was human once. There's still the little boy huddled in his mother's arms."

He flicked a sidelong glance at her in utter disbelief. "Nearly two thousand years," she continued, shaking her head at him. "How long do you think you can go on before your past finally catches up with you?"

He snorted softly. "It already has."

She shook her head. "Not even close. Because you missed the

point again. You've never had the chance to live, and you never will. Look, I wouldn't have stayed around, I wouldn't be here now unless I saw more than what you think is inside you. Don't you think it's time to give yourself a chance?"

Hunter wasn't sure he understood her words. But he understood the look in her eyes. Tenderness wasn't something directed at him. Ever. And for a moment, he drowned in it.

Hesitation filled his voice as he asked, "A chance of what?"

She took a deep breath and seemed to steel herself as she replied, "Life. The chance of living a life that's more than just war and duty and honor. A chance to be the boy I saw, a chance to be the boy who grows into the man."

"I'm not a mere soldier," he insisted, his chin lifting. "Even though I believe this has become a war."

She lifted a brow. "Not exactly true, now is it? I mean, considering you're lying in a hospital bed wounded during what could be construed a battle?"

"Point taken," he bit out not liking the reminder.

"Hunter," she began in earnest. "Listen to me. You need to fight this. With all the guts and determination and cunning you used in the arena. I can't do this without you. I need you to put things back into perspective. Survival is ninety percent will, mind over matter."

Mind over matter? How simple this sounded. He should let go. But Tori wouldn't let him do that. So he had to ask the question.

"Why do it at all?" She stopped short and frowned. "Why do you care? After the way I've treated you, you should be rejoicing in my suffering."

"I took an oath to save lives. No one ever said what kind of lives. Or that the one who'd hurt me the most would need me the most. It's called forgiveness."

No. This wasn't the way life—or death—worked. "I give no quarter. I deserve no quarter."

She crossed her arms over her chest. "True. And you'll keep on doing the same. Until you understand one thing."

"What is that?"

"You need to forgive yourself first."

Chapter Twenty-Three

FORGIVENESS.

Tori stood under the stinging spray of the shower and wondered if Hunter would ever understand. How many nights? Doubled over and unable to breathe? Telling herself how she should never have left them, how she would've been able to stop the thieves if she'd just been home. Then beating herself into a pulp because she'd been partying, having a blast, enjoying a weekend away.

How long had it taken? To even think of coping? A year? Longer, maybe. And how long had it taken until she'd been able to even think about trying to smile? To laugh. Until she'd been able to even go out to a restaurant without wanting to flay herself alive. Because her life had come to consist of going home, then going to the hospital or to the school, then going home again.

Of course there'd been the temptation. Sedatives. Happy pills. Begging for one night of respite so she could sleep without the nightmares. But she'd deserved those nightmares. Right? They'd been her penance.

Better to be dead than without them. Her family. Her loved ones. Her baby. Right?

If it hadn't been for Stacy and Kelley and a couple of other sorority sisters, she'd never have survived. They'd forced her to go to a support group. They'd set up therapy sessions and made sure she'd gone. And they'd reinforced what the doctors, the police, every analyst had said.

It wasn't her fault.

And was she coping? She smiled, still not sure about that one but finally accepting the words. What had happened wasn't her fault, at face value. Bad things happened to good people. Innocent children died every day. She was just as much a victim as they were.

Tori knew all the platitudes too.

Would she ever accept them deep inside? Hard to say. The wall would have to come down first. Or else she'd have to make a door and let someone in. Someone who'd suffered just as much, if not more.

Hunter Pierce.

In big, bold letters.

Hunter Pierce?

The man who considered her a filet mignon? With mushrooms and onions?

And yet for all his protests, he'd thrown himself in front of that dart and protected her as he'd said he would without worrying about his own life. Duty and honor?

His shining moment. Her—God she knew all about that kind of failure. Her duty to protect her family. Her mother. Her father. Beautiful. Sweet. Oh God, Kelly. No more arms wrapping around her neck. No golden halo resting on her chest. So much love in such a small package.

Tori shuddered as a piece of the wall blew away. Her fists clenched. Tears filled her eyes and mingled with the water dripping from the shower. She straightened and, in her mind, reached out. She slapped mortar down onto the broken wall. A brick. Then another. And another. And when she could breathe again, she started in surprise. The agony. A little bit less painful, a little bit easier to bear.

Because of Hunter. Because he put his life on the line for her.

Did he need her as a woman? Or did he need her as a doctor? Did he care, even a little? If so, she'd need to know the why before she even thought about framing the portal.

All of which would become a moot point if she didn't figure out what was wrong with him.

After she toweled off and threw on some clothes, Tori grabbed her laptop and went back to the lab.

Stacy joined her. "How's it going with the dart?" Tori asked.

"Gonna be a while," Stace answered. "But I found something interesting. As we know, vampire skin knits almost immediately. Seems it might go back to transcription factors in their cells. You know, we could really use a molecular biologist on this."

"Or a cellular kineticist."

"Or both," Stacy added. "Morgan?"

Tori wasn't sure. "Three humans knowing about vampires?"

"Gotcha," Stace murmured. "Last resort."

Until then, they were stuck. "Okay, you keep going. Our best bet is still to find out what Nirvana is. I'll keep trying to get Hunter back on his feet."

Hmmm. Symptom mitigation. If you couldn't beat a disease right away, you tried to live with it until you could.

As soon as he was able to eat, Hunter would become strong again. Tori hoped.

First rule, what goes in must come out. Poison went in. Now poison was coming out. And normal human blood cells weren't strong enough to fight whatever was attacking them.

But what about royal blood cells? Was it possible that Sam might be able convert blood cells to make them stronger? Could she carry some kind of innate mechanism because she was one of the first of their kind? After all, she was the strongest and oldest of them all.

Tori nearly killed herself running over to the microscope.

SAM!

Chapter Twenty-Four

HUNTER KNEW TWO INDISPUTABLE FACTS. ONE, THE SIGHT OF Sam's wrist, pulse fluttering beneath her pale skin, was akin to an oasis in the Sahara. And two, no matter how much he wanted to drink, he couldn't.

"Hunter...." Sam chastised.

"We can do this the hard way or the easy way," Tori chimed in. Her words sounded a touch eager, didn't they?

He shuddered. "You're not putting another IV in me," he shot back.

"If I didn't know how much you want my blood or how sick you really are, I think I'd be insulted," Sam retorted, rolling her eyes. "Don't make me get rough with you."

Hunter didn't know how to explain. Every time he tried, that sour, disgusting taste came back. That old, tainted blood taste. The kind he'd never ever go near.

How Casperian must be laughing.

Taking matters into her own hands, literally, Sam tore at her wrist and shoved it into his mouth. Each time he sucked he forced himself not to clench and let the blood surge back. After a moment his whole body quaked. He had to tear away. Either that or he'd be bending over and heaving into the bucket again.

"How much did he get?" Tori asked Sam.

"Not nearly enough," she replied.

They both stared at him like he was some sort of experiment gone bad. "I'm fine. I feel better."

As he said the words, he knew them to be true. He did feel a little better.

Sam simply stared. Tori frowned. "All right," he sighed. "I'll try to take a little more."

The reaction was even more violent this time, and he only got a couple of sips before he had to stop. About an hour later, though, the ants stopped marching.

"They've stopped," he whispered in wonder. Then he said the words louder. "They've stopped."

Tori came running over. "The ants?"

"Yes. Though I'm still not sure about the rest."

Hunter had rarely overindulged as a human. But he did remember the morning after he'd watched Casperian grope Antonia, knowing what was going to happen next. He'd gotten violently sick from too much wine. He felt the same now, wanting the sickness to end and impatient with himself for getting into this situation. "I haven't felt sick in nearly two thousand years. I'd forgotten what the feeling was like."

"I could tell you all payments come due eventually," Tori told him, part of her words sounding like they were in jest, part of them sounding way too sincere.

He hung his head. Feeling remorseful wasn't something he was used to. "You're right. I deserve every moment. I was very nasty to you."

She nodded. "And if I wanted to play this kind of game, we could go tit for tat. But this isn't your fault."

What? "I don't understand." After everything he'd done to her, she was being kind? No. Impossible. "Without me, Casperian disappears."

"Do you really think so?" she asked, her tone intense.

Hunter thought about that a moment. Casperian wanted nothing more than to break him and keep on breaking him. "He wants me to suffer."

She shook her head. "No. He wants *everyone* to suffer. I don't know why. Maybe it doesn't even matter. What matters is that we must stop him. I can't change his behavior. You certainly can't."

"Oh yes I can," he retorted. "I can end his worthless rotten life."

"You can," she agreed, her hand gripping the railing on the bed. "Or you can let go of your hatred."

What? "Let go? He tried to kill you!"

She shook her head at him as if talking to a child. "Haven't you ever heard that the definition of *insanity* is performing the same act repeatedly and expecting a different outcome? The Casperians of this world will always try to kill and keep on trying. Yes, he needs to be stopped. And yes, I need to figure out how to neutralize Nirvana and any other drug he comes up with. Because he can harm others. Not because we've already been harmed."

Hunter stared at her as if she'd grown a pair of horns. What was she trying to tell him? "You've lost me."

"What he's done to you is over. The past can't be changed. If you set out to stop him out of vengeance, you'll never heal yourself."

Heal? Why would she want him to heal? After what he'd done to her? "Doesn't matter. He'll be dust."

"And what will you be?" she hammered home. "Whole? The man you were before?"

Hunter frowned.

Tori sighed. "Funny, I don't think the men who murdered my family have stopped robbing houses. But I do know if I keep letting bitterness rule my life, then my life is over."

She paused to let her words sink in. "At one time this might have been acceptable. I called it justice. And I was willing to make that trade just as you are right now. What you need to understand is it isn't justice anymore."

Not justice? Of course it was. An eye for an eye. Still not understanding, Hunter stared at her. So beautiful. Her doe-like eyes filled with warmth. And—yes, he was certain—compassion. For him. "Why not?"

"Because I found out I still care about people. And people are worth caring about."

"After everything you've been through?"

She nodded. "I have a group of friends who'd lie down and die for me if they could, who forced me to stay alive when all I wanted was to join my family. You can't imagine how it feels to be cared about like that, to be loved like that." She paused and grinned at him. "And a very stubborn vampire who just saved my life trying his damnedest to do the same and die for me."

What was she driving at? His insides were a swamp. His head pounded with the steady dirge of a bass drum. He couldn't think straight.

Did she simply want him to turn the other cheek? Did she think it was possible? "Then you don't want these men to pay for their crimes?"

The doctor. The oath. Her oath. Not exactly the way she was staring back at him at the moment. He knew death when he read it. "After it happened, the only way I was able to go to sleep at night was imagining I had a red-hot stiletto and I put it through each one of their eyeballs."

Hunter backed up a bit. "Sorry I asked."

"No you're not." She laughed.

"I can't turn the other cheek," he told her, a sliver of remorse running through him as he thought of what he'd done to her. "I'm not made that way."

"I understand." She leaned her elbows on the railing to get closer to him. "And I don't think I'm asking you to. But what I am asking is if you really want to be judge and jury. I tried it that way for a while, and I found out in the end the only one who was suffering was me."

Suffering. Now there was a word he understood in spades. "Surely you don't want them to go free, do you?"

She breathed in deeply and answered in the most honest tone he'd ever heard. "I have to believe somewhere along the way they'll pay. You do the crime, eventually you'll do the time. Karma's a bitch, and all." She paused, then added, "But it's not up to me to make sure that happens. Because then it's not justice, its revenge."

Hunter paused. He wasn't quite sure he saw the difference. He'd lived by the sword. He'd been meant to die by the sword.

"I'll miss my daughter to my dying day and beyond. Every time I pick up her favorite stuffed animal my body implodes. I can barely stand."

Hunter nodded. Words weren't necessary.

She swallowed hard and fought to get herself under control. "I'll want all the moments I wasn't able to share. All the birthdays. Kelly riding her first bicycle. Digging holes in the sand at the beach." She paused and swallowed again. "The first day of high school. Proms. Oh God, her wedding day,"

Tori's voice broke, and she gripped the railing by the bed to stay upright. Suddenly he knew, really knew, her pain. As she knew his.

"I'll never know why she was taken from me. And no parent should ever, ever bury their child. Her loss will never be fair. But I made a choice, and I'm sticking with it. I refuse to wallow in bitterness. I refuse to give in to hate. Not because I'm this grand being but because I did that already, and living there was worse than dying."

Was it? Bitterness and hatred were the fuel that had kept him alive for centuries.

"For the record, it took so much more to rebuild than to allow myself to break down, I finally stopped falling apart."

Hunter had never thought of the possibility before. In his human life he'd never cared enough to fall apart. Those walls were his protection, his safety net. As far as he'd been concerned, feeling equaled weakness, so he'd stopped feeling.

She smiled. "I get it. You still think Casperian needs to be punished, and if you need to punish him, you need to be in a place to do that. But isn't two thousand years long enough to live without warmth, without caring, and, most of all, without love?"

"I don't know," he heard himself confess. "I don't know what love is."

Her smile filled with something he didn't understand. A strange, knowing warmth. "Then don't you think it's about time you tried to learn?"

Tori walked away, and Hunter closed his eyes. All these centuries, all this time, trying to prove what? That he was worthy—worthy of living. He had earned the right to his life, not by just being born but by trying to make amends for the blood on his hands. And by giving his people safety and security, by creating a society so they would know the peace he craved so much.

Hadn't he proved it all with his willingness to give up his life for those in his care? Didn't his sacrifice count for something?

He stilled. She was asking him to dig deeper. All right. But there was a problem. The night Antonia had died, he'd died. He hadn't moved fast enough; he'd been frozen, unable to comprehend. He hadn't been able to save her. For ages, he'd blamed himself for his hesitation, and it had taken those ages to realize he'd never have been able to best his new master. But now, all he really wanted was to thwart Casperian and the vampire prince who'd made him, Antu Si-Tayat, high priest of Egypt. Sam's brother.

Beware the little word *revenge*. At least in this, Tori was right. There was a difference between justice and revenge. Justice was blind. Justice was impartial. But revenge? Revenge was personal. Revenge was all about retaliation. Because there were right reasons and wrong reasons for everything, Hunter had believed he could live in the place Tori had described and rebuild himself without consequence. Now he wasn't so sure.

Chapter Twenty-Five

TORI WALKED AWAY WITH A HEAVY HEART. SHE COULDN'T BELIEVE she'd opened up this far with Hunter, exposed so much of herself to him. Deep inside she realized he'd never come around, never be able to feel the way she did. And yet she continued to care? Why?

Tori dragged Stacy into the elevator and up through the main floor and out into the gardens. She pressed a finger to her lips so Stace wouldn't say anything. For once, just once, she wanted to have a private conversation.

"What the hell?" Stace muttered. "Are you all right?"

"I'm beyond tired of everyone in that damned building knowing what's going on inside my head!"

Stacy didn't seem surprised by her outburst. "Chaz has been teaching me some meditation techniques. They help."

Tori threw Stacy a look. "I don't have the time right now, nor the inclination."

She shook. The pit of her stomach swam somewhere between her knees, yet her arms and legs twitched with adrenaline spikes.

"You're not going to go postal, are you?" Tori shook her head. "Puddle on me?" She shook her head again. "Okay, good. Let's take a walk."

The moon peeked out occasionally from behind a thick bank of clouds. Although a bit overcast, the night was cool with just the right amount of breeze to counteract the humidity. One of the last nights of a summer gone by, the kind of night where you held hands with your love and wished upon the one star you could see in the night sky.

Not exactly the night she was having.

They must've gone about a quarter of a mile before the words bubbled out of her. "Oh God, Stace. I don't even know where to begin. He's maddening. Infuriating. Exasperating. And too damned proud for his own damned good."

Stacy laughed and linked arms with her. "Sounds like someone else I know."

Damn Stacy, she was right. Did she dare go on? Could half the population in the cell hear her thoughts? Would they hate her for them?

"We—we understand each other on such a deep level. He's suffered so much. Been forced to do things I can't even imagine. He's built these incredibly high walls to protect himself."

"So have you."

"I know." Tori hesitated. "The things he did and the things he had to accept, they made him hate humanity. I don't know if you can ever forgive something like that."

Should she continue? Would letting Stacy in create a key and a lock to the portal in the wall? "I know this is going to sound like a non sequitur, but when did you first know you were in love with Chaz?"

"Oh jeez. The first time I laid eyes on him?" Stacy stopped and turned to face her. "Okay, maybe it was when he tried to drain me enough to keep me from becoming the bait that finally brought Mikhail down."

Tori didn't know how to answer. Stacy's mouth quirked, and her gaze filled with so much love, Tori didn't dare. "Maybe it was when he told me about his human past or when I heard how much it hurt that his friend and mentor needed to die by his hand." Stacy drew in a deep breath and let the air out. "And speaking of death, how about the way he felt responsible for killing his wife?" Stacy paused. "I don't know."

"I'm sorry," Tori murmured.

Stace continued, "Maybe it was when he explained his vampire purpose."

A vampire cop. A Paladin. A protector of other vampires. One of the good guys.

"Jeez, you do ask tough questions, don't you?" Tori nodded. She had to know. "These things make him who he is," Stacy continued. "So, all of the above I guess?"

"They make him human," Tori whispered. "More than willing to lay it all on the line for you, is this what you're telling me?"

Stacy smiled at her. "Of course."

She sighed. "Peter was such a shit. Damned bastard used me, abused me, and left me when I needed him most."

"He was indeed, my friend," Stacy couldn't wait to agree.

"And me? All that time. God, could I have been any blinder? All of you tried to tell me. I kept trusting him, and he kept using me. Funny, I never realized before. He kept draining everything out of me, not just my bank account."

"You have some very good friends, you know," Stacy replied in a gentle tone. "Including you-know-who."

"I didn't listen." Tori kept bashing herself. She had to so she could heal. "I didn't want to."

"But you knew the truth, deep down. I know you did."

"Yes. Funny, isn't it?" she asked as a hard-won reality occurred to her.

Stacy frowned, a bit confused. "What?"

"Peter was the real vampire."

Stacy nodded. "Now there's a truism if I ever heard one."

"But good can neutralize bad, can't it?" she asked, turning to the friend who would understand everything. Stacy didn't answer. "I mean, Kelly came out of him. Right?"

"She did, and what a blessing she was."

Tori stopped and covered her face with her hands. So much jumbled up inside. Pain. This strange excitement. Thought on top of thought. When she let go and straightened, she said, "My wall is crumbling."

"And you're terrified of what happens when it does?" Stacy replied, not looking one iota surprised. She took Tori's hands and squeezed them hard, then let go.

"Yes. That wall saved my life."

"Gotcha. But your wall also closed you in. God, Tori. Would you rather live in a 'dead zone' for the rest of your life?"

Oh hell. "What is it with everyone and the bad vampire jokes?"

"Sorry," Stace deadpanned.

"No. You. Are. Not."

She grinned. "No. I. Am. Not." She sobered slowly. "You need to come to terms with your life now, Tori. Not the one in the past."

Now? Each day was such a trial. Surviving each one a victory. Come to terms with existence? Could she?

"You need to try to understand the life that's going to take you into the future. Can you take that first step again or not? Can you trust life won't try to destroy you again? Because opening yourself up is going to open you up to new pain too."

"I know. Problem is I'm not sure I'm strong enough yet."

Stacy reached out, hugged her, and then let go. "Just remember. You've only been going through this for two years." She paused and stared deep. "He's been doing it for nearly two thousand."

"Doesn't make him right," Tori shot back.

"Doesn't make him wrong either." Stacy laughed softly. "Look at me. Who'd have thought? Defending Hunter Pierce of all people. But I think this is the point. He's still a 'people,' and you're having trouble with the concept."

"You're right."

"Never thought I'd ever say this," Stacy continued. "I still keep remembering our first meeting, when he wanted to end my life. But here goes. Hunter doesn't have that bond. With anyone. So when you think about your future, think about his past."

"I know."

"Do you?" Stacy asked, her tone a little stern but even. A teacher tone, like Tori had a lesson to learn. Softening a bit, she gave Tori a lopsided grin. "I have some research I have to finish."

"I'll be down in a few."

Stacy reached out and hugged her again. "We're sisters, Tori—by more than just the sorority—and always will be."

"Always," she repeated, meaning every syllable.

Letting go, Stacy added, "Take your time. You need to think."

Think? Yes, she did. Stacy was right. Tori walked along the path some more. But this time the night faded. She turned inward, honest with herself.

The man was stubborn, pig-headed, beyond arrogant, even beyond brutal. And to top it all off, he had some humongous issues. His arrogance. His bias toward humans. His professed inability to feel.

Okay. Those were the bad traits. The good? Vulnerable. No, beyond vulnerable. He had such a huge heart. Creating this haven for his people and caring for them as if they were his family.

And what about inside. Wasn't he just as afraid of having his wall come down? Because he wanted to be alone? Okay, there was alone and *alone*. Tori couldn't imagine how it felt to be so insular. She knew the emptiness of the confines of that wall. The security too.

Yet hadn't she sometimes chafed at the small space?

So, the question became, would either of them learn to trust the other?

Tori turned to go back into the house. Suddenly, she saw a flaming-red mane of hair walking toward her, and the face beneath the hair wasn't one she wanted to encounter.

"Hello."

Tori nodded. A storm of harsh words bottled up in the middle of her throat. She could only hope Vanessa heard what she didn't say. "Hello."

The vampress seemed contrite. She nodded to let Tori know she'd heard every unsaid word. "I just went down to see Hunter. He told me to piss off. I think he's feeling better."

"For now."

"Look," Vanessa sighed. "I'm sorry about how things went down. I'm not really known for my tact. Or for thinking before I act." She half smiled. "Sam really reamed me a new one."

"I'm not the one you should be apologizing to," Tori answered, holding onto her temper. Somehow.

"Yeah, well, Hunter seemed to think so."

"Did he now?" she asked, that strange warmth filling her insides again.

"Even though it wasn't my intention, I did kind of put you in danger," she acknowledged. "Using you as bait didn't make him very happy."

"I'll live," Tori sighed. "But Hunter might not."

Vanessa's gaze grazed the ground before lifting. "Mikhail was like a father to me," she offered.

"Must have been quite a guy," Tori murmured, wondering if familial love was excuse enough for Vanessa's actions. "Chaz said the same."

"He was."

Tori didn't think she'd ever forgive Vanessa completely. But hadn't she just told off Hunter about that very thing? The least she could do was listen to herself. "I may not be able to save him, you know."

"If you can't, I'll have to take his head. I won't let Charles do it."

"I know," Tori whispered, a sear of fear flowing through her stomach.

"Look. I know an explanation won't make up for what I've done, but I wasn't a nice person after I became a vampire. I was supposed to be a Paladin, but I didn't listen to my calling. I did some things I regret very much."

"Out of anger. For your past?" Tori asked. "Seems to be a common theme."

Vanessa nodded. "Not the time and place for the whole story. Suffice it to say Hunter and I have more in common than you can imagine. Only his chains were made out of iron."

"I'm sorry."

She made a face. "Anyway, Mikhail threatened to take me down. He should've. For some unknown reason he didn't. Instead, he gave me a second chance. No one in either of my lives ever thought I was worthy of a second chance. I want this Casperian very badly."

"I imagine you do."

"But I also have a duty to perform," Vanessa continued. She swallowed hard. "I'd like to apologize. My duty should never have been at your expense."

If she'd just told Hunter about revenge and consequences, Tori also had to remember not to hold a grudge. "No harm no foul, for me anyway. But Hunter is another matter altogether."

Vanessa let go of a deep breath almost as if she'd been holding onto it. "I understand completely. My duty shouldn't have been at Hunter's expense either. Is there anything I can do to help?"

An idea popped into her head. A tantalizing idea and one which might just work. "Actually yes, there is." Vanessa waited, a slight impatience in her stance. But the woman's face lit up, and she really did seem eager to make amends. "There's a bio-tech company called CoRRStar. They're really heavy into mitochondrial disease research."

"What kind of research?" she asked, completely bewildered.

"You wouldn't understand," Tori replied with a shake of her head. "You don't need to understand. So just listen. I want you to take Jonas with you and pose as an investor."

"A what?"

"An investor," she repeated. "I assume you have bank accounts. Access to *mucho dinero*?"

Vanessa started and threw her a sideways look. The vampress was willing to do what needed to be done for Hunter, but she obviously had reservations about trusting Tori. She answered in a slow drawl. "I may."

"Good. All you have to do is walk into their building like you own the place. They'll understand that kind of arrogance. Besides, it seems to come naturally."

Her eyebrows drew together, but Vanessa let the barb slide.

"Let Jonas be your admin," Tori continued. "I'll talk with him. I'll make sure he knows the right questions to ask."

Vanessa cocked her head, her gaze narrowing. "And why am I doing this?"

"Because I don't have time to set up meetings and go through lawyers and file nondisclosure agreements. They may have something that might help cure Hunter."

"Ahh." Suddenly, Vanessa's face cleared, and she grinned. "Now I understand."

"And if they have what I need," Tori continued. "Are you up for a bit of larceny?"

Vanessa beamed. "I thought you'd never ask."

Chapter Twenty-Six

TORI RETURNED TO THE LAB KIND OF EXCITED. AFTER VANESSA had left, she'd thought about Hunter and what she now termed "royal blood." "Stace? I think there's something unique about Sam's blood. It seems to be stronger than human blood. Or maybe it's just my imagination, but Hunter's been resting more comfortably, and if I'm not mistaken, he hasn't complained in hours."

"You know, you're right." Stacy cocked her head. "I was pretty surprised when Sam decided to go along."

"Go along?" Tori asked, a bit confused.

"Yeah." Stacy put a test tube into a rack and took off her safety glasses. "With giving Hunter her blood."

"Why?"

"Vampires have a rule never to drink from one another. It seems to create a special bond between them, one they can't get away from."

Fascinating. But Hunter didn't seem like he was attached to Sam. They shared an emotional bond, one she thought stemmed from knowing each other for so long, not an attachment. "Maybe Sam's different."

"Actually," Chaz explained, having overheard the conversation. He'd been sitting patiently while Stacy had worked without complaint.

She watched him catch Hunter's gaze and watched Hunter kind of nod in return. "Hunter is."

"What do you mean?" Tori asked, turning to Hunter.

He grimaced as if he was the last thing in the world he wanted to discuss, but he answered her question. "I was made from royal blood."

Tori flipped her gaze to find Stacy just as shocked by this revelation. "Royal blood?" she asked as she looked over at Hunter again. "Sam?"

He fell back against the bed, so Tori turned her gaze to Chaz. Chaz didn't look comfortable but answered. "No, Sam's brother. Antu Si-Tayat."

Tori and Stacy asked the question at the same time. "Brother?"

"We don't usually talk about things like this. How we come to be vampires is private, so you can imagine what I'm about to tell you is very secret. They both come from the beginnings of our race," Chaz answered, his gaze guarded.

Things made sense now. Since he'd been made by royal blood, Hunter was able to respond to Sam's blood. "I'm bound by doctor-patient confidentiality."

"Ditto," Stacy agreed.

"I'm afraid I don't know too much more than this," Chaz continued. "Sam's never shared her story. But obviously, if Hunter was made by a royal, he's stronger than most of us."

Tori nodded. Any and all information was useful, so she tucked it away and continued her work. She was certain Hunter's response was because of the royal blood, and sure enough, a couple of hours after drinking, Hunter told her he felt well enough to sit up on his own.

Not too long afterward, Sam came down to the lab to check on him, and under Tori's watchful eye, Hunter drank some more. Again, as before, he acted like he wanted to expel most of it but swallowed hard and often to dispel the urge. Then she watched as he simply waited for the upheaval to subside.

Never having been a patient as a vampire before, Hunter chafed at her constant, nagging care. "You know, I've been nicked, cut, and stabbed when I was a human. The physicians of my day placed poultices on the wounds, sewed them up when necessary, and let me drink wine for the pain. They didn't hover, asking a thousand times a day how I felt," he groused.

Tori laughed and walked over to a bench to put some slides on the microscope. She glanced over to see Sam stand by him for a long moment while she waited for her wrist to heal, but Sam also seemed to be waiting for something else. "What?" she heard Hunter ask, his tone impatient.

"No whips. No chains," Sam murmured.

Tori turned to watch them, for she wondered if there was more than just time and shared experience between them, and caught Hunter looking bewildered. "What do you mean?"

"Something for you to think about while you lie in bed and the rest of us work," Sam answered.

Was there really a bond between them? Had there been a relationship?

Hunter wasn't able to move his head quickly, but he caught her gaze as he heard the questions in his head. *Damn vampires and their abilities!*

All right then, if he'd heard those words, why not go all the way? *Are you listening, Hunter? I'm asking myself if I'm jealous. Got that?*

He frowned, and she turned toward Sam. Sam met her gaze openly, but a slight smile lifted the corner of her mouth. She shook her head ever so slightly no.

So there'd been no relationship. Tori couldn't believe the weight lifting from her shoulders. And then she chastised herself for her stupidity. How could she stoop so low when it was Sam's blood that seemed to save his life?

Then it hit her with all the subtlety of a sixty-megaton baseball bat right between the eyes. Maybe Sam's blood could save all their lives.

Tori had to keep her hands from literally accosting the vampire queen. "Sam. Excuse me, Sam?" She turned lifting a brow. "May I take another set of tubes please? Your blood is unique, and I really need to figure out what's in it, what seems to be stopping the progression of the disease in Hunter. I'm hoping if your blood works with Hunter, it may with others."

Sam nodded, then lifted a pointed brow at Hunter before holding out her arm for Tori to take more of her blood. "Of course."

Ahh. Sam was pointing out to Hunter that no one was forcing either scientist or doctor to spend their time working in the lab trying to save him.

Sorry about that.

Nothing to forgive.

Tori still couldn't get over that she could hear Sam in her head. *I'm only human.*

Sam's mouth quirked as Tori withdrew the needle. "Yes, you are."

The vampire queen walked out of the lab, and warmth welled inside Tori's heart. *I have a lot of sisters who have become my family over time. Perhaps someday, you'll feel the same.*

Perhaps.

Tori set the tubes in a rack, then walked over to Hunter. "How do you feel?"

"Embarrassed and a little annoyed at being asked the question again." His gaze softened. "How do you feel?"

"Embarrassed and a little annoyed at having my mind read yet again."

"Unintentional, I swear." He reached out a hand to clasp hers, then he let go. "Actually, I'm really annoyed with myself."

"For what?"

"Creating this predicament. I should have let Mercy set up her men. I should have scouted the best way to enter the building. I knew what was waiting for me."

Was that—had she caught a little contrition for his impatience from before? "You threw caution to the wind. I'm grateful you did."

He nodded, and his gaze warmed to the emotions running riot inside her. "I feel better," he announced. "Stronger. No one-hundred-yard dashes or anything, but if I move slowly, the sickness isn't too bad." He paused. "I'd really love a shower and some clean clothes. The scent of the dying blood..." Hunter's voice trailed off.

"I know. Total ewww." She turned. "Stace?"

"Yeah?"

"Can you and Chaz hold down the fort for a while? Hunter needs to clean up, and he's too macho for a sponge bath."

Stacy grinned. She didn't dare look over at Chaz. "Sure thing."

Tori helped lift him up and get him onto his feet. "I never said that, you know," he muttered.

She laughed softly. "I know." He swayed, and she settled her shoulder under his arm to steady him. "Lean on me."

Chapter Twenty-Seven

"LEAN ON ME."

What an incredible thought. "I'm not used to doing that," Hunter told her.

"Time to learn then, no?"

Was there a tinge of humor in her tone? Whatever it was, whatever was between them simply made his next words truer than true. "Yes. Yes, it is."

Once they were up in his bedroom and he was sitting on the edge of his bed, Hunter let her unbutton his shirt. "You know your thoughts. They're very…intriguing."

She kind of looked at him sideways. "You're sick."

He smiled. "Perhaps not *that* sick."

"Really?" She hesitated. "I find your response very…intriguing also. But first we have to get a few things straight."

"All right," he answered, wondering what her point was.

"I just don't 'just do' sex. I don't know how. So here's the turning point. The cliff, if you will. I'm not going to simply jump off for a moment's pleasure. No matter how incredible the moment is. Do you understand?"

Did he understand? What a question. "Yes."

"You've already professed a dislike of humanity. With just cause, I'll grant. But you must realize there's a difference between us. I'm not those people. And there's another caveat. What happens when the fire cools? It will, eventually. You know it will. So, are you going to end up hating me simply because I am what I am?"

"No." And as he said the word, he knew it to be true. *Veridicus.* His hatred, that burning red-hot poker of hate, refused to flame. Fascinating. Dangerous.

"All right. I believe you." She drew in a deep breath. As the air whooshed out, she asked, "So here's the next question. Are you going to just let me go, then? I mean, if we get through this are you going to wipe my mind?"

An even tougher question. Tori and Stacy were the "weakest links" in their chain. And yet here they were, working day and night, as Sam had so delicately told him, to save them all from an as yet unknown menace. "The decision is no longer mine to make."

She pulled a double take and frowned. "What do you mean?"

"Diederich—you remember him, don't you? The vampire who gave me the blood?"

"I remember him."

"He informed The Council of his concerns. The Council thought the concerns were valid. But Miklos testified on your behalf. He told them of your kindness. So did Rolf. Rolf made sure they knew about your courage." His words seemed to please her. "The Council has made a decision. Both you and Stacy have been accepted into our…world."

She huffed a puff of air, then her face fell. "That's awesome, but you didn't answer my question."

He'd hurt her again. "The decision's already been made."

"The decision by everyone else. What I want to know—what I need to know—is what about you?"

A thousand words stood ready to spill off his tongue. He didn't know how to get them out. But he could give her the truest confession of them all. "I don't know how to let you go."

"'Know how'?" Her brows drew together. She didn't understand. "Explain," she demanded.

Hunter sighed. "Every time I decide what I believe is in your best interest, I'm wrong. You would be so much safer forgetting I ever existed."

"And if I don't want to be safe?" she asked, her face clearing.

Always so confident, why did she sound so unsure? "We could fight about it…" he replied, his tone low and seductive.

"Or what?" she asked, her voice warming, deepening, turning downright husky as she realized his intent.

"Not fight."

She leaned down and kissed him. She didn't rear back in disgust as she lifted, so this meant she couldn't smell the sickness inside him and Sam's blood was helping him. "Are you sure?"

"Very," he answered, knowing this kiss, based on the truth, would be different than all the ones before. He opened his mouth, ready to be seduced, needing to be seduced, desperately hungry for the succor her caring would provide.

She didn't disappoint.

She lifted onto the bed and engulfed his mouth with hers. Her tongue swirled over his incisors, which had grown as another part of his anatomy had grown. A testament to his desire despite the sickness.

He broke the kiss, needing to know. "Why, Tori?"

She unbuttoned her shirt and ripped it off as she answered. "A gift."

He lifted and cupped his hand around the back of her neck, drawing her lips down to his mouth. When their breaths became one, he whispered, "Not out of pity."

Her eyes widened, and he knew the truth even as she told him, "Never!"

This was all he wanted to hear.

He unsnapped her bra, flinging the cloth across the bed. She shucked his pants and underwear in seconds flat. Then she swung her leg over his hips, capturing his erection right where he wanted it. Except she still had a pair of jeans on. She stilled a moment and cupped his cheeks with her palms, and he pressed a kiss into one.

As sick as he was, the need for blood still outweighed everything. Funny, his need made him sad. He wanted…he wanted their lovemaking to be special. Between the man and the woman, not the vampire and the human.

Her gaze dove deep into his. Soft and tender, yet filled with need. As if by sheer will alone, she could know the truth. He wanted what she wanted. The net. The place of safety outside the wall.

She trusted him.

He listened to the rush of her blood through her veins, the rapid beat of her heart, and for the first time in his existence, sickness or no, he didn't want to drink. He wanted her as he would have wanted her two thousand years ago. The ice warmed. Melted.

He trusted her.

Somehow, he helped her shimmy out of her jeans, and his palms slid down the soft curves of her hips, slipping off her thong. He drew her up his chest, her moist core burning a hole in his chest as he suckled her breasts. She seemed to understand he needed to remain still. But she did not and slid farther still until her core rested right over his mouth. He snaked out his tongue to tease and torture until she moaned and threw back her head, then pulled back so as not to ruin things too soon.

Hunter realized that in deference to his condition, Tori would be the aggressor. He wasn't one to argue at this point, especially not with her nipping her way across his chest and swirling her tongue over his nipples. Each lap sent an electric current right to his cock, and that part of his anatomy strained and twitched, ready to be captured. His hips pumped, practically begging for entry.

She wouldn't let him.

Instead, she slid down his body and let the slick folds of her core tease the tip of his cock. He lunged upward again, but she drew away until he finally got the idea this was her show. She would open for him, taking in just the head, and then she would pull free. He groaned with each thrust.

"Tori, please. You're killing me."

He watched her eyes soften and her gaze turn liquid as he twirled her nipples into tight buds. She leaned back, and this time she stopped teasing him, sliding down the length of his cock until their bodies were fully joined. So deep he felt almost a part of her.

She leaned down to kiss him, and Hunter felt only warmth. She was giving him everything she had without words, and he was going to take it. Because her caring was going to allow him to forget who he was, forget the need that never left him, and remember only the heart beating above his. Only Tori could make him human again.

He thrust upward into her body. She reared back and sat down so deep inside he touched her womb.

He wanted more. He craved more. He wanted to become one with her, something he'd never done with a woman in his life before. This was the cliff she'd told him about. This was the point of no return.

She leaned forward, half drawing out, and he thrust into her again. Harder and harder. Hunter could feel her contract around him. She was so close. His balls tightened with need—so was he.

Their hips pounded together. She braced her arms on his chest, seeking the fulfillment. But for Hunter, completion was not enough. He cupped his hand around the back of her neck and drew her head down to hers. She let go, and he put his lips right into the crook of her head and shoulder. Her pulse fluttered beneath his lips.

He was so ready.

One thrust. Two.

He let the real Hunter out of his cage. He let his heart expand and contract with hers. She was the light. He was the dark. They climbed to the pinnacle and released in a mighty roar together. And he won the battle.

He stepped off.

Chapter Twenty-Eight

TORI WOKE UP NEXT TO HUNTER, KNOWING THIS WAS WHERE SHE belonged. Lying in the crook of his arm, her head on his chest, listening to the steady beat of his heart. There was nowhere else she'd rather be.

"Don't move," Hunter begged. "Not just yet. Please."

Tori snuggled closer. He'd slipped out of her body, and she'd collapsed onto his chest, gasping for breath. Not once in her life had she ever experienced an orgasm like that before.

She smiled. He practically oozed contentment. She knew *she* did, so their lovemaking had to be a step in the right direction for both of them.

"What you've given me, what you're trying to do for me can never be repaid," he told her.

Baby steps. "I'm not looking for payment."

"I know," he answered, and she heard frustration in his voice. "Again, I don't want you to misunderstand me because 'payment' is not quite what I meant. You see, when I'm with you, I seem to say the wrong thing and do the wrong thing all the time."

"Not all." She grinned.

He kissed the top of her head, then sat back and shuddered, a grim reminder to them both of what he was suffering. "No matter what happens…" he began.

"Shhh," she told him, clutching at his chest.

His arm tightened. "No matter what happens," he repeated. "I want to thank you for your kindness. For caring about me. No one ever has before."

As if she didn't understand. You see, she could hear his heart beat. Not a vampire heart, a human heart. "Not necessary."

He paused, and Tori realized the importance of his next words. "I don't know how to love, Victoria Roberts. I'm not sure I'll ever know."

"Really? Are you certain? I'm not," she admonished.

"My human life all but killed any emotion, and being a vampire simply doesn't allow," he continued, drawing her even closer. "But with you, I've come the closest I can to this prize. I've never known peace before. When I fought with you, I was only fighting with myself."

Now Tori knew he was on the right track. "I know."

"There are words between us I wish with all my heart I could take back, actions I would like to undo. A simple apology will never suffice."

Tori lifted her head with a frown. What was he trying to tell her? "Hunter. What's wrong?"

"I can feel the change coming. No matter what you do, no matter how much of Sam's blood I take in, I'm going rogue. You can't stop it. Once the change begins, it can never be stopped."

"Oh yes it can," she vowed, sitting up. Determination filled her gut, steel solidified in her backbone. "I'm going to find a cure. I swear I will."

"No, Tori. You need to let me go," he insisted.

"Absolutely, positively no way that's happening. Not now."

He stilled, his tone meant to show the absolute utter certainty of his next words. "I don't want to fight Casperian anymore. You've shown me I'm worthy. Being worthy is enough."

"Not for me, it isn't," she cried, her heart clenching. Tori looked down to search the face she'd come to know so well and decided if he didn't want to fight for himself, she would fight for him. "Don't you dare give up on me, do you hear? Giving up is not allowed. Not now. Not ever."

He stared at her. Confusion filled his gaze. "I thought this was what you wanted. I thought you wanted me to accept what's been missing in my life so I can accept my ending."

She half laughed, terror and angst leaking into the sound. "You thought wrong. Again."

"Why?"

Tears filled her eyes, but she held them back. "Let's just say I'm more stubborn than you and leave it at that."

Tori jumped out of the bed. The race against time had just gotten a bit dicey. But now she had more at stake than ever before. She showered and dressed, then helped Hunter do the same.

"I must go take care of a few things in my office, then I will join you."

"You sure you're up to it?"

He smiled. "Yes." He kissed her thoroughly and let go. Once he was gone, Tori ran down to the lab.

Stacy was gone. After all, it was early morning. With a cup of coffee in her hand, she read Stacy's notes. There were only the characteristics of human blood in vampire blood once it was ingested and processed. A western blot test didn't really work because there were smaller amounts of everything, especially antigens and antibodies. Again, not enough components. Which made sense considering a vampire would need to feed on anything if necessary.

Vampire skin and most of their internal organs healed at an amazing rate due to the specialized protein in their blood. The rosary pea extract containing the poison abrin was a protein synthesis inhibitor which obviously destroyed this specialized protein. The question became, How exactly was the Nirvana working? Was the drug creating internal bleeds? Maybe. But Hunter didn't say he felt pain internally. Probably wouldn't, she figured.

But he did feel ants. A symptom like this one generally occurred when nerve endings were overreacting. Could his cells be overreacting as well? Nirvana was a trigger. And this particular trigger caused cells to speed up, go into overdrive, and die. And that's where the out-of-control mitochondria came in.

Out-of-control cell aging. Without enough human blood to compensate and with the protein that healed them becoming completely overwhelmed, vampires simply became walking corpses. As Tori thought back to her time with Hunter, she figured she knew that one all too well. Slow degeneration. The stench. The deterioration.

Through her research she found that CoRRStar Biotech had been working on mitochondrial disease. They'd created a drug that would stabilize the reduction-oxidation process, thereby halting the progression of mitochondrial death. But it wasn't a cure.

Hunter needed a cure. And then it hit her like a ten-ton bomb. The biotech company had come up with a stop-gap measure. They'd figured out a way to stop the degeneration of the mitochondria.

What if they'd also figured out a way to speed it up? But not for the human market?

Mitochondria had their own gene expression. Was it possible? Could the genes within the mitochondria be manipulated? And if so, had they found a way to do that?

Oh God. Cordell Stuart and Casperian? Was it possible?

Tori ran to her cell phone. Would Vanessa be asleep already? After all, it was daytime. "Hello?"

"Jonas?"

"Good morning."

Tori could barely contain her curiosity. "Did you find out anything?"

"CoRRStar is owned by Cordell Stuart."

"Yes, I know that already," she replied, a tad impatient.

"But did you also know he's got some pretty hefty investors but he's still bleeding cash? There was one particular source I couldn't trace."

"Casperian?"

"Possibly."

"Anything else?"

"Yeah. CoRR. Most people think its stands for *Cordell*. But listen to this. He's working on a colocation for redox regulation in the cell. Another place for the mitochondria to work from."

Tori frowned. Then she realized she'd been right. "Gene manipulation. Inside the cell."

"Looks like it."

"Then it's possible that the company found the trigger that Casperian is using to create rogues."

"Yes."

"You know, I know someone who tried to do that with human cells. She couldn't get the mitochondria to slow down." Tori began thinking out loud. "That had to intrigue the people over at CoRRStar. Maybe they figured they could use the gene manipulation to stop the cell aging once they used the trigger. And we all know a particular someone who'd only want to know the first part of the process, not the second."

"A very good possibility."

Adrenaline rushed through her veins. Now she had something solid to work with. "You're a genius, Jonas."

"I'd like to think so," he preened. "Ness and I will continue to hunt around. I'd like to see if we can track back through the finances and maybe find out where Casperian is hiding. Money always leaves a trail."

"Great. That would be excellent. Thank you."

"Not necessary. Ness always pays her debts. Tenfold."

Tori hung up and practically ran around the lab. Her mind raced ahead of her. If they could create another location in another part of the mitochondria to work from once the cell "turned on," the cell could bypass the out-of-control phase and slow down. God, that would almost be like a fountain of youth.

"Tori? Are you all right?"

What was Sam doing here?

"You were shouting again. I don't really sleep, but you pulled me out of my rest and kind of woke me up. What's going on?"

"I'm not positive yet. But if I need those 'arrangements,' how fast can they be made?"

Sam grinned. "As fast as you want them to be made."

"Good. I'm going to need cash. Lots of cash. I asked Vanessa to pose as an investor. But we may need to try to buy out Cordell Stuart and his company."

Sam frowned, obviously wondering who Cordell Stuart was, but Tori didn't have time to explain. "Why would we want to buy out his company?" she asked.

"To stop him from creating Nirvana."

"Are you certain of this?"

"Not yet. But if I'm right?"

Sam shuddered at the picture Tori created in her mind. Thousands of rogues. "Consider it done."

"I also need to make a phone call."

"Then I won't keep you."

Sam left, and Tori dialed one of their sorority big sisters, Dr. Morgan Kent, a cellular kineticist. "Hi, Morgan. Good morning. I hope I didn't wake you up. It's Tori. Tori Roberts. I need your help."

"Wake me up?" A baby screamed in the background. "Not possible. Not with twins." Another scream pierced the background. "Please tell me this is about something other than diapers, bottles, and lack of sleep." Morgan paused. "Jeez, I'm sorry Tori. I didn't mean…"

Funny, for the first time in two years, the stab through her heart didn't hurt as much. "Don't worry, Morgan. I'm okay. But I've got this problem and I need your help."

Tori rattled off the issues and where her investigation had led. Suddenly, she didn't hear anything. "Jack has them," Morgan told her. "Damn the man. He can get them to do anything. They're actually sleeping for a change. At the same time."

There was a long pause on the other side of the line. "I worked with mitochondria," Morgan continued. "You know how well everything went down."

True. Morgan was able to get the mitochondria to speed up but not slow down. "I know, but CoRRStar is working with colocation. Gene manipulation."

"CoRRStar?" Morgan asked. "Cordell Stuart's company?"

"Yeah, it is."

"I heard of him. Brilliant. But a playboy." Morgan paused a moment. "What's he doing playing with mitochondria?

"I don't know," Tori lied. She had to. To protect her friend. "Haven't been able to find out. All I've read are the papers he's published."

"Well, you can take my word for it. Doesn't work," came Morgan's emphatic reply. "I tried it. I couldn't get anything to slow the cells down once they sped up."

Tori knew all about the problem with out-of-control cells. And the possibility that Cordell Stuart had figured out how to fix this particular problem. But right now, Tori needed to cure Hunter. "What about using a neutral cell?" she asked.

"You mean, like, stem cells?"

"Yeah. Reprogram the cells, and let them replace the ones that are out of control," Tori answered.

"Jeez. You know, that just might work. New mitochondria. They could slow the process down." Morgan sounded excited as she asked, "You need my help?"

No, Morgan sounded more than excited. But a third human knowing about vampires? They would truly be pressing their luck. Unless she could convince The Council otherwise. "Maybe. Down the road. If I could just stay in touch for now?"

"Okay. You going to tell my why you need all this?" Morgan asked, sounding very disappointed.

Tori hated disappointing her friend. In her opinion, there was no one better to help. "Sorry. I can't. Nondisclosure agreement."

"God knows I know all about those damned things," Morgan muttered.

"But if it makes you feel better, I'm helping a friend," she added.

"Then that's good enough for me. There are plenty of places selling dental pulp stem cells."

Who'd have thought her next problem could be solved so easily? "Thanks. Stem cells are exactly what I needed."

"My pleasure. And if you want someone to continue the research later, I'd be much obliged."

Tori laughed. Morgan sounded like she needed something more

than just parenting. "Gotcha. You'll be the first person I contact. Promise."

"Good luck."

"Thanks again," Tori replied as she hung up. She was going to need it.

Chapter Twenty-Nine

For Hunter, becoming a vampire had been easy. Remaining human? Now this seemed to be the hard part.

He stood looking out the window of his office and knew without a doubt this was his home. He thought back on his life—but this time without shame or regret. This time he reflected with the understanding that each and every moment, each and every action, right or wrong, had led him to this place, the only place he wanted to be.

After being made, Hunter had remained in chains, fed at the will of his new master. He'd remained a gladiator and a slave. But where Casperian had been cruel, Antu Si-Tayat had taken the word to new heights.

Vampires were stronger than humans. They could bend metal and break locks. But his new master had known exactly how thick the bars needed to be. He'd known exactly how strong the chains around those bars needed to be. And he'd known exactly how to feed Venatorius so he could function but not break out.

Antu had forced him to fight human gladiator champions from around the world. The game had been that he'd had to fight like a human and not show his true power until the end. Then, at a signal, he could finish the match.

Clearly no match at all.

His reward? Just enough blood to sate his hunger from the dead and the dying.

Aside from being locked up, his guards had been vampires. Soon, though, Hunter had learned the extent of his new powers, and his guards had been no match for his fighting skills, for he carried the power of royal blood in his veins.

You were sloppy with your last kill, Venatorius.

"No more."

Antu turned to him in surprise. "Did I hear you correctly?"

Venatorius nodded. "No more."

With a roar, Venatorius pulled apart the links of the chains that bound his wrists. His master watched with an amused smile.

As soon as the iron parted, he attacked. Only his hands closed over thin air. He turned to see Antu smirk. Venatorius knew better than to fall into a game he couldn't win. He waited a moment and sprang again. Same result. Then he simply he stopped trying.

Venatorius closed his eyes. He listened to the wind. He decided if he was going to die this night, there should be peace in the act. Once he let go of the baggage, Venatorius was able to hear everything. He felt the slight shift and heard the tiny rustle of air as Antu attacked, and he avoided the sword thrust just in time.

"I belong to no one," Venatorius raged. "No one shall ever belong to me. You will never understand."

"What could you possibly know that I do not?"

He refused to answer. He simply knew he had to get out of there. He would never know what fortune guided his steps, for just as he turned to run, the blade of a knife grazed his cheek. He slid sideways, jumped, and rolled.

Scrambling to his feet, he flew with Antu's laughter mocking him. His master was letting him go. There would be another day when they would meet.

Had that day arrived?

Hunter touched the skin of his cheek where the knife had cut. His maker could have killed him at any moment. But hadn't. Why?

A game? Something to rend the tireless ennui? Could the answer be this simple?

They were all pawns. Pieces. Hunter. Casperian. Even Sam.

"I always thought you would understand," she told him as she walked stoically into his office. Still, he heard and felt the guilt, the concern, and the tiny touch of helplessness.

"I always have, Sam." Such a sad truth. The time had come to hear the entire story.

She turned and closed the door. "Where do I begin," she asked. His mouth quirked. "All right," she continued. "At the beginning."

She paced, as she always did. He found the action comforting. "To the Ancients, we were…what? Amoeba? All right, not that bad. Babies, at the very least. We were playthings, certainly. Pets? I'm not sure I'll ever know. But one thing I do know. The Ancients loved being worshipped."

She let out a millennial sigh. "They taught us so many things. Language. Mathematics. Engineering. The pyramids weren't built by chance." She flashed him a wry smile. "But as time went on and we learned, they grew bored with us. Maybe they got tired of being teachers. Perhaps we were simply too young, and we weren't growing at an acceptable pace. Our unpredictability kept them around a while, but even our capriciousness grew predictable as time passed."

"Time has a way of becoming the same, doesn't it?" he asked, knowing the inimitable truth of his statement.

"It does," she agreed. "Anyway, before they left, they made arrangements to leave their mark on our world. They chose the best of us, and they gave us the gift of their blood so we could be like them in all aspects. They gave us the gift so we could teach the rest of humanity throughout the generations."

Sam's face grew sad. "After a surprise attack in the temple killed all the vampires made by the Ancients, Antu and I were chosen as the high priest and priestess. You know, I still wonder how it all happened. I'll never know the exact truth either. I was told it was robbers. I mean come on, humans defeating vampires? Really? Even the best trained ninja can't match our skills. However, when I found out Antu had been injured, something we both know to be nearly impossible, I let go of the worry and questions. But they still haunted. I couldn't recon-cile what I knew to be fact and what had happened. I began asking again until I found out the truth. Antu had been behind the attack."

Hunter moved slowly to sit behind his desk, watching Sam rub her face with her fingers, then let her arms fall to her sides. She didn't sit across from him. "What happened?"

"He broke our most sacred law. The Ancients forbid the abuse of human life. They were there to worship us, serve us, and feed us. They were not meant to be played with or tortured."

Hunter knew all about that last part. "You're not to blame, Sam."

"Yes I am. I chose not to fight him. I chose to let his actions play out. You can't begin to understand what a mistake my cowardice became. He created his own children to guard the temple. But they were really chosen for only one purpose: to guard him. Then he began to play."

"Play?"

Horror seeped into her gaze. She turned very pale. "Games, Hunter. Terrible, horrible games of deceit and torture. You know him. You know what he's capable of."

Hunter did. He shivered.

She sighed. "I always thought he was dead. Until I ran into you," she added with a wry smile.

"I know."

"Mad with power," she muttered. "Drunk on the damned stuff, Antu simply didn't know how to control himself. And if the games he played weren't bad enough, he became a despot toward our humans."

Hunter sighed. "They weren't 'your' humans."

"I know that now," she replied, inner torment lacing her tone. "I didn't then."

"Go on."

She shuddered. "I warned Antu. I cajoled. I begged. Finally, I was forced to trick him."

"You couldn't know what would happen. With some, absolute power corrupts absolutely."

"Power," she repeated, a terrible sadness in her voice. "No, Hunter, the culprit wasn't power. It was time. Things changed. We weren't the Ancients. We weren't as strong. We weren't as beloved. And our humans—sorry, the people grew up. They worshipped us, but they didn't need us anymore. I adapted. Antu didn't."

She stared at him, her gaze begging him to understand. "I swear I didn't know he was alive. You must believe me. He must have known what I was planning. The tomb was sealed under tons of rock. I thought he'd simply let go. I would have. I assumed. And look what's happened now."

"Should I repeat myself?"

"No" She half smiled.

"So how did he survive?"

"I spent months trying to figure it out. He couldn't have survived for two thousand years without feeding, even with the sleep. There must have been an escape route built into the tomb."

"Was this why you were so frightened when I told you my story?"

"I had no idea he'd survived." Sam frowned and looked very worried. "I have a direct connection to him. And yet not one sign, not even a hint of him since the day I tried to bury him alive. Until now."

Troubling. More than troubling as he thought about it. "Do you think he figured out how to shield his mind?"

She shrugged. "I can't think of any other possibility. How else would he have managed to remain hidden all these years?"

How indeed? Hunter asked himself.

If Sam heard, she didn't acknowledge. "He's very angry with me, Hunter. He has the right. I tried to kill him. But he's not stupid. He knows an army of rogues would decimate the human population."

Hunter rose and walked slowly around the desk. He clasped Sam's shoulder and squeezed. She looked up at him, confusion, regret, anger, and fear swirling in her gaze.

"He might not care."

"Or, as we both know, Antu might be playing at another game. Games are what he does best."

Ahhh. "I thought there was someone else behind Casperian. That bastard is clever but not as bright as he thinks."

"I know." She cocked her head. "For now, leave Antu to me. The key to all of this may be as simple as taking care of Casperian."

Hunter nodded. Sam was still hiding something. But he trusted her, so he let it go.

Sam held out her wrist. Hunter lifted her arm, licking his lips. The bile rose, but he swallowed hard. Then he sank his teeth into Sam's flesh.

A few moments later she told him, *Tori is coming.*

I need more.

The door opened. Tori locked gazes with him. He expected disgust. He read confusion as she retreated and closed the door. Hunter continued to feed until Sam was forced to pull away. "This should keep you going."

"Yes. Thank you."

A surge of strength flowed through his veins, one not felt in a long time. "Go after her," Sam urged. "Tell her how you feel."

He shook his head, filled with uncertainty. "I'm not exactly sure what those feelings are."

"No?" Sam smiled. Enigmatic as ever. But even he could see the strain in her features. "I let you drink more than I should have. I must rest and feed myself now. I know what you're thinking, my friend. Don't. Trying to fight him would be suicide." She turned to leave.

"Not if I win."

"You're a fool, Hunter, but not foolish. I can't stop you. One of the most crucial gifts the Mother and the Father gave us was free will." She paused as she reached for the doorknob and turned. "You'll do what you think is necessary. You always have. Just don't forget."

"Forget what?"

"Love is necessary too."

Was it? Or did caring only cause pain?

Funny, Hunter didn't even have to go after Tori. Not long after Sam left, she came back. "I'm sorry," she hesitated. "I didn't mean to barge in."

The sight of her, vulnerable and unsure of her feelings, warmed his heart. "Did my feeding bother you?"

"Bother me?" she echoed. "No. I'm glad Sam decided to allow you to drink from her again. I wasn't sure she would."

"Why not?"

"Because we still don't know what we're dealing with here." Her gaze raked him from head to toe, the consummate doctor. "How do you feel? Any problems with movement?"

"I still get an out-of-body feeling when I move too quickly, but it passes."

She nodded. "Sam's blood seems to be a temporary fix. I'm not sure if this is because she's reintroducing the necessary transcription factors or from something else."

"Transcription factors?"

"Not important," she dismissed with a shake of her head. "But you need to remember, her blood is a Band-Aid, not a cure. And you'll only feel good for as long as her blood is fresh in your system."

"I understand."

He stared at her. What was wrong? Why was she so edgy? "There seems to be a giant elephant in the room. Care to explain?"

"Back in the lab Sam gave me the impression she's not in love with you. Are you in love with her?" she blurted, looking extremely uncomfortable now that she'd said the words.

Hunter started. "What?"

"You heard me."

He laughed softly. "I think everyone is a little in love with Sam."

"You're not answering my question," she shot back, her impatience obvious.

"You know, you asked yourself if you were jealous. Are you?" That warm feeling surged through his heart again, melted his insides.

"Of what? If you weren't sick right now, I'd just be another steak dinner."

He choked back a laugh. "Delectable," he murmured.

"Stop, Hunter," she cried, shaking her head. "Please. This on-again, off-again switch is killing me."

"All right. All right. I think everyone is a little in love with Sam. Except me."

Her features cleared. Her gaze warmed. Twin spots of pink dotted her cheeks.

He breathed out the words. "You care."

"For someone who prides himself on his intellect, you're really dumb."

Hunter reached out and snared her wrist. With a gentle tug he pulled her closer. And closer. "I've dished out all of the bad and all of the ugly I know, and you're still here. Why?"

She still seemed unsure as she fought against his pull. He wondered what lurked beneath her calm expression, for her thoughts were so chaotic they were impossible to read. "Professional courtesy."

He drew her nearer. He drowned in the same citrus scent and soft, brown gaze. "I don't think so."

Hunter finally let the moment live. "Tori, listen to me. I've never felt this way before, not even with Antonia. Roman soldiers shattered the concept before I could even really put it into words, so I may never know how to love. The rest, as you know, went downhill from there."

Her gaze snared his. Was that a spark of hope he read? "I care for you, Tori. Very much."

She angled her head as if trying to gauge the truth of his words. He couldn't lie. Didn't want to. She'd shown him his best action was honesty at the very least.

"There seems to be more at stake than even I imagined. If this is true, then there may never be another time for me to explain. I want to care. I want to give you back what you've given me. But I don't know how. Yet."

In a deep, husky whisper she answered, "I can teach you."

"You already have," he smiled down at her. "But I must learn on my own. Can you be patient with me? Can you wait?"

She didn't answer. Instead, she asked, "Will you send me away, give me the drug, make me forget you if we win the day?"

He shook his head. "What do you think?"

Her lips quirked. "I don't know."

"Never," he promised, lifting her hand to his lips.

"Even though our races should never mix? Even though we're nothing more than a meal?"

He winced, deserving the jab. "I was wrong. We need each other."

She nodded. "Took you long enough to understand."

"I do," he replied, wondering now if she would ever forgive him. "But you need to remember something important. As long as you're a part of my world, you will always be in danger."

She didn't hesitate as she answered, "I can deal."

"A chance is all we can hope for, then." As he said the words, Hunter wanted them to be real. All he was asking for was a chance. "And a new beginning. If you'll allow it?"

"Perhaps," she teased, joy shining in her gaze.

They stared at each other for what seemed an eternity, until she sobered. "There's more you need to know, Hunter."

"I'm listening."

"I was able to contact a colleague. Long story short, I think there's a way to cure you. But I have no idea if it will work. Are you willing to try?"

Hunter knew the answer before the words passed his lips. He shook his head. "I'm sorry. I can't. Casperian needs to be stopped. Now. Before he attacks the compound. My people need me. I have to save them."

Pride for him filled her gaze as well as a deep disappointment. "I need you."

"I know."

"Always the hero," she bit out. "Strength and honor, right?" His heart constricted at the bitterness in her tone.

"A long time ago I was a champion but never a hero. I've scraped and clawed and protected, lying to the mirror that my actions were for my people. Make no mistake. What I did for them I also did for myself. Don't make me what I am not—forget valiant and remember reality. Dying to save you, to save them is much more appealing than just dying."

She nodded. Her shoulders straightened. Her chin lifted.

His heart turned over in his chest.

Pride and wonder coursed through his veins as he watched her turn and walk away. And he realized. He did know how to fall in love.

Chapter Thirty

HUNTER HELD THE MEETING IN A SMALL GATEHOUSE ON THE FAR side of the property so as not to alarm the members of the cell or say no to those wishing to fight who were more valuable remaining to guard. Charles, Vanessa, Mercedes, and Ozzie. Sam needed to rest and feed; he'd taken too much of her blood. Besides, she didn't need to be here in person. He knew her thoughts on his plan.

"Normally I would have called you all together in a joint meeting with The Council. But this is my fight, and the fewer who know the better. I don't want to start a panic, and I don't want an army."

Charles stepped up to the table. "According to Tori's colleague, it sounds as if this Nirvana speeds up the aging process inside the cell, so it runs out of control. Her colleague also warned there was no way to stop the process."

"But I'm living proof," Hunter continued, "that it can be controlled with royal blood. So we have to assume Casperian knows this and he knows there isn't enough royal blood to save everyone who goes rogue. This is why we haven't seen more rogues created."

"Casperian?" Ozzie questioned.

"Some of you know my story. Some of you don't. I come from the time of the Caesars, the Roman Empire. I was a gladiator and a slave. Casperian was my master."

"Gotcha," Ozzie replied, his face a mask of distaste.

Hunter shook his head. "Not quite. Casperian is not my maker. I was made by royal blood."

"Sam?" Vanessa asked.

"No." He drew in a deep breath. Letting the air out, he said, "By Antu Si-Tayat. Her brother."

Dead silence. Of the vampires standing in the gatehouse, only Charles knew she had a brother. "Another reason for this small gathering and a request this information remain private. Agreed?" They all nodded, even Vanessa. "Good. And just so you know, she had no idea he was even alive. She thought she'd killed him."

"Killed him?" Vanessa repeated. "Now this is getting interesting. Do tell."

"Not my story. You'll have to ask her." Hunter frowned. She shrugged. "Sam believes her brother is behind everything. Casperian. The rogues. All of it. But unlike Sam, he doesn't care about anything or anyone. She fears he'll stop at nothing to exact his revenge."

"Revenge?" Vanessa asked.

He lifted a brow. "She did try to kill him."

Hunter watched his compatriots absorb this new information. They all seemed to get the seriousness of the situation. "So where does that leave us?" Charles asked.

"In the middle, I'm afraid," Hunter replied. "We do what we can. We stop Casperian first. We hunt down and find every vampire who's been given Nirvana and destroy them. Then we hope Tori and Stacy find a cure."

Shocked silence filled the room. All of them seemed ready to speak. Hunter held up his hand. "Not yet. Mercy? If you'll continue?"

Mercy explained recent events. "We were able to track down the helicopter service Casperian used."

"Helicopter?" Ozzie blurted.

Mercedes stared at him for interrupting. Good. But she also took the time to explain. "We tracked the two vampires who tried to kill Dr. Roberts. The trail led up into the middle of New York State and then simply vanished. But there was a small field nearby. The grass had been swept and bent as if by a strong wind, but there was no sign of footprints. People don't just go poof. The logical answer was a helicopter."

"And?" Hunter asked, motioning for her to continue.

"A small sightseeing service. The owner was the pilot. He looked terrified when we showed up. He shouted his thoughts at us. We gave him the drug to be safe."

Mercy unfurled a map of New York State onto the table. "There's an estate. Here," she added, pointing to a spot on the map. "In the middle of the woods. In the middle of nowhere, actually. We scouted the property once as a possible cell after the owner died. He was a recluse."

Hunter watched Charles turn ghost white. "Charles? What's the matter?"

"Oh my God. The pictures of an abandoned estate in New York. Mick sent them to me. I didn't know why. Then Pitch came to warn me. He couldn't contact Mick. Mick must've found out about Casperian and Sam's so-called brother. They must've found out he was spying on them and turned him into a rogue."

No one spoke. Mercy looked up at him. Hunter nodded. "Continue."

"Anyway, the area is too barren and too sparsely populated. We decided there weren't enough people to sustain an entire cell. But just look at the place. It's perfect for Casperian. My guess is he doesn't have many soldiers. He can't because there aren't enough people around to feed on without arousing suspicion."

Hunter shook his head at the group and held up his hand to stave off a myriad of questions. "Thank you, Mercy. Good detective work. But I can't emphasize my next words enough. No guesses. No assumptions. Are we clear?" She nodded. "Your men?"

"They've been keeping the estate under surveillance along with humans during the day. No signs of activity."

"Aboveground," Charles murmured. "But what about underground?"

Hunter nodded. "An excellent thought. Also, Casperian was made with royal blood, as was I. He is more than capable of passing through human detection during daylight hours. What I find surprising is he didn't feed off any of your human soldiers."

"That would've alerted us to him," Vanessa commented.

"True. But you all need to understand your enemy—I wouldn't put it past him. He truly believes he's more powerful than all of us combined."

Hunter looked around the table. Charles looked grim but more than ready to fight. Indeed, Charles had every reason to want retribution now. Vanessa seemed amused as always, but a fire burned in her gaze. She'd loved Mikhail just as much as Charles. Mercy stood ready to follow his orders and lay down her life if necessary. And Ozzie seemed ready to go along with whatever was decided because it was his duty. And yet deep inside Hunter could feel his anger burning bright. Mikhail was just as much a friend and mentor to him as he was to Charles and Vanessa.

Very well. "We need ten more of your handpicked best, Mercy."

"What about Creighton and the rest of our force?"

"Not yet, Charles. If we can't stop the rogues, they'll need to try to guard those who survive."

Try. Such a small word which carried such weight and apprehension. Because if their small group was unsuccessful, there would be out-and-out war. The Council would be forced to fight. Hence the warning from Miklos. *Get your house in order, or we will.*

"Sir?" Mercedes asked. "What about Tori? I mean, Dr. Roberts?"

"She doesn't have a cure yet. She's been working day and night. But we must accept the facts as they are right now. She may never have one. I'm giving two orders you must follow."

Hunter's gaze scanned the room, knowing he'd fight with none better. "Casperian is mine. And as soon as I take his head, one of you needs to take mine."

"I'll do it," Vanessa chimed in a bit too cheerfully.

"No," Charles countered. "You'd enjoy killing him too much." His gaze lifted. He nodded. Hunter nodded back. "I'd consider this request an honor."

Mercy stared at both of them. "No!" Hunter read her fear and horror and anguish. "No," she repeated. "The duty is mine."

Hunter smiled, proud and sad at the same time. In that moment he felt like a human parent. "As I'd hoped you'd say." He bowed his head. "The cell is yours to command, Mercedes. No matter the outcome, I wish to step down. Rule in my stead. Lead us into the future."

Shocked, Mercy stilled. "No sir. You can't. This is—"

"Wrong?" he asked, cutting her off. "No it isn't. I endangered every man and woman in this compound by not being truthful with all of you. A mistake of that magnitude is unacceptable."

Mercy straightened. Then she bowed. "By your command."

A great weight lifted from his shoulders. He would have only one regret leaving this world. *Tori.*

Chapter Thirty-One

Tori reached out and gulped another swallow of cold coffee. Ugh. "Stace?"

"I know. I heard you groan again. We need a microwave, right?"

Stacy looked dead on her feet. Okay, her pun was bad, and she did feel a bit guilty about the vampire joke, but tendrils escaped the drooping ponytail on Stacy's head, her cheeks were hollow, and the bags under her eyes had bags. Tori imagined she looked much the same.

"Have you been able to isolate the protein with the transcription factors yet?"

She nodded and yawned. "Yeah. But when I add it to the stem cells, nothing happens. The stem cells remain human."

Very well, it wasn't the protein which was disappointing but not unexpected. Still, something in a vampire was able to turn a human into a vampire, otherwise they couldn't be made. Hunter had called it an essence, but could it be something more, like the drug that made a human forget? What had they called it? The Lethe? Tori wondered if she'd ever figure out the answer.

But for now, she had a task to complete. Take neutral, imprintable cells and make them vampiric so they could destroy rogue cells.

Every time she tried to drill down with logic, she kept coming up with royal blood. So maybe stem cells could take on vampiric properties from royal cells.

"Stace? What about Sam's blood? If it works for Hunter, maybe it's the 'missing' ingredient. Let's try."

About an hour later, Tori kicked Stacy out of the lab. They might've both been tired, but Stacy really looked beat. "Go upstairs and get some sleep. I'm right behind you," Tori lied.

She had to keep going. She had to.

Stacy grinned but acquiesced. She tidied her workspace as she answered, "Sure you are."

Tori shrugged. "Just one more experiment. I'm going to create a royal blood plate. See if it works."

Stacy nodded. "Good idea." She yawned again.

"Are you sure you're okay?" Tori asked, feeling guilty.

Stace gave her a quick hug, then headed to the elevator. "Just tired. Besides, Chaz should be back by now."

"Back?"

"He left the house a little while ago. Scouting party, I think."

Had Hunter gone with Chaz? A chill ran down her spine. She bit her lip, glad Stace couldn't read her mind.

The elevator doors closed, and she turned back to her workbench. Her best bet, no, her only bet to save Hunter was logic, and everything pointed in one direction. Royal blood. Could it be this simple? First, Tori used a slide. Sure enough, when a drop of royal blood hit the stem cells they began changing.

Hope rushed through her. For the first time she thought she might have an answer. *Sam! I need you. As soon as possible.*

A few minutes later, Sam marched into the lab looking none too happy. "You called?"

Tori threw her a sheepish look. "I need more of your blood."

"I thought you had enough with the extra tubes I already gave you." Tori shook her head. "Seems as though I'm extremely popular these days," she groused. "Hunter just tried to drain me dry."

A sinking feeling filled her belly. "He what?"

Sam rolled up her sleeve. Tori used the moment to gather herself and took several more tubes from Sam's arm. When Tori was finished, she realized. "He's going after Casperian."

"That is his duty," Sam answered. "And his choice, a choice I must respect."

"Even though I don't want him to go?"

"You should have told him the truth when you had the chance."

"And when would that have been?" Tori fired back. "While I was culturing cells? Running gel electrophoresis on blood samples? Running chemistries to find out what chemicals are in your blood that might be killing you?"

Tori was shaking by the time she finished. Sam reached out. "I'm sorry. I was unkind."

Sam apologizing? Wow.

"Please tell me he didn't go alone."

Sam shook her head. "No. We're all in this together."

"Sort of." Simple human females didn't stand a chance in a fight like this.

"You're not simple," Sam admonished.

Tori rolled her eyes. "Thanks."

A timer went off. "I, uh, have to get back to work."

She nodded. "And I have unfinished business to attend."

Tori read her meaning loud and clear. Sam needed to finish feeding, then she was going to join the "scouting party." Tori's time had just run out. Hunter would certainly sacrifice himself, thinking he was already dying.

Tori used most of the blood Sam had given her to create plates. Then she put stem cells on them and placed them in the incubator. She had one small cluster of stem cells growing from before, created on a plate made with human blood agar. Her last. Under the indecently expensive molecular microscope she'd had Sam purchase, Tori took the blastula and added a fresh drop of Sam's blood. The cells began taking on vampiric properties. And fast. Really fast.

Heart pounding, Tori kept asking herself, Had she found it? Had she really found a cure?

She began to pace. Time, it seemed, could move with agonizing slowness when it wanted. She had no choice but to wait because even though vampiric cells grew at an accelerated rate, she still had to let nature take its course.

Which did nothing for the ball of anxiety simmering in her guts. Again and again, she went back to the incubator to check on the plates and had to stop her hand at the last moment.

Finally, a timer sounded.

She ran over, grabbed a plate, and pulled out the specimen. To her absolute amazement, the cells were growing even faster than she'd expected. She placed another specimen from the plate under the microscope again. Sure enough, they were vampire cells. Clean. Unadulterated. Ready, willing, and able to give new life. Vampire life.

Tori ran to the elevator, then ran up the stairs and started banging on Stacy's door. The door opened, and she shoved an energy drink into Stacy's hand.

"Get dressed!" she cried. As tired as she was, she started doing a happy dance. "We did it! We found it! We have a cure."

Chapter Thirty-Two

THINGS FIT, OR THEY DIDN'T. PLACES BELONGED, OR THEY DIDN'T. A Spanish hacienda sitting in the middle of the woods in the middle of New York State? Hunter shook his head. Not so much.

And yet the structure had remained unquestioned, and Hunter guessed this was because of the reputation of the previous owner and its state of disrepair. Just rundown enough to make people believe the estate was being cared for by a family who didn't care about the property or the man who owned it.

For a vampire cell? Perfect.

The stone wall around the perimeter of the property could be easily scaled, yet the red-tiled overhang would be slippery when wet. And the movement of a loose tile would be a dead giveaway for vampire hearing.

Not to mention the dead vines and leaves on the grounds left purposely unkempt. One crackle? One snap? Like sounding an alarm. Not that Casperian would ever think, for one second, Hunter would forgo the pleasure of their next meeting.

Five soldiers lay sleeping in the back, and Charles reclined in the front seat of a large, blacked-out SUV. Mercy and her men rested in another on the other side of the property. And Vanessa? She marched to her own tune, so he had no idea. But she always paid her debts, so he had no doubt she was nearby. No Sam, which concerned him but didn't surprise because he couldn't sense Antu either.

Above everything Sam hated waste. She'd made it abundantly clear she felt he was wasting his life by going after Casperian. In return, he'd made it abundantly clear this was his fight and his alone.

Mano a mano.

Why so silent, Venatorius?

Why did Casperian bother asking when he already knew the answer?

How does it feel to be the walking dead?

His nemesis certainly knew how to stack the odds in his favor. Each hour which passed made him weaker and weaker. The first flush of power from Sam's blood had already ebbed. But at least the sickness was better. He could move without his guts roiling in constant turmoil.

For how long? That was the question.

Another? How long would he be able to survive without Sam? She had to know he needed her. And yet he'd made his feelings abundantly clear. Better to die with honor protecting his home and, yes, his family than to simply waste away in chains until he begged someone to take his head.

Such a delicious picture you paint.

Delicious picture? No. The most beautiful painting would be Tori gazing at him with warmth and desire and a touch of impish delight.

Would she ever understand? Would she be able to forgive him?

Armies throughout the centuries had had their mottos. *Carpe diem*, as an example. During his time the words had been *strength and honor*. During his human life, those words had been but figments of his imagination. But now? Now he had the chance to live by them and die by them if necessary.

Hunter shrugged, not caring if Casperian could hear or see his thoughts. Casperian already knew how he felt. The vampire had listened long enough to know his true feelings about his life and about Tori.

What irony, to have finally figured out what Sam had been trying to get him to understand.

His one regret? Timing. For he'd never be able to tell Tori now. He sighed. He would have liked a little touch of Hollywood, getting down on one knee, enjoying the happy ever after.

"You're a fool, Venatorius."

"Am I? No worse than being a slave."

"You were a good one, I must admit."

Ever the arrogant bastard. *"I wasn't speaking of myself."*

"Which means you were talking about me and makes me think you have that backward."

"Do I? Very well. Perhaps slave *is too harsh a word. How about* puppet?*"*

"Puppet?" Casperian asked, and Hunter could hear his astonishment. *"How?"*

"Don't you feel him playing you? Plucking your strings at will?"

"Ahhh. We have an…understanding."

Hunter guffawed out loud, then glanced over to make sure he hadn't woken Charles. His stomach began to swim, and he decided not to laugh so hard again. Although, God knew, it was tempting.

"Indeed you do," he replied, laughter still threading his thoughts. *"Antu says jump, you ask, How high?"*

Silence.

Hunter smiled. Odd how stating the painfully obvious could be so delectably satisfying. Some things should simply be.

"Run, Casperian. Run to the far reaches of this planet. Farther, even."

"And why should I even move one foot?"

"Because I'm going to kill you."

"Me?" Shrill laughter sounded through his brain. As shrill and grating a sound as it had been during his human life, the sound was even more so now. And, he'd decided, Casperian's laugh was beyond annoying even after two thousand years. *"You're the dead man walking to his doom."*

Hunter nodded. *"I've been doing that for nearly two thousand years. And I've learned one thing. The bill always comes due. You gave me mine, now I'm going to give you yours. Pray to whatever gods you desire. But make no mistake. I will kill you."*

Chapter Thirty-Three

"CHUG IT."

Stacy stared. She shook her head, then gulped, made a face, then gulped again.

"Chaz wasn't up here when you came up, was he?" Tori asked, already knowing the answer.

"No." Stace looked little guilty, like she should've said something, but Tori understood. Always trying to protect.

Then she stilled. "Damn! They've gone after Casperian. This wasn't a simple scouting party."

"I know." Stacy stared at Tori. Terror filled her friend's gaze along with resignation. "It's what he's meant to do. Once a cop, you know?"

Duty. Honor. Such small words. Tori reached out. No others were necessary as they clasped hands.

"Hunter's gone too," she continued, drawing in a shuddering breath. "So is Sam. Normally she hangs around to guard during the day, but she didn't hear me shouting down in the lab. Maybe she did. Doesn't matter. She's doing what she feels is necessary too."

"Did you really say you have a cure?" Stacy asked. "I was half asleep, and I thought that's what I heard."

Tori smiled despite the fear filling her heart. "Yeah. I've got it."

Stacy threw her arms around her. "Oh, wow! I can't believe it!" Stace leaned back and let go. Then her friend realized why she barely hugged back. "Umm, yeah. Not so good if he goes and gets himself killed before you can save him. Gotcha."

A truth which scored her insides worse than a scouring pad. "How fast can you wake up?"

"Cold shower," Stace fired back. "Sugar. Another one of these," she added, making another face as she went to gulp some more.

Tori fished around in the pocket of her jacket and pulled out a protein bar. Stacy caught the packet in midair. "You've got ten minutes. Meet me downstairs."

"Done."

Tori ran out of Stacy's bedroom and down to Hunter's room. She threw cold water on her face, cleaned up, and threw on some fresh clothes all the while gulping an energy drink and munching on a protein bar. She stared at the chair Hunter sat in, remembering his hot gaze raking her body. She straightened as she had that day, proud and wanting him to be proud of her. Was he?

Hunter's image simply wouldn't leave her. All she could see was the moment when he'd opened the gateway to his soul and told her of his past. His image anchored her, steadied her thoughts.

"I'm going to cure you," she promised. "Stay alive, Hunter. That's all I ask."

She hurried down to the lab. Stacy joined her moments later. They nodded, knowing it was up to them to make things right.

"C'mere. Look at these." Sure enough, as Tori pulled out plate after plate, healthy vampire cells were growing all over.

"This is amazing," Stacy breathed.

"Royal blood seems to be the key. As soon as I used Sam's blood as the medium, the stem cells started changing and growing. I have no idea why."

"Guess we'll never quite understand why."

"Guess not. Does it matter?"

Stacy shook her head. "No."

"We still have another problem," Tori continued.

"What problem?"

"Vampires don't have bone marrow. We can't inject the cells and allow them to grow from the inside out. So how do we get them to work for Hunter?"

Stacy thought for a moment. Then she started laughing softly. "What else? Blood. A transfusion."

Tori wasn't sure. "You really think so?" Stace nodded. "Okay. You're the SBB. And a transfusion is as good an idea as any, I suppose."

Stacy's face fell. "All right. We get the cure ready. Then what?"

"Sixty-four-thousand-dollar question. We have to find Hunter."

"Chaz didn't even hint at where he was going." Stacy's gaze filled with commiseration. "I'm sorry."

An idea hit her, and Tori grabbed her cell, punching numbers as fast as she could. He picked up after the first ring. "Jonas?"

"Figured you'd call."

"Vanessa went with them," she said, more of a statement than a question.

"Yeah. Didn't tell me where she was going either."

"Damn," Tori bit out.

"Uh, not quite," Jonas answered. She put him on speaker. "I think she knew I was following her and let me. Ness always pays her debts."

"You know where they went?" Excitement and relief bubbled up threatening to overwhelm.

"Give or take."

Tori's knees gave out. She grabbed on to the counter to get a hold of herself. "If we get close enough, Sam will hear," she told Stace.

"If she's there."

"So will Hunter," Tori bit out. "And Casperian." She pulled herself up.

"We need extra ammunition." Tori frowned, wondering what her friend was talking about. "I've been working on an extra-strength extract," Stacy continued, walking over to a refrigerator. She nodded as she opened the door. "Damn it! It's gone. Chaz took it. Guess I'll have to make some more."

Anything that could give them an edge would be more than welcome.

"Jonas," she continued, speaking back into the phone. "We're in the lab. We need your help. We need to try to coax some cells into growing just a little bit faster, and Stacy's gonna need a hand reducing and intensifying the rosary pea extract."

"I'm on my way."

Chapter Thirty-Four

HUNTER DOZED AND DROWNED IN MEMORIES HE HAD NO RIGHT TO remember. The car seat dug into his back, and each time he shifted to get comfortable, his stomach made seasickness seem paltry. A small price to pay.

Settling back down, he let her fill his mind. Tori haunted as only a woman could with a man, nestled deep within the heart and soul. His mouth quirked at her long-legged lope, the lift of her lips when she'd thought he hadn't been looking, her outright laughter so free and easy, the sound of her voice singing, able could put the most beautiful bird to shame, the incredible sadness in her gaze at times making him want to band his arms around her and never let go.

But those were only external.

She was so utterly unique for a human. She had such heart to stand up to him, defy him, and fight for him when he deserved nothing. No, less than nothing, for in all his life—human and vampire—he'd done nothing to deserve the care and feeling she'd shown.

Was this truly love?

So new. So huge. Hunter wasn't sure. Every time he thought of her, he felt invincible. Her belief in him kept urging him on to continue, and he knew, just knew, they would win.

Charles stirred. Every part of his Hunter's psyche screamed no, the cost had to be his and his alone, and yet the man sitting next to him wouldn't let that happen. When had he earned such loyalty? How did the blood on his hands not erase that kind of fidelity?

Hunter opened his eyes to a sky streaked with the yellow, red, and gold of the setting sun. In his human life, men had worshipped gods. Hunter had seen only statues. In his human life, men had appreciated the beauty of a flower or a sunrise. Hunter had seen only the beginning of another day in hell.

Until he'd met Tori, beauty and grace had been only figments of the imagination. Warmth and love had been wisps, echoes on the wind, just close enough to grasp, then disappear through outstretched fingers.

It'd taken nearly two millennia for him to appreciate what had always been around him. Tori had become the light of his life, the shining example he tried to achieve, and yes, the love tucked deep inside his heart.

Sam had become a friend and compatriot and the one person who understood the trials and tribulations he suffered by being a vampire.

Charles, Mercy, even Vanessa had all become his friends, even though they were soldiers willing to sacrifice themselves for the greater good, for the continuation of their cell and the survival of their race.

"You okay?" Charles asked.

Hunter swallowed hard and nodded. He motioned for them both to get out of the SUV. "They'll awaken soon," he began once the car doors shut. "I cannot help feeling I should be alone in this."

Charles clapped him on the shoulder but didn't answer. Hunter already knew.

"Do you think of being a vampire as a gift or a curse?" he asked Charles eventually.

Charles didn't answer right away, then said, "Both." His friend drew in a deep breath and let the air out slowly. "At first I raged against becoming a vampire. Especially after I realized I'd caused my wife's death. I've seen terrible things, done worse because of the blood. And yet becoming a vampire led me to the one true soul I call my mate."

Hunter worried about this decision. "She'll die, Charles. Sooner than you want, faster than you think. Doesn't that scare you?"

"Yes," he paused, "and no." Charles laughed softly. "I might just die first, you know."

Hunter snorted. "Indeed."

He stared at the sky, wanting to embed the beauty into his brain the same way he wanted to embed the picture of Tori's face just at that moment when he entered her body.

"I've always thought the difference between us," Charles continued, "was something moral. I was good. You were evil. You became a vampire willingly, I didn't. That kind of thing."

"But I didn't."

"I know this now." Charles threw him a sheepish look. "What I'm trying to say is I was wrong. The character of a man never changes."

"Character? Seriously? After what I've done? I'm a murderer, a cold-blooded killer."

"Are you? Really?"

Hunter shook his head. "All right. What about Tori? What about how I treated her?"

"You have a point," Charles agreed. "But did it ever occur to you that everything you've done has led you to this moment?"

"To kill again? To become the heartless bastard I really am?"

"No!" Charles growled. "This moment brought you right here to protect and serve as you always have. Don't doubt yourself now, Hunter. I don't think things are over for you just yet."

Hunter wasn't so sure. In fact, he was downright certain. He had a job to do. Once his job was done, he could let go.

Only, Tori kept pulling him back.

No, even Charles agreed. The events of his life had led to this moment. His job was to save his people and then die.

One by one, his soldiers awoke. Each one awaited his orders with a nod of the head.

"You all know the plan. Casperian knows we are coming. He's set traps, probably created more rogues. He doesn't care about consequences. He must be stopped."

Grim faced, tight-lipped, they all agreed. "Not a single rogue lives," he continued. "According to Charles, the extract Stacy was working on is twenty times more potent. That should give you an edge. Even so, no one travels alone. If you find yourselves in just a pair, fall back. Retreat and regroup. We hunt in packs. Minimum of three."

Hunter waited while Mercy gave the same speech to her men. "No rogue lives. Are we clear?"

Each one nodded again, and they melted into the grounds just outside the estate.

Hunter looked at Charles. He held out his hand. But instead of shaking, he clasped Charles's forearm as he would have done in his own time, to show his brotherhood and to prove their bond. Then he let go.

"Casperian is mine."

Chapter Thirty-Five

ALL THE WAY UP THE INTERSTATE, TORI SHOUTED, PLEADED, AND begged. Then she cursed. Tori wasn't quite sure of the distance, but as they drew closer, she shouted even more, cursed even harder. Surely, he could hear her.

Please answer me. And yet no matter how many times she told him she had the cure, no matter how many times she begged him to answer, there was only silence.

"How far away are we?" she asked Jonas.

"Maybe five minutes or so," he answered.

Damn you, you sorry-assed vampire. I know you can hear me. Quit being so freaking stubborn, and listen. One last time, I have a cure.

Silence.

God save her from an incredibly stupid, equally obstinate vampire.

"Make a left up here," Jonas told her, pointing at a single-lane road. No street signs, few landmarks. Tori had no clue where she was. Except she was driving deeper and deeper into a forest. A part of a state park? She had no idea.

Tori complied, tires screeching. The car swerved, then straightened as she kicked up gravel and dust. She glanced over, and Jonas grinned. She looked in the rearview. Stacy simply held on for dear life. She'd apologize later.

Shadows deepened, and the breaks between the trees grew fewer and fewer. All of a sudden, the tree line broke. An opening seemed to have been carved into the forest and was surrounded by a stone wall. From above, Tori bet she'd be looking down upon a big square stretching for miles.

The wall was made of hand-placed stones with red tiles for an overhang and black wrought iron on top of those, ending in nasty spikes. Definitely a warning to keep off the property. Red tiles also covered the posts that held the gate guarding the road. The décor reminded her of Southern California, not New York State.

A broken chain hung from one of the pushed-open sides of the gate.

Tori continued slowly, her gaze darting left, right, and then center. More trees surrounded, but the grounds, although overgrown, were sparser than the woods. "Looks like they could use a landscaper here," she muttered.

"No joke," Stacy agreed.

"Eyes sharp, okay? There's no telling where everyone is. Especially the ones that've gone rogue." Tori half ducked, remembering the one who'd jumped on top of the car. "Not sure if they can smell us inside the car, but once the doors open, all bets will be off."

Hunter. Please. I'm begging you. Don't do this. I have the cure. I can heal you.

No answer. The same as fifteen, twenty, and thirty minutes ago.

"Ness says stop when you see the SUV. Don't come any closer."

"Tell her I need to find Hunter."

"She's got a—" *BAM!*

A vampire turning rogue slammed into the car. Vanessa followed and hauled the creature off the vehicle, throwing him in front. Tori hesitated. She'd sworn an oath to do no harm. But she only needed to slow the thing down, not kill it. She stomped on the gas and hit the creature, watching it fly backward onto the grass.

While Tori slammed on the brakes and threw the car into Reverse, Jonas jumped out of the car and ran over to the creature. Vanessa tackled the creature, and Jonas popped the top of the extract vial. Her guilt meter hit the max. She hated being a party to anything taking a life, but in this case, what choice did she have?

The extract and Jonas gave Vanessa the time she needed to stake the thing to the ground and cut off its head. Jonas let go of the rogue, grabbed some dead leaves, and piled them onto the thing's chest. Then he threw Vanessa a lighter.

Tori got out of the car and turned away. Even though she understood the need, she still couldn't quite reconcile the act.

"Sorry about that," Vanessa apologized, out of breath. The vampress pushed her hair out of her eyes. "Slippery little bugger."

She glanced at Stacy, who'd turned grim. Seemed Tori wasn't the only one unhappy with the method. Their gazes met. Tori sighed. Stacy shrugged. Someday she'd need to understand the word *necessary*.

"Where's Hunter?"

"Last time I saw him, he was marching up the steps to go into the house."

Tori ran to the trunk and popped it open. She pulled out the cooler with the transfusion.

"Hey, wait a minute!" Vanessa yelled as she headed toward the house. "You can't go in there alone."

"Not alone," Stacy chimed in.

"No, Stace. Stay here."

"Like hell I will."

Tori stopped, put the cooler on the ground, and rounded on her. "Don't. Start. With. Me." Stacy frowned. "He's talking to me. Right this very second."

"Who's talking to you?" Stacy asked.

"Casperian. He'll let me through. Don't you see? It's all part of the game. I'm an important piece. He needs me alive right now. But he doesn't need you. Stay with Jonas and Vanessa. Please."

Stacy stared. Tori reached out and hugged her, then let go, picked up the cooler, and started walking. She passed two more fires and heard gunshots in the distance. How the hell many more rogues were there?

Enough.

"You cock-sucking little bastard," Tori muttered.

High, shrill laughter filled her ears. *No. Not a bastard. Full-blooded nobility.*

"Ask me if I care."

No need. I already know. And to answer the second part of your statement, enjoying my own is physically impossible, enjoying others, however, most frequently. And with great pleasure, I might add.

"TMI," she answered, shuddering as she tried to keep a visual out of her head.

I didn't take you for the squeamish type, Doctor.

"Not squeamish, ass-hat. Discriminating. Or if you want me to be really clear, I'd rather talk to a drug cartel kingpin than talk with you. At least they're honest about their evil. You couch it in terms I can't even begin to understand, and then you make yourself believe you deserve praise."

Tori realized she might just get caught by a rogue if she was carrying the cooler, so she set it down next to a huge tree. And just in time, as two vampires and a rogue brought their fight a little too close for comfort. The next thing she knew, the rogue picked up her scent. But the delay allowed the two soldiers to surround the rogue and not give it an opportunity to escape.

She waited until they started circling away from her position, then darted toward the front door. The rogue kept circling, wanting to follow yet not quite sure which way to turn.

She made it to the next tree and peeked out to make sure the rogue was still occupied. "Doesn't it even bother you?"

What?

"Treating human beings like animals."

They were mine. Just like my horses and my goats and even my pigs. God, could his words get any more arrogant? *I paid for them, so they were mine to do with as I wished.*

"And you never thought to put yourself in any of their shoes? Not even for a moment? A second?"

The rogue-vampire fight got close again, and she ran to her right to avoid the melee. Then she stopped next to another tree to scan the area. Her heart clenched at a terrible screech, the sound much like boiling a lobster, and she looked out to see the rogue had been wounded. Even though they died instantly, she could never kill a lobster and always had to ask someone else to put them in the water. She'd never had the heart.

Sadness filled her as she watched another rogue become another fire. The two vampires had been victorious. Her stomach turned over. Death was the only winner here.

Why ever would I do that? Casperian asked, turning the conversation back to him. Of course. *They were chattel. Slaves.*

"They were flesh and blood, just like you, you conceited bastard."

Tori peeked around the tree. The coast was clear. She hit the afterburners, scrambling a bit on the wet leaves before building up speed. She ran through the already open front door, skidding to a halt on the atrium floor.

Her gaze traveled the house. Incredibly unique. There was a hole cut out of the second floor, so her gaze could travel all the way up to a cathedral ceiling. Wrought iron, almost like a fence, surrounded the hole and a hallway surrounded the fence. Doors were spaced along this hallway, evenly spaced, making her think maybe they were bedrooms.

Swordplay needed space. Hunter would want to take his fight into a larger area. But still confined so Casperian would not escape. Tori crept toward the back of the house, listening for any kind of sound. An archway opened into what looked like a formal dining room with a table. To her left, another archway let her see into the kitchen. She turned her attention to her right.

"He will kill you," she added, hoping to keep Casperian somewhat occupied.

Hearty laughter filled her head, even more shrill and grating, much like the vampire. The sound stopped at her next thought, and Tori smiled.

"If he doesn't," she continued, clutching the extra-strength rosary pea extract in her hand, "I will."

She approached the archway by circling the dining room, sliding against the wall to stay out of sight. Casperian knew she was there but not exactly where. She reached the edge of the opening and peeked around the corner. Hunter and Casperian were circling each other, blades drawn. Tori had kind of figured Hunter would use a short broadsword like the weapons of his time. Instead, he carried a thinner, longer blade. As did Casperian.

Hunter was, by far, the better fighter. But the Nirvana in his system gave Casperian the edge. And the longer Hunter fought, the more drained he became and the more the scales tipped in Casperian's favor.

He hadn't seen her yet but knew she was there. And she would become just the distraction Casperian needed.

Bait. Again.

Fool me once, shame on me. Right?

She ducked back and flattened against the wall. In her mind, she measured the room. Would they make a full circle?

Perhaps you should ask your hero?

Tori decided she really hated when Casperian sneered at her.

Without hesitation, without considering the move, Tori reacted. She had to. So Casperian wouldn't know what she was thinking. She pivoted and hit the afterburners again, letting loose a wild banshee scream.

And tackled the wrong vampire.

Chapter Thirty-Six

TORI LET GO AND ROLLED AS THE AIR WHOOSHED OUT OF Hunter's lungs.

Casperian's sword sliced through the air exactly where she'd been less than a second ago. Steel rang on steel as Hunter parried the blow. The cords stood out on Hunter's neck as he strained to keep the blade from reaching his chest.

Tori screamed again and jumped, using her shoulder like a football player to push Casperian away. She rolled. But these were vampires. They gained their feet long before she did, and she watched in morbid fascination as they began circling again.

"Why do you hate Hunter so much?" she asked, intensely curious. She'd always wondered. Besides, anything, even talking, would be a distraction.

Casperian didn't answer. Not until he was certain Hunter wanted to know too. "I was thirteen at the time. Seems to be a common age for boys to be told they're men."

"You flatter yourself," Hunter rasped.

She thought so too as they continued to circle. Casperian flipped his sword from hand to hand. Hunter's gaze never faltered and followed each change of possession.

"My father was told of my…interest in the male anatomy."

God, that was delicate. The man was an out-and-out brute.

"He found my…desires distasteful. Beneath a patrician of the house of the Caesars." Casperian snorted. "I hadn't the heart to tell him it was his own uncle who'd introduced me to the pleasure."

The sword rolled back and forth between hands.

"However, he decided men were acceptable as long as I was discreet. The problem became progeny. There had to be an heir. More than one to ensure our illustrious house never faltered."

Hunter feinted and attacked mid-throw. But Casperian blocked in time. Steel rang on steel, echoing through the room. Then they both retreated.

"Hunter," she called out. "He's stalling. He knows the longer he waits, the weaker you get and the more you must protect yourself. He's taking advantage."

Casperian laughed again. Shrill. High pitched. *Awkward.* Then his lips tightened a moment. Obviously he didn't like hearing his tactics broadcast. But the vampire simply shrugged, and he continued because, no matter what, Casperian loved to talk about himself.

"My father bought a golden-haired beauty from the north beyond Britannia. She had the palest eyes. Almost clear, and yet at times the most beautiful blue." Casperian chortled, a mad sound that caused the skin to ripple in distaste. "He'd saved her for himself. Maidenhead and all."

Casperian chortled again, and Tori finally realized where he was going with the conversation. "My father forced me to fuck her right there in front of him so there could be no doubt about my performance and no doubt I would beget an heir."

The vampire shook his head and looked right at her. "And you think I don't know what it feels like to be treated like an animal?"

She glanced over at Hunter. She couldn't muster even an ounce of pity. Strangely enough, though, she wasn't surprised by the story, given the time period. But pity this depraved monster? Never.

"You know, as I think back, I was rather honored that my father would bestow such a gift. After all, he really did want her for himself. He took her too, right after I did."

The left-right swing of the blade stopped, and Casperian attacked. Hunter deflected easily, but Tori could see the weariness stretched tight across his features.

"I'm intrigued," she coaxed to keep Casperian off Hunter. "What happened?"

"My father's physician announced a few months later she carried a child. My father fairly beamed his pleasure. Another slave to add to the household. One made with patrician blood."

"I will never understand man's ability to debase his fellow man," she muttered.

"A few days after we learned she was pregnant," Casperian continued, ignoring her. "She ran away. Back to her people, I suppose."

Hunter paled. Tori drew in a swift breath. "Who were her people?" she asked, already fearing the answer.

No doubt about it. This was Casperian's story, and he would answer in his own good time.

"My father had his men pursue her. Make no mistake, she was too valuable to lose. They almost caught her, not once but twice. I've never seen my father grow so cold as when his soldiers came back empty-handed. They said she fell off a cliff into a raging river; they begged my father to understand no one could have survived."

Casperian smiled. "Once my father's rage lessened, they were both demoted and whipped. Not only had they failed in their duty, they didn't bring back the body."

The ensuing silence deafened. Tori could only watch the emotions run across Hunter's face as he tried to process. She wanted to run to him and hold him and tell him he'd be all right.

Instead, Casperian continued. "Imagine my surprise to see those pale eyes staring at me from the center of a fight circle. With my—no, our dark coloring, and just the right age."

"No," Hunter whispered in denial. "Impossible."

Casperian nodded. The swordplay stopped as he dug into the pocket of his shirt. "Does this look familiar?"

The vampire drew out a red stone. A gemstone? A ruby?

"The eye," Hunter breathed.

"Yes, the eye of the horse's head. General Corvus had it in his possession. He lost the stone to me along with you."

Tori was sure she was going to be sick.

Casperian stilled. "Good to see you again, brother. Or is it son?" Casperian chortled with glee. "I suppose we'll never know."

Chapter Thirty-Seven

GOD. ALL HE COULD FEEL WAS DEEP-DOWN, MISERABLE COLD which, after a few moments, turned to ice and fire. The ants became stinging rivers of lava, and Hunter knew his time was up. He was dying. But the sickness never reached his heart. His heart was the one place no one would ever touch except her.

When she'd tackled him, Hunter hadn't been sure if he'd wanted to kiss her or kill her. He'd thought his silence would convince her to stay away. His heart swelled. That she'd come to save him meant more to him than all the years of freedom he'd enjoyed.

But his powers were sinking into the lava, bit by bit and piece by piece. And then there was the constant burning, the never-ending fire crackling up and down his through his veins. He deserved the fire and the pain, for, suddenly, his life made sense. Casperian made sense. Even... "Did you ask Antu to create me, or was turning me his idea?"

His father—or brother—frowned. "You wound with the tact of an elephant."

"So you've told me." Hunter smiled. He could not have cared less that Casperian was his flesh and blood.

"Surely you realize I have no control over what our maker does or doesn't do. I would have thought you, would realize...of course you do."

So Casperian had figured out he was trying to regroup. Fine. "Did you seek him out?"

Casperian paused as if trying to decide whether to answer or attack. "We met by chance. I didn't know what he was, just that sex with him was, well..."

Hunter didn't need to know more.

"When I did find out, I didn't care. He was the agony and the ecstasy. What is it these modern-day people say? Ah yes. He had me at hello."

Out of the corner of his eye, Hunter caught Tori inching toward Casperian. *Don't.*

Her eyes widened, and she smiled. She'd heard. Then she shook her head no just a fraction. So Hunter made sure she'd hear the rest.

You are the light of my life. You are a warrior.

Her gaze turned liquid.

I would be proud to stand by your side in any fight.

She slid closer.

"Such warmth. Such tenderness," Casperian mocked. "Surely you realize I'm going to kill both of you?"

But not this fight.

Hunter had one more attack in him. And fear—fear for the most incredible woman in the universe—to fuel his arm. He needed to get her away from Casperian.

And then he felt it. The complete and total collapse. The wall crumbled, bricks falling every which way, the dust flying. His heart choked, coughed, and sighed with contentment.

Victoria Roberts was willing to die for him.

Strange—or perhaps not so strange now that he knew about his flesh and blood—but the air seemed lighter. The darkness seemed brighter. Perhaps it was as simple as clarity. Whatever the cause, Hunter felt stronger. He attacked, and at the same time, Casperian darted away. Both moves ended with Hunter's sword but a fraction of an inch from Tori's chest. Casperian had grabbed her to use as a shield.

Tori, bless her heart, slammed her heel down on Casperian's foot. He howled, gaze flashing with anger and pain. She struggled, squirming and fighting. Casperian tightened his grip until she couldn't breathe.

"Stop," Hunter cried. "Let her go."

"Kneel to me, Venatorius. Kneel to me, and I might, just might, consider your request."

Her head lolled, and Casperian loosened his grip. He didn't want her dead just yet. She was still a toy to be played with.

Tori choked and coughed and gasped until she could draw in a ragged breath. She coughed some more, then gulped in air. Then she shook her head. "Don't, Hunter. I'm not worth it."

"But you are," he vowed.

Casperian watched the exchange, then threw back his head, laughing. He took his time sobering. "Oh my, oh my. At last. Finally. Someone has moved you, Venatorius. What an unexpected delight."

Hunter put Casperian's shrill, irritating being out of his mind. Only one person in this room merited that space. The only person who would ever hold his heart in the palm of her hand.

"I never thought I was capable. Until now." He swallowed and straightened. The tip of his blade hovered right over her heart. Her gaze locked with his as she waited for his next words.

"I love you, Victoria Roberts. Soul of my soul."

He stepped closer so his blade touched her shirt.

"I don't deserve your love. I never will. But I don't hate anymore. And for this, I thank you."

Tori made to stomp down on Casperian's foot again, but the vampire tightened his grip. Hunter frowned because his mind moved so slowly. He watched the whole movement unfold in bits and pieces of minutes instead of seconds.

Tori stepped forward instead of down. Casperian, off balance, had no choice but to fall with her. Hunter's hand tightened instinctively, remembering the tug and tear of flesh and steel, the blade going through human skin and muscle.

Again, because of his sickness, it took a moment to realize. They were both impaled. Casperian right through his heart. Surprise filled the vampire's features. As if he couldn't believe what just happened.

Hunter couldn't either. Or that Tori threw a vial at him, which he caught with his free hand. "Extra strength. You know what needs to be done," she gasped in pain.

He popped the cap. For a split second he thought about downing the contents. As he should. But she cried out, "Don't you dare, you stupid fool. I love you."

As soon as the last word left her lips, Tori lifted her hands and grasped his wrist. With one fierce tug, she pulled with all her might, and the sword went all the way through her body and all the way through Casperian's heart.

Hunter let go of the sword. She moaned but shook her head. She swallowed hard and motioned for him to finish the job. So he closed Casperian's nostrils with his fingers, opened the vampire's mouth, and poured in the extract. Then he shut Casperian's mouth and held it closed. Casperian tried to get away. He struggled. And Hunter had no idea where his strength came from.

Check that. Yes, he did.

Casperian finally swallowed, and Hunter let go. "You've killed me," the vampire whispered in disbelief.

Hunter pushed Casperian's shoulders away from Tori, and he fell to the floor. He writhed and pleaded in pain. Hunter couldn't have cared less.

He lifted Tori into his arms, knelt, and let her body slide gently to the floor. Then he made to remove the sword.

"Don't. Leave it in," she gasped. "I don't want to bleed to death."

Hunter didn't quite understand. "Don't talk. Save your strength."

"No. You need to listen. I found the cure."

"I know." He smiled though his fear. "You've been shouting the words at me for some time."

"It's in the cooler in the front yard. Get Stacy to start an IV," she commanded.

"No. Not until I know you're out of danger."

She sighed and winced. His breath caught in his throat. "Stubborn vampire. Okay, so we both die while we argue about who gets saved first?"

Stacy, Vanessa, and Jonas all came rushing in. "Get the cooler. Please. He's dying. Save him first," Tori begged. "Hurry." Vanessa simply vanished.

Then Tori turned her head to him, her face suffused with love. The same love pouring from his gaze. "Did you mean what you said?" he asked.

"Did you?"

He lifted her hand and kissed the back, cradling her skin to his cheek. "Every word. I love you."

"Ditto." He lifted a brow. "Oh, all right," she teased. "I love you too. More than you'll ever know."

Charles came running in, his face flooding with relief when he saw Stacy was unharmed. Hunter watched in camaraderie as his friend kissed his mate, hugged her, and then let go.

Chaz turned, his face growing grim as he watched Casperian gasp his final breaths. "No," Hunter cried. "He's mine."

Tori blanched, and Hunter didn't understand. "No, my darling. You can't. Not now. You let your wall crumble. Use our love to stop the hatred. Please." She squeezed his hand. "You can do this. Let Chaz or Vanessa be the cops. This isn't your fight any longer."

Mercy came running in and slid to a stop as she surveyed the scene. "I would consider it an honor."

Hunter looked down. "Do no harm," she begged. "Well, at least as much as you can in a situation like this."

He drowned in the love in her gaze, and the revenge poured out of his heart like water from a broken cup. "I love you, Hunter. The man you are in here." She tried to point to his heart but moaned as her hand fell.

He nodded to Mercy and turned right back to Tori. She was his world now.

Jonas knelt beside her. He rolled Tori onto her side to inspect both sides of the wound and breathed a huge sigh of relief. "Looks like the sword went clean through your shoulder and not so near your heart."

"I figured." She grinned, then swallowed hard. Hunter frowned. "Casperian's taller."

"We're not near any kind of hospital," Jonas continued. "I can pack the entry and exit wounds. Stitch them. But you might bleed out if anything's nicked."

"A chance I was willing to take," she replied, her hand squeezing harder as she winced in pain.

Not Hunter. Not by any means. Not by the sheer, stark terror flooding his being. "Can you help her?" he asked barely above a whisper.

Jonas nodded. "Stitching her up is no problem."

Stacy walked over and stood by Tori's other side. "Hey, girlfriend."

"Hey," Tori breathed.

Chaz, Vanessa, and Mercy lifted Tori up off the floor while Jonas held the sword immobile. They moved her to the table in the dining room.

Stacy clasped her good hand and squeezed tight. "I have an idea."

Tori stared at Stacy, waiting for her to continue as did he. "The transfusion. New transcription factors. Could make your skin seal fast. Real fast."

"She'll become a vampire!" Hunter cried, aghast. *No, no, no, no, no.*

"Will she?" Stacy fired back, her tone stern so he would listen. But how could he when his heart lodged deep inside his throat and his gut roiled in complete dismay. "One or two drops? I don't know that. None of us do. But she has a choice. Let her make it."

Hunter clutched her hand to his chest. "Would you be willing to spend an eternity with me?" Even as he asked that question, his heart took flight. The idea lodged inside his brain and wouldn't let go.

Tori smiled, his heart flying with hers as her face lit up. "What do you think?"

Chapter Thirty-Eight

TORI OPENED HER EYES TO SNOWFLAKES FLOATING EVERY WHICH way through the air. Snowflakes? Bemused, she found part of herself intrigued by the possibility. Then she realized it was the beginning of fall so it couldn't be snow. She blinked.

Ahh. Dust motes. Visible through the filtered light of the window.

Her gaze traveled farther to find beige walls. But not simply walls, for she could see every line of the grain in the Sheetrock beneath the paint. Such an intricate pattern. How fascinating. And the white crown molding. Wait a minute. White molding and beige walls? Why, she was in Hunter's room.

Still, her brain drifted as if she were lying on a float in the middle of a pool. Gentle ebbs and flows, and truth be told, a part of her didn't want to stop gliding.

Her gaze lowered. Dark hair. Cropped short. His head bowed so she could only see the top. His shoulders slumped. Her hand reached out to touch but stopped just short so she could admire her fingers, her skin, so pale, no, nearly translucent. But so beautiful. So elegant.

Wonder filled her being.

He lifted his head. His gaze caught hers, gray again, not dull and filled with sickness but soft and beautiful and proud. And filled with love. For her? *Wait a minute. What have you done with my Hunter?*

One side of his mouth lifted, yet mirth seemed beyond his comprehension. There was so much suffering and agony in his face, her heart clutched and then double clutched. And she remembered.

"The IV? It worked?"

Stupid question. Of course it had, or he wouldn't have been sitting there leaning up against the bed, now would he?

He reached out, surrounded her outstretched fingers with his, closing tight. Never to let go.

Fine with her.

He nodded, swallowing several times before he could speak. "I feared you were dead."

His voiced broke on the last word.

Dead? Right. Wounded. The sword in her shoulder. "How long have I been out?"

Tori struggled to sit up and back against the pillows and found the movement to be no struggle at all. Why? Confusion filled her brain.

"Three days."

His voice broke on the words again. She frowned, not under-standing why. "Three days?" she murmured. Damn this fog. She couldn't think straight, couldn't get her brain cells to move.

Then she remembered the rest. "Casperian," she whispered. The forest, the house, the fight all came back to her. Stacy standing beside her, holding her hand. "Transfusion. The transcription factors."

Hunter looked stricken, guilty, and mortified all at the same time. And Tori wanted to tell him not to feel this way. Her choice.

"You were magnificent, standing up to that bastard." His face tightened. "Stacy used two drops, one on each side of the wound, as soon as Jonas pulled the sword out. Your skin healed almost instantly."

Strange, she felt like herself but still felt like she was in the middle of the pool. Not a bad feeling. Not nauseating. Just mellow. And very not...her. Then she began to understand what was going on. She could feel the scratch of the fabric of the sheet against her skin. She could hear the birds chirping in the distance even with the window shut. She could see the way his lips compressed into a grim pattern, but his gaze was full of pride and strength.

Heightened senses and awareness.

He reached out to cup her hands and pressed his cheek to the back one. "I'm sorry, Hunter. I never meant to hurt you or tackle you or create more problems." His mouth quirked again. "I just couldn't think of any other way to stop Casperian."

"I nearly died when you pulled my sword through your shoulder," he whispered.

Wow. Such pain in those words, as if the heart he'd just found broke into pieces as he said them.

Tori felt terrible. Then again, not quite. "You were dying. You were reaching the point of no return. Casperian knew that. Laughed about it, for heaven's sake. He was stalling and would have continued all day if I'd let him."

Hunter looked ready to boil over as he nearly shouted, "And Charles or Vanessa or Mercy would have killed him!"

Whoa. Tori retreated into her pillows, and Hunter had the grace to look a little repentant. "I couldn't take the chance," she explained.

"Not your choice," he bit out. "I was supposed to protect you."

"Yes, it was my choice. And the street goes both ways. I love you, Hunter."

Ahh. The key. He lifted his gaze. Doubt. Confusion. Anger. Fear. What a mess. "What have we done to you?" he whispered, his tone filled with dread.

Oh. So that was what was bothering him.

Suddenly, Tori realized. Was she a vampire? The floating sensation? The ability to see such detail, hear every sound? Joy surged through her veins.

"Hunter," she breathed. "Strong. Stoic. Indomitable. We've both suffered so much. We've both known such loss. Why would you ever believe I'd give up the chance to be happier than I'll ever have the right to be?"

"Because I'm not worthy."

Tori shook her head. "You're not?"

He swallowed several times. Then the words came pouring out.

"You are...a miracle. You're an oasis in the desert, a life preserver in the storming sea of my heart; you're the shining star and the perfectly cut diamond." He paused, and the joy inside her warmed to a glow. "You deserve twenty carats." He opened his hand. "Instead, I can only give you this."

In his palm rested the ruby. No single stone any longer but part of a horse's head of gold, intricately woven, delicate, and oh so beautiful. The pendant was attached to a fine, gold chain, which he lifted in his hand. "May I?"

She sat up and leaned forward. He placed the chain around her neck and closed the clasp. Tori lifted the pendant, and her eyes filled with tears. Hunter stilled. He didn't move. Joy lit up his face. The sheer breadth of his happiness filled her.

"What?" she choked as a lump formed in her throat.

"Tears," he breathed. "You're crying."

Tori frowned. "And your point is?"

"I cannot." He repeated the words as he rose and shouted, "I cannot!"

Okay, Hunter doing the happy dance was beginning to scare her. "I don't understand."

"Thank God. You're not a vampire. Vampires cannot cry."

Both her brows lifted. "Well then, you'd better go look in a mirror."

He stopped cold. "What are you talking about?"

She reached out and crooked her forefinger at him. He approached the bed with suspicion. She beckoned so he'd lean over. Then she flicked her finger under the corner of his eye. "This."

On her fingertip rested a single tear.

"Impossible," he breathed, doubt and confusion shimmering in his gaze.

Laughter bubbled up inside her. "Guess not."

He walked over to the bed, and she scooted to the side so he could sit. He leaned down, his arms creating a prison—her kind of prison, with the kind of bars she wanted around her for the rest of her life.

"I will never deserve you. But I'm willing to spend the rest of my life earning that right."

"Oh, Hunter," Tori sighed. "You're so wrong. And to prove it, I'll ask you a question. Do I deserve you?"

"A hundred, thousand, million times over." She touched her finger to his lips to stop him from going on.

"No. You're wrong. We're beyond *worthy* and *deserve*, we're beyond all the debts needing to be paid. We've both been given a second chance at life and at love. I'm not going to waste mine wallowing in the past. Don't waste yours."

Tori saw she'd have a way to go on this one, but to his credit, he seemed willing to try. "Very well. From this moment on. Together."

"Always."

Hunter bent down until their breath mingled. "I'm not sure what's happened to us, Hunter. I feel strange, more alive than I've ever felt before. Every touch seems almost too much."

Hunter pinned her to the bed, grinding his hips against hers, slow and languid but with a touch of the devil dancing in his gaze. "Think there's a cure for this particular ailment, Doctor?"

"Oh yes," she replied, amazed at their byplay. "Very much so."

Tori pulled his head down to hers. Kisses had so many meanings. *Hello. Goodbye. Be careful. I can fix that, make everything better.* Or *there will never be anyone else in the world for me but you.*

This kiss was all those things and more.

And then Tori realized there was another unexpected development with the changes in her body. Flame on. One kiss. That was all it took. She wanted to explode right now. "Is it always like this?" she asked breathlessly as Hunter broke their kiss.

"With you? Yes."

Tori tried hard not to grin. Fat chance. "I could get very used to this kind of perk."

"So can I," he told her, bending down to nuzzle the soft skin in the crook of her neck. Then he rimmed the shell of her ear. Tori shivered and jumped. Too much feeling. She couldn't process it all.

She captured his lips and explored his mouth, grazing an incisor just so he'd know he was driving her beyond crazy.

Suddenly Hunter jumped off the bed. Jacket. Shirt. Pants. The rest of his clothes. Shucked in seconds. Tori's hands itched to run over the contours of his chest and down the ridges of his abdomen.

As she sat up to accomplish her goal, he divested her of her clothes. Now, there were slower and much sexier ways of getting rid of them, but his eagerness suited her just fine.

"There," he announced. "Much better."

His gaze filled with liquid heat. His eyes turned crystal, sharp and clear with a touch of blue tint, like the water off a Caribbean island.

"Yes," he answered. "We can honeymoon there, if you wish."

Tori had no wish except the one he currently fulfilled. He settled his entire length on her, and she welcomed his weight. Her legs parted, and she tried to get him to plunge inside. Hard and fast would be about right.

But Hunter paused. Waiting. And then it occurred to her. "Oh. Don't you have to ask me something first?"

God, this new Hunter was amazing. He smiled, barely able to contain his deviltry. "Did I forget to do that?"

Barely able to contain her joy, Tori simply beamed. "You did."

"Very well," he continued, his gaze filled with so much love, Tori thought she'd explode. "Victoria Roberts, heart of my heart, soul of my soul. Will you marry me?"

Tori paused, making a face as if she were considering his request. He answered by grinding his hips against hers. "Not fair," she gasped.

"You started it."

She relented, wishing she could tuck all of him in the furthest recesses of her being. "Yes. With all the love I possess. Yes."

"Thank goodness," he murmured, shifting back. He poised at her core, then slid deep inside. Tori bit her lip. Being filled with his body felt incredibly wonderful. "I thought I'd have to go ahead and persuade you anyway."

"I wouldn't have minded," Tori answered. Then she grunted as he pushed all the way in.

"God, you're beyond hot," he bit out.

Tori wanted to scream. She writhed, raked her nails down his back. "Yes."

"Yes, you haven't changed your mind and still want to marry me, or yes, you're burning up in there and if I don't do something about it right this very second…?"

Tori laughed, thoroughly enjoying their banter. But enough was becoming enough. She had other things needing attending. "Both."

"And you're willing to stay by my side even though I'm the most stubborn, obdurate, infuriating vampire you know?" He shifted slightly, and Tori sucked in a quick breath. "You're willing to spend whatever piece of eternity we have together? Willing continue what you started?"

"Continue what I started?" she asked.

"Of course." He turned serious. "You honor me with every breath you take."

"I do?"

"Indeed," he breathed. "Thank you, Tori. For loving me. Thank you for wanting to be my mate. Thank you for being my soulmate."

Hunter started to move, and Tori knew she wouldn't get any words past her lips. All thought ceased. Except one. *Ditto.*

Epilogue

TORI WALKED INTO THE LABORATORY THE NEXT DAY, PRACTICALLY radiant. Stacy ran toward her, then stutter-stepped and stopped.

Tori couldn't help laughing. "Damn, girlfriend. I promise I won't bite."

Stacy lifted a brow with skepticism. "Does that mean you won't or you don't want to bite?"

"Can't," Tori continued to laugh. "Not a vampire. Honest. No teeth." She smiled wide just to make sure Stacy could see. Tears of joy filled her eyes. "And just so you know, Hunter says vampires can't cry."

"Sorry," Stacy replied, visibly relieved. "I wasn't sure."

Tori couldn't help but laugh again. She wiped at her eyes and then opened her arms as Stacy opened hers. They hugged a long time. "I thought we'd lost you."

Letting go, she answered, "I'm tougher than I look. So's Hunter."

"Thank God." With her tongue firmly ensconced in her cheek Stacy added, "I'm going to need lots and lots of specimens."

Tori grinned and nodded. "I can't wait to get started." Tori sort of tried to flash her finger in the light.

Stacy stilled. Her face split into the biggest smile Tori had ever seen. "Oh my God. Is that a rock? No. A boulder? Oh my God. Really?"

Stacy yelled and threw her arms around her, and Tori thought she'd get squeezed to death. "Stace? Um, Stace? You can let go now."

"Oh. Sorry."

They stared at each other, and Tori just knew what Stacy was planning. "A quiet wedding. Nothing more. We don't want call attention."

"To what?" Hunter asked.

He and Chaz walked toward them in stride, like two models on a runway. Damn, they were fun to watch. "Anything. I'm kind of unique. You may be too. We should find out what's keeping us ticking first."

Chaz pulled Stacy into his arms. Tori peeked as he kissed the hell out of her friend. Then a gentle finger pushed her chin straight, and clear, gray eyes let her see inside. Right where she belonged.

"No," he murmured, his lips hovering. "We have a wedding to plan." Tori shivered as his tongue thoroughly explored the inside of her mouth. Her knees caved, and her insides turned to mush. *Last night wasn't enough?*

Never.

She broke the kiss and whispered, "As long as we visit a particular stone bench. I want to continue our discussion this time."

With a devilish lift of his mouth he answered, "I'd consider that an honor. Your wish is my command."

***

Thank you for reading! Did you enjoy?

Please Add Your Review! You can sign up for the City Owl Press newsletter to receive notice of all book releases!

And don't miss more paranormal romance like PRIDE AND PARANORMAL by City Owl Author, Adrienne Blake. Turn the page for a sneak peek!

Sneak Peek of Pride and Paranormal

The parking space was too tiny. There was no way my poor little Beetle was going to squeeze into the one solitary spot in front of the pub, but this was an emergency and there was no other spot in sight. My best friend, Charlotte Lucas, never went out drinking in the middle of the week. She was far too busy with her work. So I was more than surprised when I got the call asking me to meet her at The Cauldron.

My family lived in a quiet little valley in Misty Cedars, Pennsylvania, surrounded by mountains. It was the kind of out of the way place easily missed in a blink. I glanced furtively up and down the street. No one was watching, so I pulled out my wand.

"*Minorem ad quietiora*," I said, pointing at the two cars flanking either side of the parking space.

A shot of green light pulsed from the tip of it, circling both. They wobbled, just a little, like they'd been hit by a strong gust of wind, but in less than five seconds, they were suddenly each about a half foot shorter, opening up the space. I backed into the now wider spot, and after turning off the engine, I wound down the window and sat perfectly still. A parking violation was hardly a major offense, but if a Hag appeared out of the shadows, they could still cart me off to

Bitterhold for the night. Unnecessary magic in a public area was an arrestable offense. How would I ever explain that one to Mom and Dad?

Climbing out of the car, I glanced around me. Sensing all was clear, I hurried inside.

Charlotte was sitting at a high table, checking her phone when I saw her. The Flaming Cauldron was a dark basement drinking hole, with slate flooring and a magically illuminated bar that always reminded me of the aurora borealis. The magic was mostly cosmetic —there wasn't any obvious source of electricity, but there was just enough light to see and be seen.

A young warlock worked the bar—there were usually two on duty. The other was a vamp. I had no clue where she was tonight.

"Hey, Benny. No Sue tonight?"

Benny was a good-looking warlock who had his life history tattooed all over his body. More than once he'd asked me to check out some of the more personal tats, and with a show of feigned reluctance, I'd always managed to turn him down.

"Hey, Iz. Nah, she's not here. Anemia. Again." He worked while he talked and was busy stashing dirty glasses into a dishwasher under the bar. "Luckily, we're not too busy. What can I get you, babes?"

We'd known each other long enough I wasn't offended by the *babes*. "I'll take an Angry Orchard," I said. "And whatever Charlotte ordered."

"I'll bring it over," he said.

I turned and strolled past the handful of tables currently occupied by a group of young werewolves to join Charlotte. A small light illuminated the center of our table, resembling a white orchid. The small flower was suspended in the air, emitting a warm, incandescent light that became dimmer and brighter as was needed.

"You found a spot then?" Charlotte took a sip of her drink and looked over my shoulder toward the entrance. "I had to park halfway up the street."

"I, um, improvised."

Charlotte's eyes opened wide in disbelief. "You didn't. You know you're lucky you didn't get caught. This place has been crawling with

Hags lately. If they catch you using ley line magic in broad daylight where anyone can see it…"

I slid into the seat beside her. "Don't worry, I was careful. I checked everywhere at least a dozen times before I used my wand. I promise, no one saw me."

"For someone who works in the legal profession, you sure like to live dangerously."

The bar went silent, and Charlotte, who had a better view of the place from her seat, shot me a pointed look. Curious, I turned to see two Hags making their way over to the bar. Years of unfiltered ley line magic had taken its toll on their skin, which was leathery and covered in warts. Wisps of hair protruded from the top of their heads and out of their ears. Their features drooped so pitifully it was hard to tell their sex. They were bereft of any kind of shape, and only their height hinted at what they once might have been. My heart stopped. Had they been watching after all? Had they come for me?

In a shadowy corner of the bar, a hooded figure sat perfectly still, hunched over a half-full beer glass. Whoever it was, they were the only person not following the Hags as they made their way toward Benny. When the Hags were just a few feet away, the individual jumped from its barstool and sprang up on the counter, running along the length of it. Glasses smashed, and plates of food went flying as they made for the emergency exit on the other side of the bar. A bolt of white light flashed overhead; its tip wrapped around the neck of the escapee, who went down with a violent crash. Their hood down, Charlotte and I stared aghast as a female goblin writhed against her restraints but to no use. The more she fought, the tighter the restraints held her.

When the Hags reached her, with a click of their gnarled fingers, the goblin rose from the ground, hovering in midair, her hands still grappling with the rope. The first Hag turned to leave, and as she left, the goblin floated through the air behind her. The second surveyed the bar area, and with a similar click of their hand, chairs were uprighted and broken glasses mended, until everything was put back to how it had been before. The Hag bowed to Benny and then followed her companion and captive to the exit. The door closed behind them, and only then did anyone dare breathe. Everyone began chattering at once, and order was restored.

"You know, that could have been you." Charlotte picked up her glass and stared at it thoughtfully.

I buried my private fears and laughed. "Oh, come on, they'd hardly do that for a parking violation."

Charlotte shook her head. "You never know. And in any case, have you looked closely at those Hags? They weren't born like that—unfiltered magic did that to them. It'll happen to you, too, if you're not careful."

I laughed out loud. "Oh, Charlotte, really. You know I do mostly earth magic. The plants pay the price, not me. In any case, I hardly ever use the ley lines. They're strictly for emergency use only."

"Like getting a parking place? Look, just be careful. You don't want to get old before your time."

"What did she do, the goblin?" I asked, wanting to deflect the subject from me.

"No clue. Probably dealing in illegal love potions. There's been a lot of it about, I heard, and the Hags are clamping down."

I nodded. "That would do it."

Charlotte shook her head indulgently, reminding me of Mom. "Did you eat already?"

I was glad of the change of subject. I'd had enough talk of Hags for one night. "Yes, you?"

"I had a little something before I left." She looked me up and down appraisingly. "You know, I love what you did to your hair. Did you braid it yourself?"

I automatically reached for the intricate braids I'd conjured the night before, and I ran my fingers over them, checking to make sure everything was just as it should be and that the magic still held. Four longer braids fell forward over my shoulders down to my boobs and I checked the ends. I considered it was probably not a good idea to mention I'd used ley line magic rather than fussing with them myself. My sensible friend would have had a fit. "Um, yes, yes, I did. You like it?"

"I do," Charlotte said. "You're so lucky. You have perfect bone structure. You look good no matter how you wear your hair. And I wish I could wear mascara too."

"I don't see why you can't," I said.

"My mom says it makes me look like a fierce raccoon."

We both laughed at the familiar joke. It was true, though. Charlotte and I couldn't look more different. I had an athletic build, with dark-auburn hair and clear skin my sisters would die for. Not that I was the best at taking care of it, because I liked to goth it up—with purple lipstick and heavy on the kohl around the eyes. My magically-knitted leotard-style dress had a V-neck, exposing just enough boobage to tease, with long leaves of black forming the skirt, which stopped just above my knees. I hated shoes, preferring to run wild without them at home, but here I wore a pair of open-toed sandals, showing off my black nail polish and ankle tattoo of a hummingbird. Half the time, people took me for a vamp. Easy mistake.

In contrast, Charlotte was slim, but her figure was otherwise unremarkable. Today she wore a simple, off-the-shelf dress adorned with an equally neutral scarf, high heels, and a matching purse. Her blond hair was cut into a short bob, and her pale face was devoid of any makeup. It bugged her to no end, but the fact was she had sensitive skin and could only get away with a few products. We'd tried a few spells to ease her condition, but so far, no luck.

Benny arrived at our table with our drinks in hand. "Do you want to run a tab?"

"Sure."

Benny grinned at the wink I gave him and shot me one of his own before returning to the bar.

"So what's the big to-do?" I asked Charlotte once the cute warlock left.

"You'll never guess who I had dinner with last night."

"Who?"

"Charlie Van Buren!" Charlotte seemed so excited I thought she might launch from her seat.

"The matchmaking guy?"

"Yes, him. It looks like Dark Coven is let at last. My dad arranged the lease, and we had him over for dinner last night. Hell, Iz, he's so gorgeous—much better than in the magazines, and he has such nice eyes. Not to mention, he's single. He was telling us all about it, all about Wendy and the big breakup." Charlotte shuddered and covered her eyes for a moment, embarrassed. "God, you know I think I drooled all the way from Mom's appetizer right through to dessert. He probably thinks I'm a total idiot."

I laughed. "I somehow doubt that."

Charlotte grinned. "But it's true. Anyway, I managed to sneak a picture of him on my phone while he was talking to Dad in the kitchen. Wanna see him?" She picked up her cell and began swiping.

"Not especially."

Truth was, I was dying to see him, but I wasn't going to tell her that. Charlie Van Buren was all anyone talked about these days: the self-made warlock who'd made a fortune with his supernatural dating app, Magical Moments. I hadn't tried it myself, though if my mother was to be believed, it would solve all my man troubles. Apparently, it never failed—users got a love match every time.

"Yeah, I believe you." Charlotte smiled at me sideways, knowing me better. Of course I was as curious as everyone else about the new tenant of Dark Coven. "Ah, here he is." She turned her phone to me. "What do you think?"

Hmm. Charlie Van Buren was certainly hot. I could see why everyone was swooning. He had sandy-brown hair with just enough natural wave to be appealing but not overly fussy. And he was tall. Charlotte's kitchen had a high ceiling, and he was way up there in mortal danger from the pendant lighting.

"Nice," I said. "So he's only leasing Dark Coven—he didn't want to buy it?"

"It's up in the air, I think," Charlotte explained. "I think he just wanted something easy while he sorted things out with his ex."

"Lucky for the neighborhood."

Charlotte's eyes glazed over as she stared off into space. Who could blame her? The population of warlocks in Misty Cedars had thinned out over time. The east side was too suburban for most young warlocks, and since most of us were third-generation or less, we had little money. And the Hags prohibited conjuring any—unless you fancied a solitary cell in Bitterhold. It was the price we paid for sharing an economy with nonmagical beings, who my generation affectionately referred to as numpies.

"You're lucky. At least your dad is in a position to meet new people as they come and go. Once in a blue moon, Dad invites someone over from his university, but they're mostly old farts he knew when he worked there. All book nerds and bibliophiles. He definitely doesn't know anyone as hot as this Charlie guy."

I amused myself by running my hand around the orchid light, checking the redness of my fingers as the light illuminated my skin.

"Oh my God!" Charlotte's sudden outburst almost made me spit out my cider.

"Christ, what is it?" I followed her horrified gaze over to the door, thinking maybe the Hags had come back for me after all.

A group of young people had just entered the bar and were looking around, checking the place out. I recognized Charlie Van Buren at once but had no clue about the other four people with him. One thing I knew for certain: they were all magical. Their pulsating auras said witches and warlocks as clearly as if it were stamped on their foreheads.

Charlie's ready smile and eager expression made it clear he was out to have a good time, although I couldn't say as much for his four companions. Charlie traveled with two men and two women, all looked around his general age, and all were dressed impeccably well. They looked a little ostentatious in this spit-and-sawdust basement bar, and from the sneers on their faces, they knew it.

One in particular caught my eye. Charlie was tall, but his companion was even taller, and I would have been totally into him if it weren't for the permanent scowl glued to his face. Still, that wouldn't matter one bit if he were nice, because the wizard was hot—like smoldering hot. My keen gaze feasted on his broad shoulders, tanned complexion, and strong but manicured hands. I hoped to Gaia that scowl was only temporary.

Charlie headed straight for the bar as his friends surveyed the place.

"I heard this place was supposed to be happening," said the more sophisticated of the two women.

"Clearly we were misinformed," the tallest man said. He had a deep, commanding voice that made my skin tingle in the best possible way. I could hear him from our table in the corner and watched as he surveyed the place, like a lord overseeing his minions.

One of the werewolves walked by. The taller woman pulled the shorter one close and stuck her nose in the air, as if some nasty smell had irritated her. I always liked the musky werewolf aroma myself, but this lady had issues, and from the stiff gait of the others, I figured none of them liked the place. Not my type of crowd at all.

"We could go back to Charlie's place," the shortest man suggested. "At least there's free liquor there."

At that moment, the taller woman managed to catch my eye. I smiled, seeing no reason not to, but my smile was not returned.

"Too late now," said the taller man with the scowl. "Charlie already ordered the drinks. We're going to have to stay for one at least." It was his turn to stare directly at me. "You're going to have to put up with the local riffraff for one round."

I could feel the color rise within me. Riffraff indeed. "Anyone would think their poop didn't stink."

Charlotte laughed. "Or if it does, it smells of roses."

I snorted into my drink.

"This place does somewhat remind me of one of my late father's stables," the shorter woman said.

"Yes, or the pigsty. I'm definitely getting eau de swine." The other girl giggled.

"You're not wrong. The resemblance is remarkable." As he said this, the tall man glanced directly at me. I would have said something smart to Charlotte; however, I was so taken aback that for the moment I was struck dumb.

"Did he just say that? Did he just call us *pigs*?" Charlotte leaned into me, and her acknowledgement brought me to my senses.

"Just me, I think. Or maybe not. They're probably think they're being amusing. Stupid asses. Thank Gaia we don't have to talk to *them*."

Resigned to their fate, the group at the door moved over to the bar as Charlie handed back their drinks. They talked among themselves for a while but were now too far away for me to catch what they were saying.

Charlie glanced over at our table. Seeing Charlotte, he grinned warmly.

"Shit," I said in horror. "They're heading this way."

Charlotte kicked me under the table as, indeed, the group of five moved in our direction. Charlie was the first to arrive on the scene.

"Well, hello!" he said, his tone friendly as he leaned in to hug my friend. "I didn't realize you would be here tonight, or I'd have invited you along. This is a great place. I'm so glad you recommended it last night."

Charlotte's grin betrayed her delight. "I'm glad you found it. I honestly didn't think you'd be coming so soon."

"Ah, well," Charlie continued, "I have the urban family with me, checking out my new digs. I had to take them out somewhere, or they'd be driving me up the wall. They'd all just hang around and do nothing, given the chance."

Charlie and Charlotte chuckled, but I could clearly see his friends weren't impressed. Judging by their faces, one would think they'd all just trod in pig shit. I thought that kind of fitting under the circumstances. I fixed my gaze on Charlotte and tried to pretend the others weren't there.

"Everyone," Charlie said, "this is my new friend, Charlotte. Her dad is Bill Lucas, the man who runs the local real estate office and who fixed me up with Dark Coven."

His companions all nodded at once.

"Nice to meet you all," Charlotte said. "This is my friend, Izzy. Izzy Bennet."

I managed a polite enough smile, although I didn't feel it. I was surprised Charlotte could be so nonchalant under the circumstances, but then I supposed they hadn't just called *her* a pig. Satisfied, Charlie continued, "These are my sisters, Caroline and Louisa, Louisa's husband, old Hursty, and my best friend in the world, Fitz Darcy."

"Fitz? Is that German?" I asked with more politeness than I felt.

"I was born in Maine, but my mother was Pennsylvania Dutch," he replied in a clipped tone.

I spotted an intricately carved silver skull ring on his finger, which looked expensive, curious about its meaning. I also had a funny feeling I'd seen one like it before, but right now I just couldn't remember where.

"Have you lived here long?" Fitz asked.

"My whole life."

"I see," he said. "And it's the best place to be, you think?"

"Yeah, why not?" I said. "In fact, we love it down here. The Cauldron's the best paranormal hangout in the county. They have the best bands, the best people, in fact, the best of everything in my opinion."

"I suppose it rather depends on what you're used to," Caroline said. "I guess it's, um, what would you call it, Louisa?"

Louisa was the shorter of the two women. She glanced around the bar, taking it all in. "It's very, err, rustic, maybe?"

"And happening," I continued. "It might not be the most sophisticated place in the world, but it has a great atmosphere when there's a bigger crowd, and the people you meet here are great."

"I'm sure they are," Caroline said. She'd finished her drink quickly and looked anxious for the others to do the same. Her friends were at least taking their time, and I smiled on the inside.

"Did Charlotte say your last name was Bennet?" Charlie asked. He rubbed his chin thoughtfully.

"Yes. Yes, it is. Why?"

"I believe I may have bumped into your dad earlier this evening."

"You did?" I stared at Charlie with more than my usual curiosity. "Are you sure it was my dad?"

"Yes, I think so. He's a retired professor, no?"

"Why, yes, he is. How did you meet him?"

"I saw him at the bank, just as it was closing. We have the same financial advisor, and he introduced us. Nice man, your father. He seems to know a lot."

I laughed despite myself. "I suppose he does, but then he was a literary professor at Yule."

"That's so cool," Charlie said. "I sort of ran into him at the bank. He mentioned he had five daughters—are they all as pretty as you?"

I couldn't help but laugh out loud at that, and when I was done, I noticed Fitz staring at me intently. I had no idea what the man was thinking and, quite frankly, cared even less. "Shit no, my sisters are much prettier. I'm the ugly one." I half expected some kind of reaction from Fitz, but he didn't respond at all.

"You're a witch, right?" Fitz asked. "Only…"

He was looking at my clothes. "Yeah, totally a witch. Not a vamp. I'm just into goth. I get that a lot."

"I see."

"We're all witches and warlocks, and proud of it," Caroline said, her tone sharp. "I never see the need to display anything other than what I am."

"So am I," I said. "It's just a fashion thing."

"And it suits you," Fitz said. "I meant no offense."

"None taken."

Under the table, Caroline pulled on Charlie's shirt.

"Um, well, I guess we'd better be off then," Charlie said. "Lots of places to go and visit before the night is done. I'm running down the list you gave me, Charlotte. Can I buy you both a drink before we head off?"

"Err, no, it's okay," I said, not wanting the others to think we were sponges.

"Thanks for the offer, though," Charlotte added. "Maybe some other time?"

I glanced at Charlotte, realizing she had the hots for him. She probably wanted to get him all on his own, so he'd have the chance to molest her with his magical dating app. Fair enough.

"Right then, well, I suppose I'll be seeing you all soon."

"Good-bye."

They deposited their half-full glasses on the table in front of them, and I sighed with relief as, at last, they made to leave.

Charlotte still looked starry-eyed, as if they'd done us a great favor by noticing us at all. But I couldn't share her good feelings. I was still too upset by that great brute of a man and the pig comment he'd made the second he'd walked in the door. I smiled to myself. Like he was anything to talk about. Twit.

I was quiet as they left the bar, organizing my thoughts and thinking about everything they'd just said to us, especially that Fitz. The second they were gone, I turned in my seat, and for the rest of the night, we did nothing but talk about the town's newest arrivals.

Charlotte, who was a darling, couldn't stop singing their praises, whereas I, part witch, and clearly part demon, couldn't stop laughing at their nonsense. On the upside, the two of us had nothing but praise for Charlie. He wasn't just smart, he was nice. But Charlotte and I had mixed views on his friends, and though she tried to persuade me to see the good in each of them, all I could think about was the snarky comments they'd made and was well on the road to disliking them.

Don't stop now. Keep reading with your copy of **PRIDE AND PARANORMAL** by City Owl Author, Adrienne Blake.

And find more from Linda J. Parisi at www.lindajparisi.com

Want even more paranormal romance? Try PRIDE AND PARANORMAL by City Owl Author, Adrienne Blake, and find more from Linda J. Parisi at www.lindajparisi.com

---

What do love potions and banshee karaoke have to do with one of the greatest enemies-to-lovers tales of all time?

Izzy may be the only responsible witch in her poor family of misfits, and as such, she has duties to uphold. Only a hot, mysterious, and infuriating warlock is determined to get in the way.

When the rich and handsome Fitz Darcy blows into town, sparks fly.

The wrong kind...

He has earned her ire as much as her eye with his constant harsh words and acts, but what will happen when a bit of magic goes awry, and Izzy needs the help of this powerful man she claims to hate?

Will Izzy's pride get in the way of saving her family's welfare and reputation? Find out in this witty, funny, fantasy retelling of Pride & Prejudice.

For books in the world of romance and speculative fiction that embody Innovation, Creativity, and Affordability, check out City Owl Press at www.cityowlpress.com.

Acknowledgments

Thank you one hundred times over to my agent extraordinaire, Eva Scalzo of Speilburg Literary, who saved me from a massive overhaul *before* this book ever became a book.

A colossal thank you to my editor at City Owl Press, Tee Tate. You 'got' this book from the very beginning. As Hunter would say, "Gratus."

As always, a HUGE shout out and thank you to my bestie MaryAnn Johnson for loving my vampires and making sure my science was correct.

So many thank-you's. To my CP's, Chris, Gwen, and Gretchen. To my Amiga's, Nancy, Roni, Shari, Karen, Maria, Kristina and Chris. And *in memorium,* MaryKate. Every author will tell you they can't do it alone.

About the Author

As a major in biochemistry with a minor in English literature, LINDA J. PARISI has always tried to mesh her love of science with her love of the written word. A clinical research scientist by day and NJRW Golden Leaf award winning author by night, she creates unforgettable characters and puts them in untenable situations, much to their dismay. Choices always matter and love conquers all, so a happy-ever-after is a must. Linda is the current Treasurer of Liberty States Fiction Writers, a past board member of New Jersey Romance Writers, and long time member of Romance Writers of America. She lives in New Jersey with her husband John, son Chris, daughter-in-law Sara, and Audi, a Cocker Spaniel mix who had her at *woof!*

www.lindajparisi.com

 twitter.com/ljparisiwrites

 instagram.com/ljparisiwrites

facebook.com/lindajparisiauthor

About the Publisher

City Owl Press is a cutting edge indie publishing company, bringing the world of romance and speculative fiction to discerning readers.

Escape Your World. Get Lost in Ours!

www.cityowlpress.com

 facebook.com/YourCityOwlPress

 twitter.com/cityowlpress

 instagram.com/cityowlbooks

 pinterest.com/cityowlpress